THE LEAF OF A LIME TREE

PAUL TABORI

His Books:

EPITAPH FOR EUROPE
SNEEZE ON A MONDAY
THE RAGGED GUARD
THEY CAME TO LONDON
TWO FORESTS
BRICKS UPON DUST
THE LEAF OF A LIME TREE

THE LEAF OF A LIME TREE

A Novel by

PAUL TABORI

London: HODDER & STOUGHTON Limited

FIRST PRINTED DECEMBER 1945

This book is produced in
complete conformity with the
Authorised Economy Standard

*Made and Printed in Great Britain for
Hodder and Stoughton Limited London
by Wyman and Sons Limited London
Fakenham and Reading*

DEDICATION

To the memory of my father who disappeared in the Nazi hell and who was in my mind every moment while I wrote this book.

AUF WIEDERSEHEN!
WIR KOMMEN WIEDER!

Inscription, scrawled in chalk on a Parisian shop-shutter, August, 1944

AUTHOR'S NOTE

I began this book in December 1944, at the height of Rundstedt's counter-offensive in the Ardennes, and finished it in July 1945, just after the closing session of the San Francisco Conference. When I started to write it, even the optimists thought that the war might last another year in Europe—which explains why the story opens in snow and wintry weather—and when I finished it, I saw no reason to change the setting. It remains only to add the usual disclaimer that all characters and incidents are fictitious. The story has no intentions of political or military prophecy, does not try to offer a solution to the German problem, nor the re-making of Europe. It is simply a tale of guesswork and make-believe; but for all that, you may as well take it seriously.

P. T.

I

OUTSIDE THE TALL WROUGHT-IRON gates the sullen crowd pressed close together. There was safety in numbers and vicarious courage in feeling the next man's breath steaming in the bitter cold. There was little sound; now and then a murmur ran through the ranks as they pressed against the railings. The roads and footpaths leading up to the clearing were black with people as they thrust purposefully forward, converging on the entrance to the park. Darkness was falling rapidly but the snow remained white; white and cold it stretched to the horizon except where the pine forest framed the pale carpet with its regular pattern of trees.

Across the park they could just see the house—long and low, the two wings seeming to merge into the taller trees while the centre part stood out with its fluted columns at the entrance and its glass doors. It was dark and desolate; menacing, it crouched like a beast of prey about to spring. Its very presence beyond the broad expanse of the formal garden, with its gradually rising terraces, its covered flower-beds and the pond in the middle, seemed to speak to the multitude, telling them to keep away, boasting of privilege and power.

But then one man in the crowd, his tall thin body covered with a weird assortment of rags, his feet wrapped in sacking, his fingers blue with the cold, suddenly noticed that the central part of the gate he clutched was shaped in the form of a swastika. For a moment he traced the crooked cross and felt the frozen iron burning his skin. Then he called out in a high, quavering voice: "Hoist me up!"

An old man, next to him, his nose running, his haggard face drawn and pale, said: "But the lodge . . . there might be some of them in there. They'll shoot you."

The other did not reply but began to climb the gate. And now there were willing hands to help him; he reached the top quickly, swung himself across and slid down on the other side.

"See," he cried, "it is simple. I'll open it for you. There is just a catch inside . . . it isn't locked."

He stepped back a pace; and the explosion sounded immense

and shattering as if the woods and the snowy fields had dissolved suddenly. The man who had stood there a moment ago, disappeared as if by magic. His scream in the second before he was torn to pieces was drowned in the shrill, animal wail of the crowd. Bits of masonry, parts of the gate and the iron railings flew into the air and were thrown with violent force against the tightly-packed ranks. A dozen at least went down and suddenly there was an empty space around them as the others, at first stunned by the detonation, jumped back. The old man who had warned his companion, stood alone near the broken stone pillar of the lodge-gate, clutching his arm and staring at the stump where once had been his hand. He was whimpering softly and so deep was the silence following the explosion that his snuffling, soft voice could be heard clearly. Then he slumped forward, lying in the snow which had turned black and red. A woman, kneeling at the head of a man whose legs had been blown away, lifted her head and stared at the house; then she cursed in a hoarse, dull voice while with a stupid mechanical gesture she tried to prop up the dead man.

But now the others came forward again; though some had taken to their heels, others, more tenacious, carried the writhing or stiffening bodies from the little clear space and deposited them under the bushes near the curving road. A small knot of men formed immediately in front of the ruined gate but no one passed its line. They stood there and talked in low voices as if they had a secret to share.

II

INSIDE THE BIG HOUSE WHICH was silent and seemingly blind, the lights burned in a room on the first floor, directly facing the gate. But except for a small rectangle, the windows were covered with bullet-proof steel and even this peephole was hidden by a metal flap.

It was a large room, furnished with taste and elegance, a successful combination of a study and a bedroom. The furniture was perhaps a trifle too substantial, the ornaments too lavish, but the total effect remained far from displeasing. It was the room of a man who knew his own mind; who had very determined ideas about comfort and convenience. The only pictures on the walls were very large photographs; the one over the mantelpiece showed Adolf Hitler in one of his characteristic poses, one hand hooked into his belt, the other thrust out in the Nazi salute. Hoffmann, the court photographer, had carefully removed the wrinkles and deeply-etched lines; it was a coarse but almost youthful face, scowling with concentration and just a tiny bit ridiculous.

In front of an ornate desk—mahogany with gold fittings—a man was sitting, going swiftly but methodically through the drawers. In front of him two small piles grew. Notebooks, stiff sheets of official-looking papers, photographs, letters; without pause or hesitation he sorted them out. Then he gathered one heap and went to the open fireplace in which huge logs burned with a clear, aromatic flame. He thrust the pile of papers well into the fire and watched it burning for a few moments. Then he returned to the desk, neatly stacked up the second pile and stepped in front of Hitler's picture. He turned it round; behind it there was a pin-point opening in the oak-brown wallpaper. He inserted a narrow, tapering key and turned it twice to the left and twice to the right. A door swung open; he thrust the papers into the safe and locked it. Just as he was turning away, the sound of the explosion outside rent the air, but this man did not flinch or betray the slightest sign of nervous reaction. He walked the length of the large room until he came to a small alcove which held a table and two chairs.

In one of the chairs a man was sitting. He was wearing an S.S. uniform with silver facings and a row of medal ribbons. He was dead. The man who had burned the papers passed close by and brushed against him but did not seem put out by his contact with a corpse. He opened a built-in cupboard in the alcove, took out a small suit-case and a flat, long box. He carried both back into the main part of the room, drew up a chair to a dressing-table placed near the bed and lit the cluster of bulbs around the large mirror which would have been more in place in a theatrical dressing-room. So would have been the flat box which he now opened for it contained a complete set of make-up material that would have made any star of screen or stage green with envy—especially in this country of shortages.

But before he touched the variety of objects in the box,

the man looked into the mirror, studying his face intently as if he were seeing it for the first time. It was a handsome face by any standard; a thin, straight, high-bridged nose, and blue eyes as clear and untroubled as any child's; the forehead perhaps not as high as he would have wished—but then he had read somewhere that a domed forehead did not necessarily mean great intellect—soft fair hair brushed severely back, fitting the skull like a cap of silvery gold; small ears, close to the head; a strong, cleft chin. Only the lips were rather narrow and the moustache a darker gold, almost a light-brown.

Beneath this face, set on a strong column of a neck, there were broad shoulders. The man was tall and well-proportioned; there did not seem to be an extra ounce of superfluous flesh on his athletic body. He was wearing the full-dress uniform of an S.S. general with three rows of decorations on the chest and the Knight Cross of the Iron Cross hanging on a broad ribbon around his neck.

He stared at the face in the mirror and suddenly made a grimace at it—a grimace which created tiny wrinkles at the corner of his eyes and made his lips even more of a narrow slash. It was the grimace an accomplice might give to a master criminal after a particularly successful *coup*. But the next moment the face was smooth and impassive enough.

He rose and with a swift, sinuous movement took off his coat. It was stiff and heavy with all the braid. Next he removed the trousers with the broad strip of silver along its sides; and he stood there in a singlet of creamy silk. His boots he had removed earlier; and now he was wearing soft leather slippers. He gathered the clothes and went back to the alcove.

The dead man had been shot through the heart at close quarters. It could not have happened long before for there was still a faint acrid smell of gunpowder in the air and the body showed no sign of stiffness. The tall fair man bent down and swiftly undressed the corpse. He had some difficulty with the trousers and once his hand slipped into a patch of coagulated blood which left a sticky smear on two of his fingers. He wiped them on the shirt of the dead man and continued with his work. In five minutes the corpse was dressed in the uniform of an S.S. General. It was a somewhat tight fit but not too noticeably so. The dead man's clothes were next gathered up and placed carefully on a hanger in the built-in cupboard. The tall fair fellow stepped back and surveyed his handiwork. He appeared to be satisfied. The other man was older and his face was frozen in a singularly unpleasant smirk; he was clean-shaven and a sabre-cut criss-crossed his left cheek. He was wearing a large signet ring on his left index finger; this the other man tried to pull off now but it had grown into the flesh and would not budge. He shrugged—the fire would take care of that, he thought—straightening the corpse, he closed its right hand around a heavy gun and then returned to the dressing-table.

III

"MINES . . . THE SWINE . . . mines against his own people. . . ."

The woman who had tried to lift up the mutilated body of her husband, was repeating these words again and again. A thin-faced man who knelt beside her, said:

"His own? What have we got in common with him? His Excellency Horst von Falkenau, S.S. General, *Gauleiter* of . . ."

"But mines. . . ." The woman could not get rid of the word as if it had been stamped into her brain. "On a battlefield, yes . . . but this. . . ."

"He would use poison-gas if he thought it convenient," the thin, middle-aged man said. "He would let loose man-eating tigers if he had any, just to save his own skin."

"How do you know he is still in there?" asked a second man, whose head was wrapped in a ragged green shawl. He looked as if he had toothache for his face was puckered with pain.

"We have been watching the roads and the railway," the thin-faced fellow replied. "And we had a guard right round the park. He won't get away."

The wounded were being taken back to the village; some of the people had sledges, commonly used to collect brushwood but now with much care they made beds on the narrow slits of wood. The village was only a mile away. But the dead were left there, laid out in the snow. This was no time to stop for burial. The explosion of the mine had scared and shaken them but it had not turned them from their goal. Already half a dozen men had hurried off on a purposeful errand.

These were thin and sickly men and women; the years of war had taken toll of their health and nerves. Death had rained upon them from the sky; death had slunk around their homes, demanding the tribute due to bad and insufficient food, leaking roofs, inadequate clothes. They had suffered long and the price for their blindness and wickedness had been a terrible apathy. There had come a time when they no longer believed in anything—neither in the blatant propaganda dinned into their ears by the high-powered machinery of Dr. Goebbels nor in the words which came to them from outside their borders, from the free world. There had come a time when they feared nothing, for no death, no mutilation could be worse than this kind of life which their leaders had decreed upon them. They were unarmed and they had no leaders; and when the pressure was suddenly removed, when the military defeat of the Reich had become a reality, their reaction was like that of a long-repressed steel spring, suddenly released from unbearable pressure. They wanted revenge; and in most cases they were cheated of it.

But here was one of the men who had been just as much their enemy as he was an enemy of all the enslaved and outraged people outside Germany. For years they had watched his rise to power and riches; the large estate, the house—once the property of a *Reichswehr* General who was caught plotting against Himmler—the shining long-bonneted cars, the hunting stables. . . . All the things they were told to renounce for the Fatherland; all these things this man had in abundance. And when he became *Gauleiter* of this great and one-time prosperous district, his hand lay heavily upon them. He took their sons and their daughters, he made them work long, back-breaking hours on little food; ruthlessly he squashed the least murmur of revolt, the slightest sign of disobedience. The work, the deprivation they did not mind. It promised them victory and then the world would be theirs. There was no turning back, they were all accomplices or comrades, however they looked at it, in this vast and risky business of conquering the universe. To the very last moment they held fast to their faith; and it was the only belief that existed for them, so perfect was their isolation, so total their blindness. But they hated him because they felt that he despised them, that they were less to him than the dirt under his well-polished boots. When he spoke to them, he never repeated the slogans that had been devised to make them feel that Germany and her future was theirs. To him they were the serfs, the helots, the scum of the earth; every sentence a whip, every word a nail; and even the thinly veiled sarcasm burst through occasionally, leaving them furious and yet bewildered.

Others, the lesser fry, let them escape. Much would still be needed to shake their faith in the Fuehrer who had been betrayed by his advisers and subordinates, for the dark myth was already stirring under the earth and only long, patient years could stamp it out. But here was one, this *Gauleiter* of theirs, who belonged to neither category—he could not be dismissed with contempt like a petty crook; nor could he be lifted to the level of martyrs and saints.

They did not tell the soldiers of the conquerors that they knew his hide-out. The occupation was still incomplete; the remnants of *Reichswehr* and *Volksturm* were still being chased towards the last hide-outs. This was a matter they wanted to settle themselves; a personal affair like a duel. And so they came, armed with little more than pitchforks and a few rusty rifles; they came to this clearing in the pine-forest, to surround silently and swiftly the house in which they knew their enemy was trapped.

The little group of men who had disappeared soon after the explosion came into sight again on the right side of the high stone wall that surrounded the park. With sticks and hoarse shouts they were driving half a dozen horses in front of them. Noble, thoroughbred animals, high-stepping, with delicate necks and arched withers. Their breath streamed in the cold air; now and then one of them shook its head and neighed as if in questioning surprise. The men drove them on relentlessly, skirting the wall. They crowded the horses towards the open gate; and when they reached the shattered railings, gave each of them an extra hard blow, reinforced with a sharp thrust by a pointed piece of iron.

The horses reared and plunged forward. One, a bay gelding, got only a few yards ahead when a mine exploded under its hooves. It was lifted up by the explosion and thrown a yard or two where it rolled over on its side. It was not yet dead and it tried to raise its head before the last stream of blood gushed from its chest and it fell back, twitching convulsively.

The other horses, stampeded by the detonation and the fate of their comrade, galloped wildly towards the house. But one by one they set off the mines. One by one they shuddered and fell and were dead; all but the last of them, a black mare with a white star on her forehead. She was only wounded in one leg and in the loins; painfully she tried to lift herself only to fall back again and again; her neigh was accusing, sorrowful and prolonged—until one of the men lifted a rifle and put a bullet through her head from a distance of a hundred yards.

The horses had cut a wide swathe through the hidden minefield, an irregular path which ended almost at the wide stairs. But now another group of men arrived, dragging some muzzled hounds with them that snapped helplessly but furiously at their legs and hands. The dogs, too, were forced through the gap and blows rained upon them until, maddened, they bounded forward the moment they were released. Most of them shared the fate of the horses; more mines were detonated and more gaps cleared across the park. But by a miracle a few of the dogs escaped; they rushed up the terrace, whining and barking, sniffing at the broad oaken door, crying for admittance.

And now a small group of men and women began to advance; slowly, cautiously, testing every inch of the ground with an exploring toe.

A woman cried out suddenly:

"Look!"

Heads jerked up, following her pointing finger. From one of the second-floor windows a thin snake of smoke wriggled into the still air. Then, lower down, an arrow of flame shot out.

"Hold back!" cried a voice at the back of the crowd. "The whole place may be mined . . . and if he has set fire to . . ."

For a moment the mob paused. But then they started to surge forward again, forgetful of the danger. The smoke and the flame were like signals for an advance. It seemed as if the defences of a fortress had crumbled and there were no more barriers. They forgot the explosion at the gate, they forgot the mines set off by the horses and the dogs. Perhaps it was the lust of loot that drove them forward: perhaps they hoped to snatch their intended victim from the fire that was too easy a death for him.

IV

WHEN THE HORSES WERE driven into the park, the man working deftly and quickly at the dressing-table, lifted his head. He rose and stepped to the peephole. His fists clenched as he watched the horses plunging to their death. He had known and loved them all; no one was allowed to ride them beside himself except his well-trusted groom. They had been far closer to him than any human being. But he only stood at the window for a few seconds. He shook his head as if to free himself from the memory of the sight: and even when the black mare neighed out its agony, only a slight flush on his cheek betrayed his emotions. The flush was soon hidden under a thin, skilfully applied layer of paint. He paid no attention to the baying of the hounds, the scattered explosions. Unhurriedly, with every movement purposeful, he continued his work. Under his deft fingers his face was transformed; without changing the main outlines, it became blurred, unimportant, ordinary; a face you would not look at twice, a face that might belong to a small clerk or a dull-witted peasant. The nose now was shapeless, the lips wider, weaker; the chin fatter, rounder. The wig he slipped over his fair hair was a perfect fit; it made his forehead even lower and his ears were now sticking out a little instead of lying close to his head.

All this had been achieved with little touches here and there. The man who was about to disguise himself knew very well that the only effective make-up or mask was the one based on the natural outlines of a face, built upon the existing features; the less difference there was between the original and the "new" face, the better the result. Any startling addition, any serious distortion would only call attention to its owner. As long as it remained nondescript and ordinary, it was a safe face, one that would never stand out in a mass of normal human beings.

It took him less than ten minutes to achieve the desired result; but then, he had practised this often enough. He closed the make-up box and placed it in a wicker basket that stood in the middle of the room. He sprinkled some wood shavings over it and then left the room with a lighted candle in his hand.

All over the house there was a trail of gunpowder and paraffin, of wood shavings and paper spills. He smiled sardonically as he remembered that his companion who sat so stiff and pompous in his resplendent uniform in the dressing-room, had helped him to prepare these. Methodically in every room he touched the candle to the end of the fire-trail and watched the flames spring into life.

Once again he returned to the dressing-room. He discarded his silk underclothes for a torn singlet; he put on a shabby, patched suit with a garish muffler around his neck. He needed no overcoat; his shoes were cracked and tied with string. He had suddenly become stoop-shouldered and seemed to shuffle instead of walking with a resilient, springy gait. A few minutes' practice and he would be perfect in this new bearing. He looked around once more, slipped three small, flat keys into his coat-pocket and then held the candle against the wood shavings on top of the wicker basket.

The sudden burst of flame stabbed at his eyes; he stepped back and almost lost his balance. But he had one more act to perform. He took a small gun from the drawer of the dressing-table and fired a shot. It reverberated loudly in the enclosed space; the bullet buried itself in the woodwork just above the fireplace. He put the gun into his pocket and backed towards the door.

As he reached the first landing on the stairs leading to the basement, he heard the shout of the woman outside—the cry that showed that they had noticed the fire gradually getting a grip inside. He nodded as if to congratulate himself on the perfect timing and hurried down the stairs. A huge kitchen, deserted, cavernous—at the far end a door leading to a scullery and then a series of vaulted cellars. The last one ended in an iron door. He slipped one of his small keys into the almost invisible keyhole, turned it and stepped into the open air.

The cold hit his body a blow through the thin clothing. He stood for a moment flattened against the wall, then he began to run. He caught up with the rear of the crowd which was swarming over the broad stairs of the terrace. The front ranks were already battering at the door. Someone cried out that they needed more space. Four men lifted a huge stone urn from the balustrade and used it as a battering ram.

"Hurry!" a sharp, clear voice rose. "Hurry or we won't catch him!"

At last the door splintered under the onslaught. An almost solid wall of smoke, met the attackers and made them stagger back. But they were so determined and eager that some of them plunged into it, holding handkerchiefs or a coat-sleeve against their mouths. The man who had come from the house was careful to keep in the rear ranks. The light had started to fail; and no one bothered about him. Here on the ground floor the fire had not yet taken a steady hold but the upper stories were already blazing. For a moment the man in the shabby clothes and the garish muffler permitted himself the luxury of a smile. He did not enter the house; and one by one those who had gone in returned into the open, defeated by the heat and the smoke.

"Too good for him," a woman screamed. "An easy death."

Cries of abuse, virulent hate, obscene curses mingled with the crackling of the fire. The man in the muffler joined in the chorus. It gave him a special, perverse pleasure to denounce himself, to shout mad, disjointed words at the house that had been his home for seven years. As if this bawling and roaring completed the destruction of Horst von Falkenau, the man he wanted to kill so that he might be reborn. His own voice surprised him; for a little while he was a detached observer, watching himself and portraying the other, stiff figure, enveloped by the flames, the *corpus delicti*, the proof that Horst von Falkenau was dead.

Gradually the crowd retreated; they stood watching the burning house, giving up any attempts to penetrate the curtain of flames. A feeling of anti-climax seemed to come over them. Their ranks thinned; one by one they slipped away as if they had finished their business. It started to snow and the wet, fat flakes began to douse the fire. But by the time the steam of expiring flames started to rise over the blackened walls and the collapsed roof, there was only a handful of people about. Perhaps they had nowhere to go; perhaps they just wanted to taste their partial revenge to its final dregs.

But the man in the muffler had disappeared long before then.

V

HE KNEW THE WOODS WELL, HE had hunted over them many a time and was familiar with every path and every clearing. There was only about three miles to go and he had a plausible excuse ready should he meet anyone. His destination was a gamekeeper's lodge and he reached it just as the moon rose above the tips of the gaunt firs.

He crept to the back and threw a pebble against the kitchen window which glowed pink with the curtained lamplight. There was a little pause and then the back door of the cottage opened. The light cut a broad swathe into the darkness; he had drawn aside but the figure of a woman, tall, splendidly feminine with big breasts and broad hips, was clearly outlined in the brightness.

"You are late," she said. "You . . ."

She stifled a scream as he stepped forward.

"Who . . ." she began but he silenced her with a quick gesture.

"You don't recognise me?" he laughed. "Perfect. You ought to be the best judge, Anna, whether I have changed sufficiently to fool them all. Where is Karl?"

"He is gone to town, trying to barter a hare for some sugar. But he might be back any moment and . . ."

"I won't stay long. Is everything ready?"

"It has been ready for three days. Why did you wait so long?"

"That fool Kemmerich only turned up last night. And I needed him."

"Is he . . . is he . . ." She faltered over the last word.

"Yes, he is dead. With a fine funeral pyre. Did you see the fire?"

"Only the distant glow. I wondered. . . ."

"Come on." He touched her arm and immediately she clung to him. Her softness, the rounded warmth of her body was not flabby nor shapeless; a big woman, she had the grace and well-proportioned beauty of Greek statues. Yet her skin was rough to his touch and her eyes deep-set and burning, as if she had not slept for a long time.

For a moment he held her in his arms, delighting in her closeness and her firm flesh. Then he freed himself.

"I must go, Anna. There is no time to waste."

He led the way to the barn just behind the lodge. It was empty. He pushed at a section of the partition in the back and it swung clear, revealing a considerable space behind it.

"Karl still doesn't know?" he asked.

"No. He has never been in here since he came back."

"Good." He switched on a torch. Inside the partitioned space there was a car. It looked shabby and battered; but its engine had been tuned regularly every fortnight or so; in the back there were ten cans of petrol. It could do a hundred and twenty kilometres flat out; and the tyres, though coated with dust, were brand-new. He had planned this ever since the day of the Allied landing in Normandy; and he congratulated himself once again upon his foresight. Evidently Anna, too, was going to be sensible; though it would make no difference however she behaved.

But no, he was wrong; for after all, she was a woman. As he bent over the open hood, he heard her say:

"Horst . . . please, take me with you."

He replied, without looking at her:

"We have been over this a dozen times, Anna. I can't. I'll send for you at the earliest possible moment."

She did not move; but her voice was violent even in its low pitch:

"You won't send for me, I know. But if you took me . . . I could help you. Anything you wanted. . . . Please, Horst . . . don't leave me here. I can't stand it. A half-crippled husband . . . the hunger and the cold . . . all that is coming. Why can't I be with you? Why . . ."

He straightened now and turned to face her.

"You know, Anna," he said reflectively, "this is quite the longest speech I have ever heard you make. But it doesn't change anything. We would never get through. I would only throw away my life for the sake of the few hours or days we could spend together."

He closed the hood and slipped behind the wheel.

"Let me get through," he called to her for she was blocking the way. She did not step aside. He switched on the ignition and turned the wheel. Gently, cautiously the car moved forward. Only when the front fenders almost touched her, did she move back. He drove across the barn, into the open. There he switched off the engine and waited. Slowly she emerged from the dim interior, her shoulders bowed, her somewhat heavy face frozen in agony. He got out, a little stiffly, and went to meet her.

"It's all over," she whispered.

"Nonsense," he said. When he kissed her, he felt the tears upon her warm, generous lips. She was rigid for a moment, then she clung to him, her mouth close to his ear.

"Good-bye, Horst," she said softly, almost with resignation.

"Good-bye, Anna," he said. A moment ago he had slipped the gun from his pocket and now he had pressed it against her left breast. Before she had even time to look down at the alien hardness close to her heart, he fired. The recoil of the gun, however slight, gave him a distinct blow. For a fraction of a moment Anna was still erect in his arms, then she went limp and he laid her down in the sandy ground of the courtyard. A single wave of blood welled up from her body, staining her dress and spreading in an irregular shape; her eyes were open and her lips trembled a little. But when he bent down to her, she was already dead.

He looked at his own clothing to see whether it had become soiled. But there was no trace of blood. He hesitated whether he should close her eyes; they were so wide open, so obviously staring. But he decided against it. He got into the car, backed a few yards and then drove from the courtyard, through the lodge-gates, across the clearing and on to the narrow secondary road that led to the *Autobahn*.

VI

BEFORE HE REACHED THE highroad, he stopped the car under some overhanging trees. It was getting dark and he almost fell over a jutting root. He opened the near-side back door and fumbled for the parcel. It was there where he had put it more than six weeks ago. One pull and the knot loosened. He switched on his torch and placed it so that its beam could not be seen outside the car. Without hurry he stripped again to his skin. It was cold and he shivered; but in five minutes he was dressed again: decent underwear, dark shoes, grey socks, a blue suit, double-breasted, a discreet tie. The labels were all correct—and a London tailor, not from Savile Row, but still, a good name. He felt his inside coat-pockets; yes, the papers were there. He gathered his cast-off clothes into a bundle, wrapped them in the paper and string that had held the new things—it was marvellous how little the suit had creased—and walked a hundred yards into the undergrowth until he found a hollow. He wrenched off a rotten branch and dug a small hole in the snow. In went the parcel and he shovelled snow over it until it was well covered.

Shading the torch with his hands he made his way back to the car. There was a thick, dark overcoat in the back; he slipped it on and nodded when he found the fur-lined gloves. He reached across the wheel to find a small button on the dashboard which he pressed. He went back to the rear of the car and flashed his torchlight briefly upon the number-plates; yes, the little gadget worked well enough. A *Corps Diplomatique* "CD" had appeared on the left and the original number was covered by a different, low-figure one.

He waved his arms and stamped his feet to get warm before he re-entered the car. For a moment he felt a strong craving for a cigarette, but he resisted it; you could not tell who might be around in these woods and it would be a little awkward to explain what he was doing here—though not beyond his talents, oh certainly not, he reassured himself.

Ten minutes' drive brought him to the *Autobahn.* Its broad white surface gleamed in front of him, endless, hypnotising, almost vocal with its temptation of smooth, endless speed. He increased his own, however, gradually; and when the sweet even song of the engine rose to a crescendo, he lowered the window at his side and felt the ice-cold night air rushing in. A bowler hat, correct and stiff, was on the seat beside him; at the same time as he had removed his shabby clothes, he had also taken off his wig and he felt tiny drops of ice coagulating on his hair.

The *Autobahn* was practically deserted. Once or twice cars flashed by going in the opposite direction, but the breadth of the road was so great that he hardly noticed them. A swift and triumphant exultation rose in him; he laughed and sang as his foot pressed closer and closer to the floor of the car and he felt the wheel answering to his fingertips. This was what he had always wanted: the intoxication of speed, unshared with anyone, the night and the sense of power. If he could have driven on to the end of his life, with just this comfort and this sense of might, it would have been perfect heaven. The complications and difficulties, the stupidities and resistances always arose during the stops when the engine had been silenced, when he had to mingle with others, when he had to pretend and compromise, accept authority and distribute benevolence. Nothing could harm him while he was rushing on, almost winged. Nothing could stop him except his own will.

He was timelessly happy, conscious of his own strength, his own well-disciplined, perfectly co-ordinated body; its muscular leanness, its potential, murderous strength. He had slept little in the last three days, but the wind and the night had swept the last vestige of weariness from his eyes, his brain. Fleetingly he thought that it could not last for ever, that the night would end and he would have to meet people again, carry on the comedy though in a different key, on a different plane from in the years before; but at the moment, with the song of the rushing air still in his ears, morning seemed to be far away. And indeed, it would be many hours before dawn came.

For a few seconds the image of Anna was projected upon the screen of his mind. He saw her, not dead and staring on the sandy, snow-covered ground of the courtyard; he saw her against a summer landscape, Ceres or Freya herself with her heavy corn-blonde hair in heavy braids around her head. It was a pleasant picture and one which he wished to retain. He did not think of her death; he had no regrets and he had long forgotten the uneasiness of cowards' miscalled conscience. It was so natural, so self-evident to him that he had had to kill her; he did not pause to question the deed, to analyse its preliminaries or consequences. Consequences? That fool of a husband would return and find her there. What could he do? Half a cripple; and the woods full of deserters, riff-raff not yet rounded up, hiding from everybody and their own terrors. Perhaps Karl would rush to the *Gauleiter's* house, only to find that it had become a burnt-out shell. Perhaps he would just hold a lonely wake; he had loved Anna in his fashion, which was a fool's and a weakling's way.

He who drove now through the night had decided to kill her when he had entrusted her with the secret of the car and all the other preparations for his escape. It was regrettable that he had had to trust her; the killing had followed as a natural consequence. Too much was at stake to think about one woman, or even a haremful of them; too much for himself and for the work that awaited him and the others. He liked to think that he had foreseen every eventuality and provided for any chance or accident. Many a time he had been complimented on his perfect foresight, on his superb command of details which never prevented him from seeing the vast entity of a plan. Well, the supreme emergency had come and it had not found him unprepared.

He cocked an ear to listen to the smooth purr of the car and was satisfied. If he could have found a different way, he would not have killed Anna. It was, in a way, a pity to kill her; for she had more life in her than half a dozen of those city women whom he had met in the drawing-rooms, at the balls and receptions to which he went because they, too, were his battle-grounds. She had a splendid vitality; a gamekeeper's wife, just think!—but then she was scrupulous about her own appearance and personal cleanliness. A woman in a million, he thought, forgetting for a moment that she was dead. But once he had decided that trusting her with the car and the rest was the easiest, most efficient way to make his getaway—he had also signed her death warrant in his mind and never given it a second thought.

He glanced at his wrist-watch—bearing the name of a Prague maker—and saw that it was half-past one. Then he braked hard; half a mile ahead there was a road-bridge crossing the *Autobahn* and red lamps glowed along the lower part of the balustrade. Someone, to make sure, was waving a red lantern, signalling him to stop.

He drew up at the exact point where two motor-cycles were barring the road. He saw the armbands over the riders' leather jackets; he lowered the window and heard a deep, drawling voice say:

"Military police. Your papers please."

He reached into his coat-pocket and handed over a small bundle to the man who had spoken. The military policeman pushed back his goggles. His face was young and puckered with responsibility; like a child playing at "coppers."

"*Herr* Reznicek?" he repeated, looking at the identity card and comparing the photograph with the face dimly outlined above the steering-wheel. His German was heavily accented as he asked:

"What is your destination?"

"Leipzig," replied Horst von Falkenau. He rather welcomed this encounter; it was the first test and he was quite confident of its outcome. "Then on to Cologne."

"You are travelling all the way by car?" asked the military policeman.

"No . . . only as far as Leipzig. I hope to get a plane from there. As you see, my papers are made out for any mode of travel I wish to choose."

Had he been a little too high-handed? You never knew with these Yanks. Perhaps he'd better add something.

He did so, in English:

"I have rather urgent business with the Control Commission for the Southern Zone. About the repatriation of some of my countrymen. Then I'll have to go on to France."

The American tapped the passport against one open hand.

"We are only checking up along this stretch of road," he said, also in English. "How long have you been driving on it?"

"About three hours. I started from Berlin shortly after eleven."

"You haven't been stopped before?"

"No, you are the first patrol I have met along this road."

"And you haven't noticed anything . . . unusual?"

He laughed—this man was evidently fishing for some information which did not concern "*Herr* Reznicek."

"No . . . why? Should I have noticed anything?"

The American bent closer. He had a broad face, pink with cold; Horst noticed one gold tooth as he smiled, a little embarrassed.

"There was just a chance. . . . You see, we're looking for a Nazi. One of the S.S. bigwigs. Had a tip he might have got hold of a car and be making for the south. Course, our radio-cars are patrolling the *Autobahn*—but he might have slipped off to one of the secondary roads and re-entered it again. If you had noticed anything, I suppose . . ."

"Naturally I would tell you. The vermin must be exterminated . . . the sooner, the better."

He reached out his gloved hand for the papers with such a natural, unhurried gesture that the military policeman gave them to him without any hesitation.

"Well, I hope you catch him," von Falkenau said. "Good night, sergeant."

"Good night, Mr. Reznicek," came the reply and the car shot forward. The barrier a few yards further down was open and he drove through, accelerating a little. He was elated over the first victory he had won, but at the same time a little worried. He cast his mind back, trying to decide whether he had left any trail behind—whether something had gone wrong with the fire he had arranged so carefully—whether, by some chance, it could be for himself that the hue and cry had been started. But resolutely he suppressed this line of thought. It would never do, he told himself, if he analysed everything, if he tried to see danger in every inflexion, every gesture. The guiltiest man can get away, he argued, if he keeps up the smooth and natural mask of innocence; nay, if he even persuades himself of his innocence. Or at least that he is doing the right thing. And about that Horst never had the slightest doubt.

Soon the small cluster of lights was left behind him and again he was alone with the broad ribbon of the road, the snow and the wind. He cut down speed; it would be much better if he reached Leipzig in the small hours of the morning. Then another quick change and a visit to the post office. After that he should be safe enough.

Snow started to fall again, thickening and whirling. He set the windscreen wiper in motion but it could not quite keep up with the swift flurries. He had to slow down but he did not mind this slight delay. There was plenty of time. He lit a cigarette and inhaled deeply. It was pleasant to relax.

Suddenly like a monster, a nightmarish creature emerging from the dark, something huge and evil appeared in front of him. Headlights blinded him—it seemed that the car, travelling on the wrong side of the road and at considerable speed, would crash head-on into his. With a half-unconscious effort he wrenched at the wheel, feeling the car jump under him and go into what felt almost like a spin. The next second the impact jolted him against the steering-wheel. For a moment his face was very close to the windscreen and he watched it splinter. Something hit him a tremendous body-blow; and he lost consciousness.

He could not have been knocked out for more than a minute or so. When he opened his eyes, he found himself tilted against the steering-wheel; something hot was trickling into his eyes. He reached up and held his hand under the faint dashboard light: it was blood. He tried to move and discovered that his limbs were unbroken though he felt bruised all over. He kicked the door open and half-stepped, half-fell into the road. He picked himself up gingerly. His headlights were still on. In that last second he had managed to turn the car towards the high bank along the side of the *Autobahn*; actually one of the wheels had started to climb it. If he had not had so much presence of mind, he would be dead now, he thought, and sickening rage filled his whole being. That clumsy, criminal idiot . . . driving at such speed in the midst of a snow-storm . . . and on the wrong side of the road when the *Autobahn* was broad enough and . . .

But he stopped suddenly. He seemed to remember . . . in that second before he lost consciousness and as the other car flashed by. . . . Weren't there several cars? As if in pursuit of the first. . . . He remembered hazily the American military policeman's words: ". . . he might have got hold of a car and be making for the south. . . ." Who except a madman or someone flying for his life would drive at such breakneck speed?

He shrugged, suddenly calmer though a little groggy. It would be just as well to inspect the damage. Perhaps his luck held; perhaps it was all superficial.

The snow had stopped now but it was very cold. He felt the blood coagulating and almost freezing upon his forehead. He found his torch and bent down to inspect himself in the driving-mirror. It was only a small cut though it had bled profusely. He moistened a handkerchief in the snow and dabbed at it. The cold stung his skin like nettles. He formed the handkerchief into a wad and tied his white silken scarf over it. "The hero home from the wars," he murmured with a twisted smile. He dusted his coat and straightened his tie. Now for the car.

A little effort and all the four wheels were back again on the road. He opened the door and got back into the driver's seat. He switched on the engine. There seemed to be nothing wrong with it. But when he put his hands on the steering-wheel, it would not obey his fingers. It was loose, flabby like a spineless animal. He let out the clutch and eased the car forward cautiously. Immediately it went into a skid. He narrowly avoided crashing into the bank again. He stopped with the car turned half round. He got out again and spent a long time on his hands and knees trying to locate the damage. There was no doubt about it: the steering had gone hopelessly wrong. Perhaps the shaft was broken; perhaps even one of the axles was affected. He had some tools in the box; but they were hopelessly inadequate for such a job.

A sudden wave of fury took hold of him. He cursed the clumsy fool, fleeing from his enemies, who had brought this disaster upon him. He hoped that the other man would be caught, that he would die a messy death. How did he dare to endanger his, Horst von Falkenau's escape, to upset his plans? Whoever he was, he could not be of the same importance as the *Gauleiter* of . . .

He had planned everything, he had foreseen every eventuality. The trail was prepared for him across half Europe. He had committed two murders to make it fool-proof. And now here he was, in the middle of nowhere, helpless and baulked because a madman. . . .

He shook himself and forced his thoughts into some sort of order. Walk to the nearest town? As far as he could remember it was at least ten miles away. He had a couple of suit-cases he could not abandon; and looters were everywhere in these chaotic days. And in any case, if the car was closely examined . . . those double number-plates . . .

There was only one thing to do. He removed the suit-cases, noticing at the same time that his blameless bowler was badly crushed, prised open two of the petrol cans and poured their contents over the bonnet, the seats, the roof. He retrieved his maps and the torch; then he lit a match and dropped it over the well-soaked upholstery.

A flame sprang up and he retreated to the far side of the road. In a few moments the whole car was blazing, a fantastic bonfire against the whiteness of the snow and the black trees of the embankment. The heat was so intense that he had to move back a few yards and even so it seemed to singe his eyebrows. He watched the fire with a queer intensity. He had always liked fires. This was a very pretty blaze. And it would also serve as a beacon. Anybody who passed here was bound to stop—and he would get a lift.

VII

HE DID NOT HAVE TO WAIT VERY long. Less than ten minutes had passed when at the bend, a few hundred yards from where he stood, headlights swept the snow with their dipped beams. He could not make out what sort of a car it was; but he stepped forward again—the blaze was much less intense—and waved his hand. With screeching brakes the car slid to a stop.

Horst von Falkenau walked up to the window on the driver's side. It was half open and when he glanced down he stiffened. A gloved hand was holding a gun and the gun was pointed at him.

"I beg your pardon," he said in German. "I have had an accident."

A man's voice replied; a deep, pleasant voice. It spoke German with a strong accent but he sounded fluent enough:

"Your papers. And keep the other hand up."

"But I assure you . . ."

"No tricks, mind you. I want to see your papers."

Horst laughed and then handed over the required documents. The man—he could still not make out his face—switched on the small roof light. He was in uniform. An American and an officer, von Falkenau told himself. This was good luck indeed. Then he noticed that there was a second person in the car—a woman.

The man at the wheel screened her almost completely from sight, but Horst could just make out the curve of a cheek, tender and slightly flushed by cold, and smooth brown hair under a peaked cap. Was the hair brown? He could not be sure. His mind wandered, preoccupied with this ridiculous problem, when he heard the other man's voice.

"I am sorry, *Herr* Reznicek. I see that you are a member of the Czech Control Commission. Your papers seem to be in order. What can I do for you?"

"Can I lower my hands now?" asked von Falkenau with a fleeting smile. "It is a rather uncomfortable pose. . . ."

"But of course. You will understand that one must be careful. There are still quite a few Nazis whom we haven't rounded up."

"I know," said the other man wryly. "That's the cause of my accident."

The woman spoke now—for the first time. And her voice was such a complete surprise that Horst's head jerked involuntarily. It was a husky voice, young yet with a somewhat harsh quality. It had a trace of . . . what? Tears? Bitterness? Some recent grief? It was tantalising—like a deferred pleasure, pain mixed with sudden relief. It was so unlike Anna's whose broad, drawling Bavarian he had always disliked, so unlike any other woman's. She must be beautiful, he decided, though he could still see very little of her.

"Peter," the woman said, "I am getting cold. Can't you drive on?"

"But we can't just . . ." A little acidity crept into the man's voice.

"I am sorry to incommode you—I—I am afraid I don't know your name though you know mine," said Horst, leaving his sentence dangling in the air.

"Captain Whitney," the driver replied. He made no move to introduce his companion. "You said just now that you have had an accident?"

"Yes. My car was struck and set on fire by one coming from the opposite direction, on the wrong side of the road. I think it must have been someone fleeing. I was told a few miles further down by a military policeman that they were searching the neighbourhood for some Nazi criminal."

"They have caught him," smiled the American. "He is dead. Saves a lot of trouble—a costly trial and all that." He added, a little wistfully: "You don't speak English by any chance, do you?"

"I am afraid I don't," replied Horst without a moment's hesitation. "French, if you prefer it."

"Good God, my French is even worse than my German . . . isn't it, Helen?" But the woman did not speak. She had now leant back so that nothing of her could be seen except a gloved hand playing nervously with a large, shiny handbag.

"In any case, my car was destroyed," continued von Falkenau. "I managed to save my suit-cases and I wondered whether you could possibly give me a lift to the nearest town."

The American was silent for a moment. Then he said:

"Yes, of course. Hop right in. There is space for your suit-cases in the back."

A minute later they were on their way again. The car

was a spacious station waggon with plenty of room. Horst selected the seat behind the woman called Helen. Whitney had put out the light and the car was dark once more. For a mile or so none of them spoke. Then the American asked:

"Where were you bound for when this accident happened?"

"Leipzig . . . then on to Cologne."

"You are in luck, *Herr* Reznicek," Whitney laughed. "We are going to Leipzig and can give you a lift that far, if you wish it."

"That would be very kind."

Silence again. It had been easier than he thought. These Yankees were simple people—though of course, his papers had been prepared by one of the most skilful experts of the S.S. forgery centre. But even so—it might have been a non-military car that passed first—not that there were many on the roads—and someone more suspicious might not have bothered to stop at all. These two intrigued him—an American officer and a woman—what nationality was she? Her accent had not sounded American. But he could not be sure. A shrewd move, he patted himself on the back, to have denied any knowledge of English. These two would sooner or later start to speak their mother language—perhaps the girl did not know any German—and give him some useful information.

But as the miles flashed by, those in the front seats remained disappointingly silent.

Once Whitney half-turned and said:

"Cigarette?"

"Thank you."

He took one from the flat case offered to him. As he lit a match, the tiny flame flickered in his cupped hands and he held it a few seconds longer than necessary. But no, she was looking straight ahead and he saw no more of her than her hair. It was brown, he decided now; a warm, natural, rich brown like a squirrel's summer coat.

He tried to make conversation.

"Do you like driving at night?" he asked.

"I don't mind," replied the American. "Remarkable, how quickly they repaired the roads, isn't it?"

He assented politely and the conversation lagged again. With annoyance he thought that after all his stratagem had been a failure when he heard the girl's husky voice, very low, barely audible:

"No, Peter. Stop it."

"O.K., Snow Maiden," whispered the man. "I do declare that you are the most unreasonable creature I have ever met."

"Please, Peter. Let's not start it again. Especially not in front of a stranger."

"He doesn't know English . . . you heard him saying so yourself."

"How do you know that he has spoken the truth?"

"Great Scott, Helen, you are suspicious of everyone. His papers were in order. And why should he lie?"

"I don't know. I just thought . . . oh, perhaps I am just tired and cross. Not nice to talk to."

"*Very* nice to talk to. Any time."

"There you go again!"

"Is it a crime to . . ."

But now the unexpected happened. She turned her head slightly—Horst cursed the darkness—and spoke to him:

"Are you staying at one of the hotels in Leipzig, *Herr* Reznicek?"

Her German was much better than the American's, though her construction of the sentence was a little stilted.

"I had a room reserved at the Astoria," he replied quickly. "I hope they'll keep it for me—it's rather difficult these days."

He wanted to add the question: "Where are you staying?" but thought better of it. However, she volunteered the information herself, but first she asked:

"That's the big one in the Blücherplatz, isn't it?"

"Yes. Do you know Leipzig well?"

"I stayed there once for a fortnight. There was quite a nice golf course at Gaschwitz. Do you play golf?"

The stupidity of these Anglo-Saxons, he thought. How should a Czech be interested in golf? A crazy game, hitting a small ball and walking miles to follow it.

"I am afraid I don't," he replied.

"We are staying at the Kaiserhof," she said. "Perhaps we'll see you."

This sounded like an invitation. What was she up to? He heard the American growl:

"Don't carry the United Nations business too far, my dear."

But Horst von Falkenau was not worried about this last

remark. In that brief dialogue there had been plenty of food for thought. "We," she had said. Was she the American's wife? His mistress? His fiancée? If he could only see her face. . . .

There was a long, silent period again. They were approaching Leipzig now; soon they would turn off the *Autobahn* into one of the trunk-roads leading into the suburbs. Horst relaxed. Everything had gone well. He was almost glad that he had lost the car. Those number-plates. . . . He ran through the programme again. Register at the Astoria, take a bath, refresh his "mask," have some food and a few hours' sleep; then have his luggage taken to the railway station's cloakroom. He mustn't go to the Frankfurterstrasse before dusk. The house between the two pastry-shops. The double knock. How silly it sounded, all this melodramatic spy story stuff! But then, the people whom he needed were still adolescents. Werewolves indeed! His lips curled in a sneer. It was all very well for the rank and file; playing cowboys and Indians, existing on the food of cheap myths, the drink of the legend of blood. But those who had to survive because their survival meant the coming of the much better organised, a thousand times better planned, new Newest Order—they disdained the childish masquerades, passwords and isolated acts of despair. To kill a few Yanks in ambush, to string up a burgomaster who was willing to serve the Allies, to cut a few telephone lines or booby-trap a dozen jeeps—what did it all matter? Perhaps it helped to let off steam; but the real work, for the time being, was to be done outside the Reich. That was why he and the chosen few had to get out—quickly, safely. They would come back . . . oh yes, they would! And he smiled again as he thought of the men and women who had driven *his* horses and *his* dogs across the mined park. They would pay for it, they would pay for everything. His smile was an ugly thing and not fit to be seen by anyone. But it gave him satisfaction to grin behind these two representatives of the victorious Allies—this girl and this man, enclosed in some private hell of their own, quarrelling evidently and both unhappy. Why? Perhaps she did not want to sleep with the American or perhaps the American had hurt her in some way. . . .

He wished he could see her face.

VIII

WHEN THE CAR STOPPED IN front of the Astoria, the girl did not get out. Of course there was still no street-lighting; the city had had a terrible battering from the air and the brief street-fighting had done additional damage. But the hotel was standing and as Captain Whitney tooted his horn, two old men came shambling out.

Horst von Falkenau shrugged and lifted his suit-cases on to the pavement.

"Thank you very much," he said. "It was most kind of you to give me this lift."

"Glad to," said the American briefly. They shook hands. Horst waited for a second or so to give the girl an opportunity to speak but she remained silent. He bowed in her general direction and then called out to the two decrepit porters to take his bags. Though he guarded his voice, it sharpened unconsciously; once again he was a man, well used to command, speaking to the scum who had to jump at his behest. But the two old men could no longer jump at anybody's behest; and as Horst followed them into the hotel, he saw the American car make a U-turn round a large heap of rubble. For a moment he caught a glimpse of the girl's profile, but it was too brief a moment, too fleeting a glance. Tantalised, he entered the hotel hall.

There was something about the receptionist which made Horst guess that he had not so long ago removed the swastika from his buttonhole; but then, the purge was only a few weeks' old and not terribly thorough. Probably the man—elderly with a frozen smirk on his narrow face—had worked for the Gestapo as hotel porters, receptionists, bellboys and chambermaids have done all over the Reich, all over Europe where it was necessary. Certainly he was obsequious enough.

"*Herr* Reznicek? Yes, we have received the telegram. On the second floor. I regret to say that at the moment we have no running water in the rooms—but you will find three bathrooms on the same corridor. And no electricity—but perhaps an oil-lamp will do. Thank you, *Herr* Reznicek. If you would sign here, please. I'll send up the luggage immediately."

He had to walk upstairs—of course the lifts weren't working—and he amused himself by remembering the last time he had been at the Astoria. Fat Schlesemann of the Gestapo was there, after one of his periodical generals—Schlesemann specialised in shortening the lives of *Reichswehr* bigwigs—Hinkel of the Foreign Office and that *Luftwaffe* colonel—what was his name? He could not remember. They had a very good time. The three girls from the *Schauspielhaus*—Hinkel's tastes lay in a different direction—and a good deal of French champagne. . . . Yes, it had been a welcome escape from all the stupid administrative worries of his *Gau*. He had chosen the Astoria deliberately in order to test his new "character" but until now he had not noticed a single member of the old staff. True, his last visit had been over a year ago and people died, were sent to concentration camps or killed in air raids . . . a year made a lot of difference. Why, look at their own little party! Schlesemann, he heard, had been slaughtered by half a dozen escaped Russian prisoners of war—the silly fat fool would insist on visiting Buchenwald for a little private entertainment—Hinkel had committed suicide, and the *Luftwaffe* colonel—now he remembered his name, such a nice chap, Otto Wittenberger—had been shot down and killed in East Prussia. Only he was alive of the four—but that was as it should be.

The water was lukewarm and the bath-tub chipped; after the marble pool he had had installed in the *Gauleiter's* residence, it was certainly a sordid experience. But he had brought a few cakes of his Yardley soap and enjoyed a good long soak which took the cold and stiffness out of his joints. He watched his body in the soapy water with satisfaction; not an ounce of superfluous fat, none of those bulging muscles some of his friends had developed; he was still good for another twenty-five years of reasonable virility. As he soaped his back and felt the water gradually growing chilly, he decided that he wanted a woman—the sooner the better. Irritatingly he heard the girl's voice as she spoke in the dark car. "There was quite a nice golf course at Gaschwitz . . ." Bah! Probably a silly English goose with protruding teeth and a complexion like a chipped brick. If only he had seen her face. . . .

He returned to his room and spent fifteen minutes with a small flat box that fitted into the bottom of his smaller suit-case. Then he was ready once again to face the world. He rang down to the reception desk. Could they serve a meal in his room? Well . . . anything would do. What? Potato-soup, a sausage and a rhubarb-tart? Well, if they could not do better for an Allied diplomat. Oh, they had a bottle of wine? All right, but it must be in ten minutes.

The waiter served his meal silently but rather clumsily. Horst gave him a sharp glance.

"Are you new here?"

"Yes, sir," the man—youngish, with a nondescript face and shifty eyes—replied in a heavy Bavarian accent.

"Have you been a waiter long?"

"No . . . not very long."

"In the army?"

The waiter mumbled something indistinct and busied himself with the soiled dishes. Horst finished the tasteless meal in silence. But the wine was good, surprisingly smooth. It sent a glow through his chilled body. He felt in a genial mood.

The waiter put everything on his trolley and asked:

"Will that be everything, sir?"

"Yes."

The man turned in evident relief towards the door. But he was only half-way when Horst called out in a sharp commanding tone:

"*Staffel, halt!*"

The waiter froze in his tracks. His back was poker-stiff; the napkin in his hand, pressed against the seam of his shiny, frayed trousers, seemed a white flag of surrender.

Von Falkenau spoke softly:

"So you were in the S.S., my friend?"

The other man swung round and almost fell on his knees. His whole attitude was one of supplication, of desperate entreaty:

"*Mein Herr*, you wouldn't . . . you won't tell them. . . ."

"Why are you so afraid?" Horst asked while he lit a cigarette and crossed his legs. "There were plenty of S.S. men who have nothing to fear. . . ."

"I have been in hiding for three weeks," the waiter said, his words tumbling over each other in desperate haste. "I—I lost my nerve. I was in the *Spezialdienst* . . . and even the other S.S. men hate us. If I were found . . ."

"Hm—the *Spezialdienst* . . ." Horst mused. He knew the

Special Service well enough. Thugs, every one of them, the executioners of the party. The *élite* of hangmen. A very useful body; but now it must be rather embarrassing to have belonged to it.

Aloud he said:

"I won't give you away . . . it's none of my business. But you'd better watch yourself. Your nerves are all shot to pieces. If you want to survive, you must be calm."

The former S.S. man raised his eyes for the first time and gave him a quick, suspicious look:

"Why do you say that?" He had dropped the "sir" and there was something menacing in his voice.

Horst pulled on his cigarette and smiled: "You shouldn't stop and stand at attention if someone calls out: '*Staffel, halt.*' And you should have an answer ready to every question."

"You . . . you really won't give me away?" asked the man, relapsing into humility.

"Why should I? I am concerned with getting food for my people, not with prosecuting war criminals. I haven't time to waste on such foolish errands."

The waiter came closer and said in a whisper:

"You . . you aren't one of us, by any chance?"

Horst stared at him.

"Why—whatever do you mean? You must have found out my name and nationality; I bet you looked at the register downstairs."

"I—I am sorry, sir," mumbled the other. "I have made a mistake."

"I should say you have. And you'd better watch your tongue—or I might change my mind."

When the waiter had left he undressed and got into bed. His last thought before falling asleep was that if he needed someone for any dirty job, the S.S. man was a likely subject for a little blackmail.

He slept for six hours and woke refreshed and alert. He lit the oil-lamp at the side of the bed and lay for a few minutes staring at the ceiling. In twelve hours he would be on his way again, *Herr* Reznicek safely buried and a new identity covering his remains. He had taken every precaution and his tracks had been obliterated. The loss of the car was a nuisance but with the new set of papers awaiting him in the Frankfurterstrasse he could easily get transportation. And once he was across the French frontier . . . no, he would still have good reason for watchfulness, but much less cause for anxiety. Not that he was particularly anxious; he was quite certain that no harm could come to Horst von Falkenau, that nothing and no one could hurt him as long as he was sure of himself.

He rang down to the desk and was informed that breakfast was not served outside the dining-room. He dressed and packed; then he descended to an abominable breakfast of *ersatz* coffee, black bread and an infinitesimal blob of margarine.

He paid his bill and asked whether his luggage could be taken to the station. The first trains had started to run a week ago, so much he knew; but he would have to get his travel pass first from the Control Office in the Town Hall. One of the ancient porters appeared with a wheelbarrow, almost as decrepit as its human appendage; Horst told him to watch the suit-cases all the time, promising him a good tip. Then he set out for the Town Hall.

IX

ONE OF THE PASTRY-SHOPS WAS gone, a fire-bomb had gutted it and only the charred shopsign, leaning at a crazy angle across the front showed what it had been. But between it and the next *Kaffeestube* the narrow-fronted, high-gabled brick house stood untouched. Its front door was locked, its windows blind with cardboard in the place of the long since splintered glass.

Horst von Falkenau looked round. The street was deserted; the curfew hour long past, the sheep-like civilians kept indoors. How his countrymen loved to obey regulations —except, of course, when their stomachs were concerned for then they broke them cheerfully and often efficiently! He knocked twice with a short interval between the knocks and waited.

The big city was silent, licking its wounds, bleak and without hope. A few hundred yards from where he stood millions of books had been burned—this time not by the S.A. men and without singing. Well, perhaps it was all to the good. When they came back, they would need no books. The Germany he and his fellow-plotters wanted would need only steel and blood. Gutenberg had been a German but he must have been one of those degenerates of mixed, foreign blood; and Horst disapproved of his invention wholeheartedly. What did it give the world, this spate of printed matter? Dangerous thoughts and ideas for most people above their proper station.

He repeated the signal; and he heard soft, shuffling steps approaching the door from the other side. He wished he knew more about this "refuelling station" or "Post Office" as it was called in the underground parlance. But it was Kemmerich who had made the arrangements, and Kemmerich had not a very long time to live after he arrived at the *Gauleiter's* house. Kemmerich, the smart, the faithful! Kemmerich who was convinced that they would travel the underground route together! Well, he had had a fine funeral pyre, one of Germany's historic mansions going up in flames with his flabby, paunchy body. . . .

The door opened and Horst faced an indistinct shape. It must be a woman, he felt instinctively and her voice, frightened and hurried, told him his guess was right.

"What do you want?" she asked.

Instead of a reply he pushed past her, drew her back into the narrow hall and closed the door behind them. He saw in the dim light coming from a door on the right that it was a young girl, bundled in a shawl, her white puffy face seemingly floating disembodied above the dark covering. Her eyes were dull, her hair lank and lifeless. God, they have put an idiot in charge, he told himself in irritation.

"What do you want?" she repeated.

"Kemmerich sent me," he said, "Show me the safe."

She stared at him and did not speak.

"Can't you understand German, you fool?" he snarled at her. "Kemmerich. The safe."

She still remained silent.

He shook her so that her teeth rattled. But she was like a limp rag in his hands and when he let go, she folded up at his feet. Resisting an impulse to kick her, he stepped into the room on the right. It was a shabby, disorderly room, crowded with cheap and ugly furniture and dominated by a large four-poster bed in the corner farthest from the boarded-up window.

Three candles were burning on the table which also bore the remains of a meal—a small piece of bread, some potatoes, a jug of water and a slice of sausage. He heard the soft whimpering of the girl behind him but paid no attention to her. The bed was occupied by a tall gaunt woman. Her jaw was tied with a white cloth, her hands were crossed on her breast and two small coins were placed upon her eyelids. She was dead; he had no need to step closer or examine her to know that.

He turned and saw the girl in the doorway, saw her open her mouth as if to scream. In a flash he was upon her, clapping his hand over her mouth. Her body trembled uncontrollably; he lowered her into a chair, and standing close to smother any outcry if necessary he asked:

"Who is she?"

"M-my mother," stammered the girl. Though her face was swollen, her body was very thin and her wrists like a small child's.

"When did she die?"

The girl burst into tears; heavy, racking sobs shook her narrow shoulders.

"Two men . . ." she said, swallowing hard. "Two men came yesterday. They—they killed her. . . ."

"Two men?" Horst's mind raced ahead of his tongue. "What sort of men?"

The girl shook her head.

"I don't know. I was out . . . queueing for water. When I came back, I found her on the floor. She spoke a few words —about the men and what they wanted . . . then she died. I—I can't bury her. What shall I do? What shall I do?"

Her voice was dull now and her question did not really expect an answer.

But Horst was not concerned with her grief.

"Where is the safe?" he asked. "Show me the safe!"

She shook her head.

"I don't know where it is. Only mother did. And she is dead now . . . dead . . . dead. . . ."

Horst left her and started a search of the house. It was not a large one and fifteen minutes later he had found the false partition in the small room on the second floor, ripped the thin laths down and focused his torch on the cavity. The safe was there, squat and smug, like a Chinese idol; and it was empty.

For a few brief moments as he stood there in the empty,

cold room, he was depressed with a sense of utter and final defeat. Napoleon, he thought, must have felt the same way after Waterloo. His carefully prepared plans had pivoted around this house in the Frankfurterstrasse, around the safe with its three bare shelves. There should have been money there—English pounds and American dollars—there should have been a passport made out in the name of Frederick Rickman, an American citizen of Danish origin whose identity had been built up elaborately and absolutely foolproof; not to speak of other, important documents. It was all gone. Someone had double-crossed him. The enormity of this crime filled him with hot anger; he clenched his hands and felt the blood welling over his whole body so that he had to wipe the sweat from his forehead. Whoever it was, had to die; and if it took him all his time and all his energy, he would find out. That he, Horst von Falkenau, one of the real key men in the Plan should be put into danger, should have to improvise and adopt desperate measures because two fools or knaves . . .

Was it Kemmerich who had babbled? The fool was dead but he never could hold his liquor and was an incurable skirt-chaser. Yet he could not have known what was waiting for him in the *Gauleiter's* mansion; when he came there, he was certain that Horst would take him on the trip to freedom and new activity. It would have been against his, Kemmerich's, vital interests to betray the secret of this house in the Frankfurterstrasse. Who else then? While he slammed the useless door of the safe and replaced the thin partition, in an automatic gesture of hiding his tracks, he mentally ran over the list of the initiates. Bredauer? No, he was already in Switzerland. Michler? No, the idiot was caught in the Ruhr pocket where that foxy, slippery customer von Papen surrendered to the Yankees. Arnold? He would not have the gumption. Who was it then? No, it was idle to guess and cudgel his brains; he must try to get something out of that stupid lump of flesh downstairs and then recast his plans. And suddenly he discovered that he did not mind having to stay in Leipzig for a day or two. This extension held certain possibilities . . . and he heard the "invisible" girl's soft voice: "We are staying at the Kaiserhof. . . . Perhaps we'll see you." Yes, he decided, it was definitely an invitation. An invitation it would be churlish not to follow.

Grim and thoughtful he descended the stairs. He found the girl, swathed in that shabby, ragged shawl, still sitting at the edge of the four-poster, still staring with dreadful intensity at the dead woman's face. She did not look up when he entered, but he grasped her shoulders and turned her roughly to face him.

"Did your mother say anything about the two men?"

She shook her head.

"Try to think," he insisted, his voice a little gentler, almost coaxing. "It is very important. They killed your mother. You want them to be punished, don't you? Try to remember ever scrap . . . a word might help. . . ."

She frowned with concentration; evidently she was trying to recall the last words of the dead woman.

Then she sighed:

"No . . . only she said . . . something about a ring. A ring with a snake on it. A big ugly snake. She kept on saying, the snake, the snake on the ring . . . but I couldn't understand."

The ring with the snake. It sounded pretty hopeless. Once again he shook her as if to jog her memory but he knew it was no use. Her dull eyes had lost the least glimmer of intelligence; now she was fondling the corpse's hands, chafing them, bending over the still body and whispering broken endearments, pausing now and then as if to wait for an answer.

She did not move when he hurried from the room and closed the door behind himself. She was lost in the world of her private grief. Would she remember him? Would she be able to describe him? Perhaps it would be better to silence her—as he had silenced Kemmerich and Anne. . . . But no, he felt sure that in her poor bewildered mind he and the two men would be mixed up . . . and in any case, her description of the lone visitor to the ramshackle house would not be of much use to anyone trying to get on his trail. For the moment he was a little tired of killing; he had to turn his attention to other things, husband his energies for a more important purpose—his own survival.

As he stepped from the house, he looked around again. The street was dark and deserted and he walked off towards the railway station. He had a few hours in which to make up his mind, to invent a reason for a call on Captain Whitney and the girl called Helen whose face he had never seen.

X

PETER WHITNEY PAUSED, HIS hand lifted to knock at the door. He had a long, lean face and his forehead was bisected by a deep frown of anxiety. Nervously he straightened his tie and pulled down his uniform jacket. He felt, foolishly, as if he were to face the general whose irascible energy one had to approach on tiptoes. The whole thing was so silly—and he had thought that Helen was different from other women, that she had more brains and less intuition than the majority of her sex; that her instincts never got in the way of her thinking processes. Not that some of her instincts were not the right kind—he had been just fooling when he had called her "Snow Maiden" in the car. . . . But—he felt stumped, exasperated like a man accused of some crime so monstrous that he could not even find the arguments to defend himself, because the charge was so absurd. Not so long ago it had all been smooth sailing and now—just because of that stupid argument . . .

He knocked.

Helen's voice, cool, with that throaty, slightly hoarse undertone which made it the most thrilling voice in the world, answered:

"Who is it?"

"Peter."

"Just a minute. . . ."

There was an emptiness at the end of the three words, as if she had wanted to add something and had changed her mind at the last moment.

Peter heard tiny noises behind the door; soft rustlings and the clink of a jar or glass; then she called out:

"You can come in now."

She was sitting in the rather shabby arm-chair in front of the fireplace. She had taken off her uniform and was wrapped in a sky-blue dressing-gown—padded and warm, it offset her short brown hair and dark eyes to perfection. Her creamy throat rose from the broad collar, proud and yet vulnerable; and he saw the small hollow, soft and smooth, which he had kissed not so many days ago.

"They promised a fire," he said. "Only the man who is

supposed to bring the wood is so old and infirm that it may take him hours to stagger up with it."

"I am not too cold," she said. "And I want to have a nap anyway. I thought you were tired, too?"

He straddled a carved chair and stared at her thoughtfully.

"Are you still sore?" he asked.

She made a small, tired gesture:

"We have been arguing for three days, Peter. I want some rest. If I am to drive on to-morrow . . ."

"There is no need for you to go on to-morrow," he replied sullenly. "Your furlough lasts another fortnight. And I can't see why you are in such a mighty hurry to get back to Paris."

"Must we go all over it again?"

He heaved his long, lanky body from the chair and caught her hands.

"All I know is that a month ago we were practically engaged and now you want to run away."

Her voice became a little sharper. She freed her hands and crossed her arms over her breasts, as she answered:

"I am not running away."

"Sure, the busy Miss Fleming!" he sneered. "Without you the Krauts would all run wild. And all the brats would starve."

"Peter!"

He was at her side in a moment, grasping her hand as he slid down on the carpet.

"Darling, I am sorry. This wrangling gets me down. But I . . . I never thought that you would turn out to be a prig."

She wrinkled her small, straight nose at him as if he had said something very funny. But he plunged on, fumbling with the words, in haste, that he should not be interrupted:

"I could imagine many reasons why I wasn't the right guy for you. You are beautiful, you know all the important people, your social background is entirely different from mine—hell, I am just a fellow who studied law in night school and then got a lucky break—you have far more brains than any woman I've ever met. But I never thought that ideas would keep us apart; that because we had different opinions about something that has really nothing to do with our lives, you would call it off. It's . . . it's unreal. I can't come to grips with it. If I told you that I have changed my mind and . . ."

She smiled; and it was almost too much for Captain Whitney. He had often tried to decide whether Helen was lovelier when her lips were closed and the soft, delicately drawn curves were in repose—or whether her smile was the most wonderful thing about her. Now he knew that it was the smile—but what good did it do to know? He felt like the hero of a magazine story; two-dimensional, bound by the conventions that make magazine heroes. But we are real people, he told himself; and he could puzzle this out if she gave him a chance.

". . . it would have made no difference," Helen was saying. "I would have known that you were pretending. It was better so—that we found out in time, before it was too late."

"But for Christ's sake, Helen . . ."

There was a knock at the door and an old man staggered in with a small pile of logs. He deposited them on the hearth, and retired to bring some paper and matches: lowering himself stiffly on to his knees, he made an ineffectual attempt to kindle the fire. Peter watched him absent-mindedly for a moment or so, then he pulled him to his feet and told him to go—he would attend to it. He built the logs into a triangular frame, pushed some kindling and a few spills of paper underneath and then struck a match.

The flame sprang to life and instantly the room seemed to be smaller, more intimate, more like home. He looked up and caught Helen staring at the flames creeping towards the pointed ends of the logs with an expression on her face he had never seen before.

"A bright new penny," he said. "Or shall I make it a dime?"

She started as if she had come back from a long way away and said softly:

"I was thinking of Hans Langer."

The flames could not get a real hold on the half-dry wood; Peter spread a sheet of the *Stars and Stripes* to give them the necessary draught. He asked with a light-hearted banter that was not real:

"And who may he be? You forget, my darling, that I cannot keep step with all the men in your lurid past."

But she did not smile.

"Hans is dead. He killed himself in the spring of thirty-nine. He was the finest pianist I have ever known."

"I am sorry. Why—why were you thinking about him?"

She shook her head as if to chase away her thoughts. "I just wondered what would have happened if he had not died." She turned to the tall, slim young man with a gesture of trust and appeal. "I would have married him."

"He must have been a pretty wonderful person," Peter conceded, feeling a fool. If only her moods did not change so quickly! Here he was, all set for a grand scene of explanation and reconciliation—but she was thinking of someone else, someone dead for six years. What sort of a girl had he picked for himself?

She continued in the same low voice: "Hans was an Austrian. He happened to be in London for a series of concerts when the Nazis marched into Vienna. His parents and his sister were taken to a concentration camp—only he did not know. For over two years he waited, hoping to get news from them. His father was a Socialist deputy and that, of course, meant a sentence of death. But they kept him alive for two years in Dachau before they finished him off. His sister—she went mad and his mother died soon afterwards. Then someone was released and got to London. At first he did not want to tell Hans, but of course he soon wormed the truth out of him. That was a fortnight before our wedding. The same night he wrote me a letter and took the cyanide he always carried on him. . . ."

She fell silent but in the silence he heard her words echoing: "A fortnight before our wedding . . . he wrote me a letter . . . cyanide. . . ." He tried desperately to feel an interest in this shadowy Austrian but he could not even feel retrospective jealousy. The man meant nothing to him—how could he?—but evidently he meant a lot to Helen.

"Are you still in love with his . . . memory?" he asked.

"He had wonderful hands," she said but it was no reply to his question. "And a funny, crooked smile. He loved all people and thought that music could heal everything. But he was not strong enough. I've often wondered whether he loved me enough—or whether I loved him in the right way? Perhaps if I had he would not have killed himself. . . ."

"But that's sheer lunacy—to torture yourself, six years later, with the 'might-have-been'," argued Peter. "He is dead, poor fellow—but you are alive and it would be a wicked waste if you sacrificed your life just because a man suffered and killed himself—a man who could not take it. . . ."

She turned her dark eyes on him and he fell silent, embarrassed. She looked at him with a friendly, matter-of-fact interest as if she saw him for the first time.

"Poor Peter," she sighed, "I am a wicked puzzle, am I not? How long have we known each other?"

"Six months," he said in sudden deep wonder. "Six lovely months. We met just after . . ."

He could have bitten off his tongue. He was a clumsy idiot—but perhaps she had not noticed. But of course she had!

"Don't be so elaborately tactful," she smiled. "You mean, just after my father and Tim were killed. I am not a child and I can bear to talk about them without flinching. Wasn't it the most fantastic fate . . . that my father and my little brother should be murdered on the same day, sixty miles apart . . . murdered by two lumps of high explosive coming from the stratosphere, uncontrolled, undirected. . . . If you put it into a play, a poem, a story, no one would believe it. What reason was in their death? An elderly man who had served his country and the ideal of justice all his adult life . . . and a small school boy who was just learning to read? What reason, what meaning, what——"

He did not move while she hid her face in her hands and her body trembled. He had tried to console her before and knew that it only made things worse. And he remembered his father's advice—the old doctor in the small, dusty Middle West town—about a "good cry" being the best cure for every heart-ache. So he waited and after a while her trembling ceased and she wiped her face in the sleeve of her dressing-gown. Her hair was tousled and her face a little red where her fingers had pressed into the soft flesh.

"I am sorry," she said. "And just a moment ago I was bragging about my courage. You should not defy the gods of sorrow, Seneca said—though this is a heck of a time to quote Seneca or anybody else. Give me a handkerchief, Peter."

He gave her a big khaki one and she blew her nose.

"Granted," he said after a little pause, "you have every reason to hate the Germans. I didn't know about Hans Whatsisname—but I knew about your father and your kid brother. I knew of your father before I even met you—long before. Believe it or not, I read one of his books about international law . . . and found it hard going because he was all the time miles above my head. But I kept on slogging at it and in time discovered what he was driving at. He must have been a very fine man. As for the kid . . . Yes, you have every reason to hate them. But just because we don't hate them in the same way—just because you deliberately came to Germany to see that vengeance . . ."

"Not vengeance," she interrupted. "That is futile and only creates new evil. I asked for this job because I wanted to see how justice was done. Grim and full justice, but not private revenge. This is too big a thing for individual hates and passions. And one man or one woman—what can you do? Still, I wanted to see and wanted to help. . . ."

"Helen—darling—we are not taking part in a Brains Trust discussion on What To Do with the Germans. . . . Remember me? I am real flesh-and-blood and so are you. So please, try to realise. . . ."

It was no use. She went on: "I asked you how long we had known each other. Six months . . . it isn't a very long time."

"You can get to know and love a person in a day, an hour, a minute," he said fiercely. "Surely you are not going old-fashioned on me? Long engagements and 'we must be sure, dear, 'and . . ."

"No, Peter," she smiled. "I am not that old-fashioned. But that was just what I meant. That you don't really know me. What do you know about Helen Fleming?"

"I know enough to want to marry you."

"You know that my father was a K.C. and that I have civilised table manners. You know that I took a job with UNRRA because . . . well, I have told you why. And I have told you a little of my life and ideas . . . but never enough. I am very bad at talking about myself, Peter dear. But I must try to make you understand. . . ."

He nodded. "All right, shoot. Whatever you say, I love to hear your voice."

She frowned disapproval and moved a little closer to the fire which was now burning well.

"You should have seen me when I was fifteen," she began. "Except that I had no braces on my teeth, I was the perfect type of the awkward 'in-between.' Daddy was much too busy and much too absent-minded to pay much attention to me at any time—except when I caused trouble which was seldom—and Mother—well, she was so beautiful and so popular that she did not mind a bit if I stayed at school, safely tucked away. I was leggy and awkward and did not make friends easily. . . ."

Peter lit a cigarette and offered her one, but she shook her head. "Go on," he said. "And I do wish I had met you when you were fifteen. I would have put a big 'reserved' sign around your neck."

"I was at a frightfully progressive school," Helen continued, "co-educational and the very last word in child psychology. The kids all talked Freud and decided to tell their parents the facts of life. They rather despised me because they said I was full of inhibitions and refused to sublimate them, whatever that meant. But I was happy enough because about that time I fell in love with an idea. . . ."

He stirred restlessly. "Ideas again!" he murmured as if she had told him that she had become a Mormon or taken to secret tippling.

Helen hugged her knees. This memory must have given her delight for she smiled at her fifteen-year-old self.

"It was a wonderful idea because it was so simple and yet I thought it would fill my whole life and give a purpose to everything I did. You know, my great-great-grandfather was a wicked freethinker who corresponded with Tom Paine and had met Voltaire. He started the Fleming library and I had the run of it ever since I learned to read. Daddy, I suppose, thought that most of the books were too stodgy-looking to tempt me. They were, but at thirteen I got fed up with *Peg's Paper* and tackled a good many of them. That started the trouble. . . ."

"But this idea with which you fell in love, as you put it," Whitney interrupted, "what was it all about?"

"Oh, that . . . Simply this: that there were other people in the world besides my own; that human beings were intensely interesting and that I mustn't waste any time before finding out about their loves and hates, their thoughts and dreams. It must sound funny to an American who cannot help meeting other races, nationalities in that melting pot of yours. Why, New York alone is a continent. But for a young English miss who was brought up on the presumption—and even our progressive school could not help it—that the rest of the world is populated by assorted dagoes, froggies, man-eating Russians and other Slavs with unpronounceable names, it was a pretty revolutionary thought, I can tell you.

. . . Perhaps because I found the prospect of boating parties, afternoons at Lord's, shopping expeditions to the Army and Navy Stores and Harrod's a bit too tame—in any case, I revolted."

"Successfully, I hope?" enquired Peter.

"Now don't sneer!" she protested. "I was a wily child. I only asked to be sent off to a finishing school. Have you got that time-honoured institution in the States, Peter? Mother, of course, had been to one in her youth and emerged with a perfect finish. So she approved and Daddy, poor dear, just didn't care. I was packed off to Geneva. I stayed exactly six months at Madam Horrense's high-class establishment."

"And then?" the young American asked. "Did you elope with your music teacher?"

"No, much worse," Helen said, and lifted her hand in a quick, characteristic gesture to her forehead, trying to rub out a tiny frown between her straight, faintly quizzical eyebrows. "I got a job with the League. Of course, I had to lie about my age, but by that time I had grown out of the awkward stage and the nice old man who interviewed me might have entertained certain hopes of my all-too-gullible innocence. He was quite a nuisance—but I moved into an impeccable hostel and walked home every day with the other girls."

"You mean, you got a job at sixteen-and-a-bit?" stared Peter. "That must have jolted Sir Clement."

"Oh, it did. At least it shook Mother to the core and she sent him to Geneva. It was February and she could not face the trip herself—which was lucky for me. I could always twist my father around any chosen finger." She held up her hand meditatively staring at the rosy fingers as if she could see someone being wound around them. "Anyhow, in two days I won him over to my side. He visited the hostel and spoke to my boss, a very sensible Scotswoman who knew more about dope-pedlars than anyone in the world. You see, I was working in that particular glamorous department. There was nothing glamorous about it for me—not at first. And Mother insisted that I should come home every Christmas and for my summer leave. But in three years I managed to get up the ladder and when Miss McCallum retired to her rock-garden in Dundee, I got her job."

"Girl makes good," mocked Peter. "But I still don't

see what your colourful and unorthodox career has got to do with our particular argument. . . ."

"I am sorry, Peter," she smiled. "Autobiography is almost always boring—unless one is a good liar. I had a wonderful time with the League. After the first three years I travelled a lot—Egypt, South America, the Balkans, the Far East—collecting material for our reports, doing 'field work' as an archæologist would say. Only I didn't have to deal with ruins and ancient civilisations but with the seamy side of modern life. From drugs I went to the white slave traffic. . . ."

"My God, Helen," protested Peter in comic despair, "you sound like a gangster retailing his various activities. Why on earth should a girl as lovely as——"

"I was still in love with my idea. I was still intensely concerned with people. And I had my fill of them—good, bad and indifferent, men and women, black, yellow, brown and white. I suppose I should have been afraid a hundred times of very real danger, but I never came to any harm. I picked up languages; I had a few dozen proposals—there, I owed that to my self-esteem—and I remained uninterested . . . until——"

"Until Hans Langer," the American finished the sentence for her. "But he was a German," he added, "and you loathe all Germans, don't you?"

"He was an Austrian," Helen said softly. "And I don't loathe them all. Only I know them. You don't."

"But for Pete's sake, I've been fighting them for three years. . . ."

She kept silent.

"Is it because they killed your father and young Tim?" he asked. "Is it . . ."

Before she could answer, there was a loud knock at the door. Peter called out in annoyance: "Who is it?"

The door opened and a muddy, tired-looking dispatch-rider entered. He saluted smartly and asked:

"Captain Peter Whitney?"

The American got to his feet.

"Yes. What is it?"

"Would you sign this, sir?" The dispatch-rider held out a sheet of paper fixed to a stiff board and handed Peter a large envelope. He signed, tore open the envelope and drew a single sheet from it. He read it and frowned with vexation.

"What is it, Peter?" asked Helen.

"Message from Regional H.Q.," he replied. "Thank you, corporal," he turned to the dispatch-rider. "No reply."

When the be-helmeted corporal had left, he took one or two turns down the room and then said:

"I must report in Nuremberg to-morrow morning. That means leaving almost at once."

"But you were to have a furlough . . ."

"Cancelled. It must be something pretty important. Old Leatherguts is considerate enough under normal circumstances. I am sorry, darling. Look—this can't take more than two or three days. Why don't you come with me?"

"How could I? My travel orders are for Paris. I have no business in Nuremberg."

"Well then . . . there is no date fixed for your arrival, is there? You might have spent another week or so in Berlin if you hadn't managed to straighten out that business of yours so quickly. Won't you wait for me here? I'll be back as soon as possible . . ."

"But Peter . . ." Then she saw the agony in his face. "All right," she said. "I'll wait. Though Leipzig is a very dull place."

"Without me you mean?" he eagerly fished for encouragement.

"With or without anybody," she replied. "I'll wait for you here—but mind you, it doesn't mean that I . . ."

"All right, all right. But we haven't really threshed it out. And if you are really serious, I'll promise to change my ideas. All or any of them. You are worth it. Henri of Navarre said Paris was worth a mass. Well, Miss Helen Fleming——"

"Stop it, Peter. And you'd better hurry. Old S. doesn't like to be kept waiting. How are you going?"

"The Transport people will give me a jeep or something. Probably an ancient one which will shake me to pieces. And you aren't a bit sorry for me, are you?"

"I am, Peter, honest I am."

But when he bent down over her rounded, vibrant face, she eluded his lips and he went from the room, muttering to himself. And Helen looked after him as if he were a stubborn but lovable child, always up to some mischief. If Peter had seen her glance, he would have been even more depressed.

XI

FOR MORE THAN AN HOUR Horst von Falkenau tramped the dark, desolate streets. He had to have a plan and a fool-proof one; but for the moment no glimmer of light appeared. There were other stations on the underground railroad, other caches of money and documents. His identity as Karel Reznicek had been well established but there was too much at stake to risk the slightest slip. The real Karel Reznicek had died a few weeks ago; and as long as he avoided anyone who had known him well, he was safe. But this left too much to chance. If he could have collected the contents of the safe in the Frankfurterstrasse, nothing could have stopped him on his way. Once again the flood of rage filled him; he vowed that if it was the last thing he did, he would exact revenge upon the two men who had stolen what was his pass-port to safety. Any moment he might be faced with danger, unnecessary and . . .

Danger—something clicked in his brain at this word and he laughed out loud. The next moment a torch was flashed into his eyes and a gruff voice in English demanded to know what he was doing on the streets after the civilian curfew time.

He produced his papers; two American military policemen examined them carefully.

They apologised curtly, adding: "It isn't safe to be out after dark, Mr. Reznicek. There are still deserters and looters about—fugitive S.S. men and similar riff-raff. Where are you staying?"

"At the Astoria. But I have checked out already. I am expecting to leave for Cologne later to-night."

"Well, I advise you to keep indoors until then. There is a waiting-room at the station."

He thanked them, boiling with rage inside; and then realised that he had forgotten his pretence of not speaking English. It did not matter but it showed that he was getting a little careless. And small things counted more than . . .

He stopped suddenly. Yes, that was it. It should work. He could see no reason why they should not fall for it. That lantern-jawed, young American did not look like a fool;

but he was an American and therefore an adolescent, Horst von Falkenau decided. And the girl . . . well, she was an unknown quantity. But if it did not work—even then he had not risked anything and might gain a lot. He was not given to self-analysis but now he paused to examine his soul—whether it was not the tantalising glimpse he had got of her hair and the back of her head that made him hit upon this particular plan? Then he found that it made no difference. Whatever the impulse, he must try it.

He went back to the Astoria.

The man behind the desk looked at him in surprise. His narrow face was now devoid of the frozen smirk which had irritated Horst when he first saw him.

"I have changed my mind," Horst said briefly. "I am staying on in Leipzig. Could I have the same room?"

"I regret . . ."

He folded a pound note and slid it across the desk. The clerk took it, unfolded it. His fingers trembled a little.

"We have had reservation for to-night. . . ."

"Has your guest arrived?"

"No, but the Berlin train is three hours late and . . ."

"Then you can put him into the billiard-room—or the hall for all I care."

He took the key and said: "My luggage is at the station. Here is the ticket. See that it's fetched at once."

As soon as he was in the room, he pressed the bell against which a tiny sketch of a waiter was set in the wall.

It was quite fifteen minutes before the man with the flat, grey face and the shifty eyes appeared.

"*Mein Herr?*" He stopped on the threshold, frozen in painful surprise.

"Come in," said von Falkenau, "and close the door."

"We don't serve meals after ten . . ." the waiter began.

"I am not hungry," Horst interrupted him. "What's your name?"

"Fritz Hu . . . Goltz," the man replied sullenly.

"You ought to be more careful in remembering your new name," smiled the ex-*Gauleiter*. "What *is* your real one? Huber? Huster? Huhnemann?"

He had been watching the waiter narrowly and so he was well in time to counter his attack. There was a brief tussle and then the short, sharply pointed S.S. dagger flew into a distant corner. The other man nursed his wrenched arm with a puckered face; he looked as if he were ready to burst into tears.

"That was very silly, Fritz," Horst von Falkenau said softly. "To use a dagger is an un-German habit. Not worthy of the *Herrenvolk*. And if you had stabbed me—would it have made things any better?"

The waiter, forgetting his assumed role, slumped in a chair. He was still massaging his aching arm.

"Who are you?" he grunted with sulky hate in his voice. "Why don't you make an end of it? You can denounce me—I don't care."

Horst placed his fingertips together and considered the problem judiciously.

"Now that's a very interesting point," he said. "Why don't I? Not because I like your shifty eyes or pasty face, my friend. Not because I am generous. But because you can be useful."

"You . . . you devil. . . ."

"It is silly to call your betters bad names, Fritz. Is it Huber? I don't like Christian names."

"Huber," the other confessed unwillingly. "But no one knows. And if I only had time . . ."

"Fritz Huber," von Falkenau mused aloud. "The name seems familiar. Haven't we met before? Where was it? Oswiecim? Bergenbelsen? Maidanek? Nordhausen?"

"I was at Nordhausen," the pseudo-waiter said defiantly. "But that's none of your business. I did as I was told. So did tens of thousands. Tell the military police. Tell anyone who wants to know. I am quite willing to die. I've had enough of this hiding and lying. My family is dead—in Dresden. That night, sixty thousand were killed. But finish it—don't——"

There was a little silence. He had covered his face and his fingers trembled. Horst noticed absent-mindedly that Huber's nails were cut very short and scrupulously clean. He cleared his throat and said:

"I am not a philanthropist, my friend. You were a guard at Nordhausen—didn't you command the special detachment? You see, I remember. I have no intention of denouncing you unless you turn stubborn."

The S.S. man took his hands from his face. He stared at the tall, fair-haired man with puzzled, hopeful eyes:

"I don't understand," he said. "You spoke of Nordhausen. Were you there . . . as a prisoner? I looked at the register downstairs. You are a Czech—and you are free. So you can't be a collaborator. But if you were a prisoner at Nordhausen—you ought to hate me and . . ."

"I was at Nordhausen. Not as a prisoner. I came to inspect the camp in 'forty-three."

Huber narrowed his eyes. He searched the other man's face. Slowly recognition dawned.

"Why, you are . . ."

"No names," Horst interrupted. "You see, I trust you. The fact that no one would believe your word against mine might have something to do with it—also, I assure you, I would kill you quickly and nastily if I had the slightest doubt of your loyalty. This disguise of yours is ridiculous. You must not stay in Germany. I am willing to get you out of the country—if you obey my instructions in every particular."

"But *Herr Gene* . . ."

"My name is Reznicek—for the present," von Falkenau said firmly. "You'd better think of me as *Herr* Reznicek—unless you want to come to a violent and unpleasant end. As I said, you must not stay here very much longer. Hundreds were in Nordhausen who might recognise you—in the street, in a shop, in the hotel."

"But what can I do."

"A good deal. First of all I want you to memorise a little text I am going to draw up for you. Then you are going to ring the Kaiserhof, ask for Captain Whitney and speak your little piece. Not right now," he added, "but when I give you the word. Can you get to the telephone if I call you?"

"Yes, there is one in the waiters' pantry," replied Huber. "But I don't understand. . . ."

"There is nothing for you to understand—nor to worry about as long as you do exactly as you are told. If you don't—well, I needn't stress that point. Come up to this room after you have made the telephone call and wait for me. I should be back by one o'clock."

He took a piece of paper and scribbled half a dozen lines on it. He gave them to the S.S. man.

"Read them," he said. "Read them aloud. Don't try to change your voice—don't make it too dramatic or artificial. Just speak your lines as naturally as you can. Let me hear you."

Fritz Huber read out the few sentences. He stumbled once but otherwise he got through them well enough. The words sounded strange and almost meaningless in the dim, cold room.

"No, you fool," said Horst von Falkenau. "Here, let me show you what I mean."

His performance was faultless. Nothing melodramatic, nothing forced—yet the right emphasis was there, credibly sinister and grim.

"Now try again."

The other man tried—for half an hour Horst coached him, mercilessly exacting until he got every inflexion right.

"I wish I had more time," he dismissed Huber. "Stay near the phone and don't get panicky."

He slipped into his overcoat and put on his gloves. As he opened the door, the S.S. man spoke:

"You really meant it . . . about helping me abroad and all that? I am a good driver and a mechanic and . . ."

"Just the right man for me," smiled von Falkenau. "Don't worry . . . you can be too useful to me—I wouldn't break my promise."

As he walked downstairs, he was whistling. It was a phrase from Dvorak's New World symphony—for he was well pleased with himself and once more perfectly self-assured.

XII

HE STOPPED FOR A MOMENT outside the Kaiserhof and then drew back into the shadows of the dimly-lit entrance as Captain Whitney came hurrying out. He could see the American's face clearly; it looked tense, worried, unhappy.

Horst von Falkenau hesitated for a moment. Then he heard Whitney call out:

"Driver? Is there a jeep-driver out here?"

A bulky figure detached itself from a bigger blur and stepped into the yellow circle of light:

"I am here, sir."

"All right, let's go," Whitney said. "How long do you think it will take us?"

"It depends on the roads, sir," the driver replied. "Three hours if it's a straight run—nearer six if we get held up."

Whitney cursed briefly and added: "Well, come on. We might as well get it over."

The jeep, now visible as the headlights were switched on, moved off. Horst von Falkenau remained motionless for a few minutes. It was better than he had hoped. If he could prepare the girl's mind, lay the foundations of his plan. . . . But what if Whitney did not come back? He was audacious enough to trust his own powers of improvisation. The English thought it was their privileged speciality—to turn makeshift means to good purpose, to snatch victory from defeat. . . . Well, at least he could show them that they were wrong. Maybe some of the Germans did have a rigid mind, only able to follow a prearranged plan, stick to a well-marked road—but there were exceptions.

He pushed through the swing doors and marched up to the reception desk.

"Captain Whitney, please," he said to the elderly, dignified clerk.

"I am sorry, sir," the receptionist said. "Captain Whitney left only a minute ago. He had to drive to Nuremberg."

A garrulous old fool, Horst told himself. If he were not, he would not have added the gratuitous piece of information. To Nuremberg, eh? He displayed great concern.

"But I thought I would find him in. . . . When is he coming back?"

"He didn't tell me," the clerk replied, "but I—I happened to hear that he expects to be away for three days."

"That's impossible!" Horst von Falkenau hid his delight behind a mask of indignant disappointment. "It—it is a most serious matter and . . ."

"Perhaps you would care to come back to-morrow and see Miss Fleming," suggested the receptionist, falling into the neatly-laid trap.

"Miss Who?"

"The lady with whom Captain Whitney arrived. She might be able to give you further information."

"I doubt it," sighed Horst. "But I may as well try it. However, I cannot wait until to-morrow morning—my business with Captain Whitney is far too urgent. Could you ask the lady whether she would see me now?"

"But *mein Herr*, it's well past midnight . . ."

"Just ring her room and tell her that *Herr* Reznicek wishes to see her on an urgent matter."

"But . . ."

Another note changed hands; the elderly man shrugged and turned to the old-fashioned telephone on the wall behind him.

Horst withdrew tactfully; he did not want to overhear the conversation which was quite lengthy. At last the receptionist beckoned to him.

"Miss Fleming will see you in ten minutes," he announced. "She wasn't asleep yet. Her room number is three hundred and five."

"Thank you. Could I make a telephone call in the meantime? Have you got a booth where I could find some privacy?"

The clerk pointed to the far corner of the spacious, dim hotel hall. Horst rang up the Astoria and asked for Fritz, the waiter. He gave the S.S. man new instructions, making him repeat them several times until he was certain that he had got them right.

Then he followed a diminutive page up the staircase, covered with a threadbare carpet. He dismissed the boy at the last turning and paused for a moment in front of the white door with its gilt number. He knocked and heard her well-remembered voice telling him to come in.

XIII

FOR THE GREATER PART OF HIS adult life, Horst von Falkenau had been a leader of men. Often they hated him, but even those who suffered worst at his hands, could not deny a grudging admiration for his single-minded ruthlessness, his cold and detached grasp of details and command of essentials. What they could not forgive him was his aloofness; he destroyed them, with the same contempt and sense of superiority that a man would employ in crushing an ant-heap or squashing a fly on a table-cloth. The loyalty he inspired in men was compounded of fear and puzzled hero-worship. His physical courage bordered on lunacy and enhanced his reputation of bearing a charmed life. As he rose higher and higher in the hierarchy of party and state, this Lucifer-like detachment and pride increased rapidly. He had never failed in any task, never suffered defeat in any undertaking; perhaps because he had supreme skill in selecting and winning appointments that suited his temperament and talents perfectly.

Some of his enemies in the Party—and he had many—compared him to Robespierre, the Sea-Green Incorruptible. But the comparison was quite wrong. He had none of Robespierre's emotional instability; affection and hate he could control in equal measure. Some said that he was nothing but an automaton, a mass of conditioned reflexes; that something colder and purer than blood must flow in his veins and that his brain was armour-plated. Few knew his early history; the official publications spoke vaguely of his leadership in a *Freicorps* in Polish Silesia, of his invaluable work during the early days of National Socialist revolution, of his enthusiastic services rendered to the Fuehrer in the days of beginning.

In his forty-five years there had never been a woman whom he wanted and did not get. At first it had been his physical attraction, the face of a dissolute Greek god and a magnificently fit body that gained him all the embraces he could wish for. Later when he became "the most eligible bachelor of the Third Reich," he did not even have to stretch out his hand. He was not a Don Juan, for the nobleman of Seville and his ilk had to work for the conquest of beauty while Horst von Falkenau more or less let women happen to him. He intrigued and infuriated most of them and they slept with him in order to discover his secret. They never did. He was fundamentally bored with women who only attracted his senses; he had no patience with their so transparent, traditional guile and coquetry. He thought them shallow and silly; no woman had a brain worth picking, he said, and the Madame Curies, Sonia Kowalevskas or George Sands were freaks of nature who, at the best, were intellectual hermaphrodites. His sexual appetite was healthy but much subordinate to his work and his ambitions. He took his ability to attract women for granted and never stopped to analyse it.

Sometimes, as he travelled across Europe, pruning the New Order, stemming an incipient revolt here, visiting a concentration camp there, building the bulwarks of the Reich that was to last a thousand years, he found a woman whom he desired because she was lovely. Often such women were bound to hate him because of his nationality, his position, all the things he stood for. But if he wanted them, he plucked them like ripe fruit from a tree; loathing themselves, despising their weakness and their helpless surrender, they gave themselves to this man of violence and evil—and at the most they felt that they were mortifying the flesh, abasing themselves in atonement for sins they never committed as they became von Falkenau's mistresses.

For all his contempt and superior egotism, he had developed a perfect mask to hide his real opinion of women. If it cracked now and then, it made them only more anxious to penetrate behind it, to remove it completely. They never succeeded, for the veneer was more than skin-deep.

Now, as he paused for a moment in front of the door of a woman he had imagined but never seen, he felt fully confident of mastering any difficulty that might arise.

She got up as he entered and the impact of her beauty was of an almost physical force meeting him. He stopped just inside the door. His lips felt dry and involuntarily his tongue slipped out to moisten them. Then he bowed and said:

"Miss Fleming? It is most kind of you to receive me at this late hour. I am sorry to disturb you."

She did not speak and he was a little taken aback by her silence. The short, auburn hair, the dark eyes, the straight, small nose and the full lips made it impossible for him to take his eyes off her. Desire, violent and dominant, rose in him; at the same time he was impatient to hear her voice again.

When she spoke, it gave him a shock. It was cold and unfriendly. "You are *Herr* Reznicek, aren't you?" she asked.

"Why, of course, but . . ."

"The man whom Captain Whitney gave a lift?"

He tried to joke. "Would you like to see my papers? I assure you, they are in perfect order."

"I am sure they are, *Herr* . . . Reznicek."

The little pause between the two last words did not make him uneasy. She could not possibly know his real identity; if she did, she would be afraid, for naturally he would have to kill her. The very idea of death in connection with her filled him with distaste and violent protest. But if she did not know . . . what was she driving at?

"Is there anything wrong?" he asked, perfectly composed.

"Just one thing," she said and sat down, gathering the folds of the long, silk dressing-gown around her. "You told us that you did not speak English. And yet now you seem to have become remarkably proficient. I don't think it's a language which you can learn in a day."

"Oh that," he laughed, relieved that she came out into the open and that he had something tangible to deal with. "I must confess my little deception. But I had two good reasons—I was just as little sure of Captain Whitney and yourself as you were of me, and also, I admit, I am rather bashful about my English. It is a very difficult tongue for a Czech to speak."

But she was in no way mollified by his facile explanation.

"You seem to speak it very well—and you haven't a Czech accent."

"It would be strange if I had. I learned my English in Shanghai from American sailors and a Welsh nurse. Together they gave me an accent that, I am afraid, defies analysis. But surely, Miss Fleming, you are not angry with me because of this? I meant no harm, I can assure you."

She looked at him and her eyes held shrewd appraisal of the tall, slim man with the very fair hair and the regular features. There was something oddly familiar about him but she could not decide what it was. Helen had the experience that most people have, more frequently than anyone she knew: the sensation of having been in a place before, of having spoken certain words, made certain gestures before, of having met a person in some other life, on some other planet. Even though she read all that Bergson had written about the "false memory," she still found this feeling uncanny whenever it came over her.

Was he speaking the truth? He stood there, smiling, perfectly at ease and Helen, with an odd sense of relief, decided that he was not lying. Why should he? Peter was a very thorough young man and if he had examined this fellow's papers, they should be all right.

She smiled and he felt that the reprieve had arrived almost at the last moment.

"You are right, *Pan* Renzicek. I am sorry if I sounded rude and suspicious. But who can help being just these things in this country? Won't you sit down?"

"Thank you."

"Cigarette?"

He took one from the box she held out to him and stared down at her hands, small and brown; strong hands with the nails rounded and without any polish. Working hands with the skin a little rough. Then he lifted his eyes and found her looking at him with still the same appraising, searching glance.

"Any more secrets?" she asked. "Any other hidden talents?"

"None at all," he replied. "That is, no personal ones I'd like to discuss."

She was silent again and he was comforted by her silence. Not a chatterbox, he thought. And she knows her own mind. Perhaps she even has got one. Though with women one never knew. They might start out all cerebral and then one moment panicked them into a stampede of instincts.

"I wanted to see Captain Whitney," he continued a little stiffly. "I am told he has left Leipzig. Do you know when he will be back?"

"I am afraid I don't," she replied. "He has gone on official business and that may take an indefinite time."

"But you—you are remaining in Leipzig?"

"That is possible."

He rose; he felt that he had to stand above her, to get the positional advantage. Also, he began to be restless. This was not getting him anywhere—and Fritz with his telephone call was due in ten minutes.

"Miss Fleming, we are complete strangers and there is no reason for you to trust me. As a matter of fact, I don't think you trust me at all. But I came here to-night to warn Captain Whitney of serious danger. . . ."

"Danger? But I don't understand. He is perfectly capable of taking care of himself."

"Probably—on a battlefield or even in that dangerous city, Chicago. But not here in Germany where all danger comes from under the ground, from the sewers, the ruined cellars, the burnt-out forests. This is a country where people kill for the joy of killing even to-day—only they wear no uniforms and accept no code. . . ."

"You mean the Werewolves? Surely they fizzled out soon enough. . . ."

"No, I mean something much more serious. Miss Fleming, to-night I sat in the hall of the Astoria. I was tired and must have dropped off to sleep. I was wakened by some sudden noise, but the next thing I heard were two voices. They talked in Russian."

"Russian! But that's absurd."

He smiled and she thought, how white his teeth were. He looked much younger when he smiled. But she tore her eyes from his face as he asked, a little insolence creeping into his voice:

"Why should it be absurd? There are plenty of Russians in Germany."

She was a little confused. "I didn't mean that. You said something about danger—and then you mentioned Russians."

"Perhaps you'd let me explain. I understand Russian as my mother-tongue—I spent almost two years in Moscow—and these two men could not see me. They talked about some plan which had to be carried out and I would have paid little attention to them except that they mentioned two names."

"What names?"

"One was the name of Captain Peter Whitney. They said that he might know something that he was not expected to know; and that they had to take care of him. I didn't very much like the tone in which they said this. It was evident that they wished to do him harm. Yet I would not have taken it seriously but for the other name. They spoke of General Vlassov."

"What? The . . ."

He nodded quietly.

"Yes. I take it you have heard of the quisling army which this man formed. The Nazis never dared to employ it against the Russians—Vlassov's men were used for garrison duties and as guards in concentration camps. They were all criminals, the riff-raff of Eastern Europe; White Russian adventurers, the scum of exiles, a good many of them recruited straight from prison. But they served their purpose. When the collapse came, Vlassov was nowhere to be found and his so-called army melted away. But these two men seemed to be in touch with the Nazi underground and Vlassov. It would be a clever plan, a very clever one," he added reflectively.

"What plan?" the girl asked. "I still don't understand you."

" A little later the two men got up and moved away," Horst continued. "I tried to follow them but by the time I reached the door, they had disappeared in the darkness. But I think I heard enough to guess their game. You see, if some Russian-speaking man should kill an American, it would create a—how do you call it?—a delicate international situation."

"And you could not find out anything about these two men?"

He spread his hands in a typical Continental gesture.

"I am distressed . . . but no. Except one little thing. One of the men—they were with their backs to me—had his hand hanging down the side of his chair. He wore a ring. A ring with a large snake on it."

She laughed. He jumped to his feet, his face working, his eyes furious.

"If you don't believe me . . ." he began.

"Please . . ." she struggled with her laughter and managed to control it. "Do forgive me, *Herr* Reznicek. I was incredibly rude. Only the whole thing sounds so melodramatic, so much like a bad thriller—one of those stories with corpses cluttering up the landscape, sliding panels and a Master Spy of ninety-seven different disguises. And the ring with the snake was the last straw, so to speak. No doubt you meant well. . . ."

These English, he thought, speechless with rage. They have no imagination. They are stupid and dull. Now this beautiful woman who should be alert and impressionable—she was laughing at him, laughing at his perfectly constructed story. Personally he thought that bringing in the ring with the snake was a masterstroke. It tied up the two men who had robbed the safe in the Frankfurterstrasse with the two imaginary Russians of Vlassov. It . . .

"I am sorry," he said stiffly. "Perhaps I had better see Captain Whitney after his return."

"Yes, you certainly must tell him the story," she giggled. He could have struck her then—but as he stood there, staring and uncomfortable, the telephone rang.

He waited for her to move. "Excuse me," she said and reached for the receiver. He watched her, tense; but she turned her back to him as she announced her name and asked who it was speaking.

She had covered the receiver with one small hand and he

could not hear Fritz's voice. That it was Fritz he had not the slightest doubt; nor did he fear that he would fail to perform his task well.

Helen Fleming replaced the telephone and swung round. Her face was pale and her lips trembled a little. Horst von Falkenau looked at her with pretended concern.

"Bad news?" he asked.

She moistened her lips before she spoke. "It—it was horrid," she said. "Some man . . . obscene threats . . . he spoke of Peter as if he . . ."

Horst resisted any triumphant exclamation of "I told you so!" He had to be doubly careful now. The girl rose and moved restlessly through the room, then turned and came to face him.

"You—you were right," she whispered. "I am sorry that I laughed at you. I must warn Peter . . . I must somehow reach him."

"Could I help?" he asked. She shook her head but he added: "Please, let me help you. Until Captain Whitney returns . . . you must have someone to protect you."

That brought back a little smile to her lips.

"Protect me? Mr. Reznicek, I assure you, I can look after myself. You forget that Germany is a conquered, occupied country. I can simply go to the military authorities if I want any help. Don't be hurt—but I can't presume to accept your offer. No doubt you have more important things to do. When are you leaving Leipzig?"

"Not for a week or so," he answered. "And you must remember that I know these gangsters and their methods. I have lived among them and I know exactly how their minds work. Now—for instance—in your place I would have made an effort to have that call traced. The military authorities are excellent keepers of law and order but they won't give you a guard twenty-four hours a day. Also, you have no proof and they might be just as sceptical as . . ."

"As I was. You must forgive me. It is difficult to realise even after six years of war that real life has turned into a cheap adventure story or into what the Americans call a cliff-hanger film—one of these interminable series in which the heroine is left in dire peril at the end of each instalment."

He did not understand a word of what she was saying, but it did not matter. The first step had been taken, the cornerstone laid; and this was the time to leave her to puzzle and fret.

He rose.

"It is very late," he said. "Forgive me for keeping you awake so long. I am staying at the Astoria and if there is anything I can do, you must let me know. And please, ask Captain Whitney to get in touch with me as soon as he returns."

"Thank you for coming to warn him," she replied gravely. "And I'll give him your message. I don't know exactly when he will be back . . . but perhaps we'll meet before that."

This was better than he had hoped; and as he bent over her hand and his lips touched the smooth, faintly scented skin, an audacious and staggering idea came to him. It was so startling and unexpected that he had to thrust it aside—he would give it attention when he was once more alone. His smile as he straightened was self-confident. He took his last glimpse of her into the corridor and the dark, cold street: straight and slim with the auburn hair above the broad blue collar of the dressing-gown. Yes . . . it was a wonderful idea and he could see no reason why it should not become reality.

XIV

THE SAME SMILE WAS ON HIS lips, the same idea in his mind —though more definite and far better developed—when the telephone rang in his room next day about noon and he heard her husky, tantalising voice.

"*Herr* Reznicek?" she asked. "I hope you got back to your hotel without any mishap. I . . . I wondered whether I could see you to-day?"

"Yes, certainly," he replied. "That is, if it were possible in the evening. I have much to do during the day."

"But of course, you must be very busy. I have a tin of coffee and if you would care to call after dinner. . . ."

"The coffee sounds wonderful. Nine o'clock?"

"Yes, that will be fine."

Horst stretched luxuriously and yawned. He had nothing

to do except lie in bed and play with his idea. Such a beautiful idea. He was almost grateful to the two men who had robbed the safe in the Frankfurterstrasse. He almost welcomed the cataclysm that had made the *Gauleiter* and S.S. General Horst von Falkenau a fugitive. He felt like the hunter stalking a sixteen-pointer stag, or as a cryptographer when a cipher begins to fall into place and the jumbled letters begin to make sense.

In his mind he went over every word she had spoken last night, every gesture and intonation. He had a photographic memory and it was not difficult to visualise her, to invoke her voice. There was no risk, he decided. Perhaps it was just as well that he had to keep the identity of Karel Reznicek. After all, he knew a good deal about Karel Reznicek. He had shot him with his own gun after . . . But why think about unpleasant details? There was every reason to suppose that no one who had known Reznicek really well was alive. Yes, the *Spezialdienst* and Himmler's boys had seen to that. And what better cover could he have than . . .

There was a knock at the door and Fritz Huber, the ex-S.S. man came into the room. He carried one of Horst's suits draped over his arm.

"I had them brushed and pressed," he said, standing to attention at the foot of the bed.

"Good." Horst lifted himself on one elbow and reached into the pocket of his coat. He pulled out a one-dollar note and flipped it across the bed. "Here, change it somewhere where they give you the black market value."

"Thank you, *Herr* . . . Reznicek. Thank you very much." The waiter's gratitude was sincere and eager. "Do . . . do you want me for anything else?"

"No, not to-day, Fritz. But I'll probably need you to-morrow. Report to me at nine o'clock to-morrow morning."

"*Jawohl, Herr Ge . . . Herr* Reznicek."

With half-closed eyes von Falkenau watched him picking up his boots and some soiled linen. Fritz Huber had been quite useful. He had the quality most valuable in subordinates: unquestioning obedience. He was not bright enough to betray his superiors. He was just bright enough to carry out orders. If these had been normal times, he would have kept Fritz handy for special jobs. It was almost a pity that he would have to die—and die before long. Still, he might be far more useful in death than alive. And what did one

Fritz Huber count compared to Horst von Falkenau? If five thousand had to die to keep him, von Falkenau, alive, it would not be an unjust proportion.

Leisurely he shaved, washed and dressed. Downstairs at the desk he enquired where the headquarters of the Allied Control Commission were. He was given detailed directions and decided to walk over to the big university building where the Commission was established.

He had to wait half an hour and was not in a very good temper when at last the officer in charge, a harassed and middle-aged British colonel, was ready to receive him.

He produced his papers which the colonel examined perfunctorily and explained the accident that had robbed him of his car. He had to get to Cologne and then to Paris, he said; could he have a priority seat on the first plane early next week? In the meantime he had business to transact in Leipzig; and he produced other documents which provided full excuse why he should not explain this business in detail. He also needed ration cards and a chit to ensure that his room at the Astoria would remain at his disposal.

"Yes, of course, of course," muttered the colonel, "you can have your mess-tickets and your hotel-room appropriation . . . but as for transport, I am afraid you will have to make your own arrangements. The planes are booked up for three weeks to the west. Now if you wanted to go to Prague or even Moscow . . ."

"Cologne, colonel. And then Paris," he reminded the other man tactfully. "Unless I circle the globe, I have to travel west and not east. Do I understand that if I can find an unrequisitioned vehicle, I have your authority to use it?"

"If you can find one," the colonel smiled grimly, "you are welcome to keep it. But you won't. We have combed out every garage and depot in town. Here is a requisitioning order and some petrol coupons. You must exchange these when you leave German territory."

"Thank you, colonel," Horst said. And he thought: it is easy, easier than I thought. If this is their care and vigilance . . . but then, there were other, more dangerous foes he would have to face sooner or later than this little bureaucrat in a colonel's uniform. He knew the type: they were not infrequent in the *Wehrmacht* and their souls were the same under whatever clothes they wore. Now

Helen Fleming, of course, was an entirely different proposition. She had laughed at him and then, with Fritz's well-timed telephone call, he had made her believe his story. But would her belief stand up to the cold, reasoned scrutiny of daylight? He wished he knew what she was thinking at this very moment.

He would have been reassured and even flattered if he had been able to read her thoughts. For after he had left, Helen took a long time going to sleep even though she was desperately tired. She had replenished the fire and curled up in the arm-chair, her feet tucked underneath her long warm gown. She could not make out this strange Czech; and because she was puzzled by him, she could not dismiss him from her thoughts. Always it had been like this: she liked to read people as a book, from cover to cover, no paragraph skipped, every page explored. But this tall, fair-haired man was like a magazine from which pages had been torn out or glued together; whenever she came to an especially interesting passage, she could not find the continuation. And that made her almost angry with him.

She had known quite a few Czechs. There was Hrdlicka, the fat, comfortable chief of the Prague Narcotics Bureau; heavy-lidded, blue-eyed and blue-jowled. A jovial exterior hid a shrewd brain, alert and entertaining. He had produced some wonderful results when that Armenian gang chose Czechoslovakia for its distributing centre. Poor Hrdlicka—he died in Theresienstadt like so many good men. And there was Samoryn, of the Foreign Office, tall and melancholy, rather like a blood-hound, who had the most wonderful tenor voice and with a little gentle encouragement would sing the folk-songs of the Tatra, until one felt like crying because of the glory and despair, the passion and resignation in those songs. . . . She had met them all: pilots and journalists, civil servants and artists. But none of them was like Karel Reznicek. In most of the Czechs, even the artists, she found something passive and slow, something of the deep, yielding yet unconquerable quality of the Good Soldier Schwejk. But no one could compare this man with Schwejk; his nervous vitality, his faint superciliousness, even his smooth, lightly accented English set him apart from his countrymen whom she had known. Perhaps —perhaps he had some German blood in him as so many patriotic and anti-Nazi Czechs had.

Suddenly she felt ashamed. It was playing the old Hitler game, trying to put nations and individuals into watertight compartments; declaring that all Jews must be dark, hook-nosed and predatory—that all Frenchmen were flighty, promiscuous—that all Spaniards were hot-blooded and lazy. Still, it was convenient to enclose people in a circle of national habits and characteristics—and as for Karel Reznicek, it would have made things easier if she could have put him in the right pigeon-hole, declaring to herself that he was just like X, the Czech leader-writer whose eyes the Nazis had put out or Y, the composer who had walked five hundred miles without shoes to cross Poland into Russia. . . . Much easier, much more convenient. As she closed her eyes and felt weariness creeping up her relaxed body, she saw his face, the straight, high-bridged nose, the blue eyes, the strong, cleft chin. It was perfect like a mask; and suddenly she wished that she might penetrate behind it. It was no longer the general, pleasant desire she always felt about new people, new faces; restless until she had discovered their secrets, read their characters. It was something deeper, far more personal—and she shivered a little because it was something unknown and never experienced . . . or was it? She had felt something very similar when Hans Langer first told her his story. It was pity mixed with love; love not yet fierce or possessive, but gentle and therefore all the deadlier.

But it was absurd. She had only met the man once, face to face; that time in the car he was just a voice, a dark shape. She knew nothing of him except that he had come to warn Peter—and now she tried to place him side by side with the young American. It was unfair for they were too dissimilar for any comparison; when she thought of Peter, Helen felt old, far more mature and experienced than he could ever be. But as far as Karel Reznicek was concerned—she thought that behind his regular features, his clear blue eyes, there was an ocean of suffering and cruelty, of wisdom and laughter.

She slept badly and when she woke in the morning, again she thought of him. She did not believe in resisting her impulses and so she rang him. She had a good excuse; there was much more, she was sure, to his story about those Russians and the danger to Peter Whitney. It was her duty, she told herself sternly, to find out whether his story could be trusted—in spite of that horrible voice in the telephone.

XV

IT WAS NOT DIFFICULT TO MAKE him talk. They sat in the warm room, almost cosy with its curtained windows and shabby arm-chairs, sipping coffee she had brewed herself over a spirit lamp. She wore her uniform; for some reason she felt that it would give her dignity, make her less vulnerable—though she could not have explained what threat she feared. He was dressed in a well-cut grey suit with a tiny badge in his buttonhole and his hair glinted in the diffused lamplight with a metallic sheen.

He told her of his youth; how he studied law at Prague University because he wanted to follow in the footsteps of his father who had been one of Masaryk's trusted friends and a judge of the Supreme Court. He spoke of the first years of the young Republic which developed into one of the most democratic and progressive in the world and led the other countries of the Little Entente in trying to create a system of security in Central Europe. He spoke of boating trips on the Váh where the lumberjacks brought down their huge log-rafts from the forests of the Tatra; of long hikes in the Carpathians; of summers spent in the primeval pinewoods of Carpatho-Ruthenia. He got his degree and started to practise in a Prague suburb. His father died just after Munich, his mother soon followed him into the grave.

"They were fortunate," Horst von Falkenau said and his voice expressed just the right degree of grief and stoic renunciation. "It was much better that they died. I had one young sister, Mlada; and because of her I could not leave Prague. When the Nazis marched in, I joined the underground. They were exciting days, rather like playing Red Indians—only this time the torture and death was not make-believe but very real."

Helen had listened to such stories many times before. Some of her London friends at parties, charity bazaars and dances, avoided the men who had escaped from Hitler's hell. With the egotism of youth and the unavoidable insularity of a free nation, they shunned what was unpleasant and tragic. "Oh dear," one lovely creature sighed to Helen, "there is that Captain M. Do let's slip away before he starts to tell us about the three concentration camps he has been in. . . ." Or: "No, I won't dance with Major F. All he can talk about is the Gestapo."

There was too much of it, too much horror, bloodshed, violence. In spite of rockets and flying bombs, of columns in the papers and a flood of books, the Terror Beyond the Water was still unreal and unbelievable to the well-brought up British maiden. Disgusting, too—like talking about the functions of the body or the mating of animals. They could not help it; few if any of them had crawled miles in the snow or hidden in a cesspit to escape the tramping jackboots.

But Helen was different. Because she had spent much of her adult life listening to "foreigners," prying into their fascinating, alien existences, she was not repelled nor bored by the monotonous flood of torture and execution. She heard the same stories over and over again and did her bit to make those men and women forget the nightmares that stalked their waking and sleeping hours. She could give little else except sympathy, being a good listener, helping over the awkward pauses, the gaps in the blighted memory, the catching of breath, the clenching of fists, the perspiration and the empty look as the picture of systematic evil came into the brains of these people.

And so she listened to Horst von Falkenau who was telling her the story of Karel Reznicek. He knew the tale well for the real Karel had been betrayed by someone whom he loved and to whom he had talked freely. He told the story as if he were acting an important, star part—and he had always been a good actor whatever some of the critics and most of his colleagues had said in those far-off days of the nineteen-twenties. He *was* Karel Reznicek just as he had been Egmont and Don Carlos, Wallenstein and Dr. Faust, Hamlet and John Tanner.

"I was first arrested early in 'forty-one," he continued and stared at his hands as if their sight gave him reassurance. "They just picked me up as I came out of a cinema with Mlada. I was taken to Gestapo headquarters and questioned—the usual method. I saw an old Jew beaten to death and it made me resolved to pay back the swine even if it cost me my life. They had nothing against me except the fact that my father was the friend of our great President. Then the S.S. captain tried to trick me—he left my *dossier* on the table and went out of the room. But I noticed that he had marked the page; he would have known if I had moved it an inch. I did not look at it. I pretended to be stupid and he fell for it. They let me go."

He interlocked his hands and pressed them until the knuckles showed white. She said:

"You need not tell me if it—hurts . . ."

He looked up with a quick, grateful, candid glance.

"But I prefer you to know . . . because I know you will understand," he said and she could not help feeling flattered. This was, for some reason, a different story from all the others she had heard. Perhaps because of the quick, enormous vitality of the man, every word painted a picture, every sentence sketched a vivid scene. "I was free to continue my work for another six months. Then came the Nazi attack on Russia. It gave us an enormous encouragement—for we knew that sooner or later the Red Army would reach Czechoslovakia; yes, we believed in the Russian victory even as they reeled back under the first German blows. But in Czechoslovakia they started man-hunts. They needed slaves right behind the front. I was taken on the street with hundreds of others—we were marched to the barracks and told that we had volunteered to fight against the Bolshevik hordes. . . ."

There was mockery in his voice, a sneer at the farce of German pretence; and he felt a warm, inside glow because he was giving such a marvellous performance.

"We were sent to Poland—in cattle trucks, seventy men in each waggon, without food or water for days. It was the beginning of the fighting, the Polish army was not yet broken . . . I tried to escape. But I was caught, beaten and sent to Lwow to await execution."

He paused again, but it was not a dramatic, artificial pause; it was smooth and natural like a full stop at the end of a rounded sentence.

"How did you escape?" Helen asked.

"I didn't," replied Horst. "The Russians marched in four days later and I was released. The Germans had simply forgotten about me."

It was one of the mistakes that had cost the Nazi Reich quite a bit in money, lives and nervous annoyance, thought von Falkenau. Reznicek had proved a nuisance—the real Reznicek, that was.

"I went to Moscow and worked at broadcasting and

translating," he continued. "But I wanted to fight and Russia was not yet at war with Germany—though everyone knew the war was coming. I wanted to get to England, but the only way was by going half across the world. I set out late in 1940. I got stuck in Shanghai and sailed back to Europe just before Pearl Harbour. I had to get back. I had heard that Mlada had been sent to one of the soldiers' brothels in Poland after my escape, and that she had killed herself. I had every reason to . . ."

Once again he paused and this time she remained silent. It was better not to prod these men who had so much to remember, so much more to forget.

He went on after a few minutes; sketching the rest of his adventures: his training in England where a soft-living lawyer had to become a tough soldier; his first parachute jump, his varied adventures in the wooded mountains of Slovakia; his return to England, the subsequent missions to the Slav countries; meetings with Tito's stern men, with Albanian guerrillas, Slovene patriots, Russian intelligence officers, Bulgarian anti-Nazis. The map of the Balkans came to life from the barren Karst to the fir-trees of Zakopane, from the Transylvanian forests to the ravaged plains of the Ukraine.

"I was constantly on the move," he said. "Again and again they told me I should rest, but I could not. I was bitten with the bug of danger and restlessness. There was so much to do! And then, just before the last battles, I was again dropped near Prague. I was there when Benes arrived; I lived through those final, feverish days when it seemed touch-and-go whether the city, my city, Mlada's city, would be destroyed. That was the end—the crowning end."

Yes, it had been the end for Karel Reznicek who never finished his last mission. He was caught, tortured, killed; and his papers, those perfect credentials giving him the powers of an ambassador-at-large reached a *Gauleiter's* mansion—just in time. . . .

His throat was dry when he had ended, but again the feeling of triumph warmed him. He softly put his palms against each other—for he had deserved applause and there was no one to clap, no one to appreciate his performance except himself.

The girl stared at him with a queer expression on her face. Then she said in a low, choking voice:

"I feel ashamed."

He lifted his head suddenly, surprised at this reaction.

"Ashamed? But why?"

"Because I am a woman and there is little I can do. I wanted to do a lot—but sitting in offices, going on tours of inspection, drawing up reports, listening to people—what does it all amount to? I never went hungry, I was never really cold or ragged. Because my father and my young brother were killed by rocket bombs, I thought I had suffered and won the right to . . ."

She turned away and said:

"I am ashamed because I thought myself important and hugged my hate of all those swine as if I had really fought them . . . as if I had made the slightest real contribution to their downfall. . . . But you . . ."

He had not hoped for this. The recital of Karel Reznicek's life and adventures had only been a first step in the plan he had evolved. He thought of the English girl as cold and unemotional, someone who had to be coaxed into life, into the warmth of fire slowly, gradually. For a moment he was taken aback because it had been quicker than he had expected—but he was a good actor and a practised performer; the hesitation was only slight and she never noticed it.

Gently, lightly he put his hands on her shoulders. She winced a tiny bit at his touch but it was because of its suddenness, his fingertips could feel that. Gently and slowly he turned her towards himself. But the rest was swift and almost cruel. As he felt her lips, cool and a little salty from the tears, yield and tremble with a quick, spontaneous flame he forgot that he was playing a part. This was real and it did not matter whether Horst von Falkenau or Karel Reznicek was kissing her; he knew that he could do with her whatever he wanted or chose to do.

XVI

THEY LOOKED AT EACH OTHER and they were no longer strangers. She had become younger, more vulnerable in those few seconds; and he kept a tight hold on himself. He knew that he could still spoil everything; he was working by instinct, without signposts. There was so little he knew about this girl; far less than she knew about Karel Reznicek. But his instincts had never played him false; there had been so many women and he remembered a line he had read in a pocket anthology he took from a British officer's kit who had been shot while "trying to escape." How did it go? "The Colonel's lady and Judy O'Grady are sisters under the skin. . . ." He had never understood the reference to the woman called "Judy O'Grady," but he had guessed the meaning of the line. And whatever the theorists, the overcomplex practitioners of love wrote or said, it was true—with only minor gradations or shades.

And so he kept silent, withdrew his hands and waited—waited for her to give him a clue; it was up to her to bar or release, to fulfil or withhold. But she, too, was silent at first; and in her eyes there was pleading and fear, uncertainty and yet something sure and swift. She did not choose the easy way of turning away; she had courage, that girl, Horst told himself. It would have been easier if he could have spoken his own language in which he knew every shade of caress and wooing. Still, if she kept silent . . . but she broke the tiny, uncomfortable pause:

"Would you like to have some coffee?" she asked.

He stared at her and felt hot under his collar. He still knew almost nothing of her—only the feel of her lips, her tears, her voice, her face—but this he had not expected. Was it to cover her embarrassment or did she really think that a Continental man would speak or think of coffee after he had kissed a woman for the first time?

She was lifting the coffee-pot, half-turned away, and he saw that her tears had started to flow again. Here was a clue he had been waiting for. He took the pot from her and put it down firmly.

"No, I don't want any more coffee," he said and kept her fingers imprisoned in his hand. "And please, don't cry. Why is it that women take love so tragically? It is a gay, a beautiful thing. Only you mustn't theorise about it—so I won't say anything more about it. But you do know that I love you . . . that I had fallen in love with your voice in the dark, with your hair, for I could see nothing else in that car, with . . ."

She turned to him again and though her lips smiled, her eyes were serious:

"You mustn't talk like this. I am not in a tragic mood. I also thought that I wasn't a conventional person—but suddenly I felt so old-fashioned. It's all this," and with her free hand she made a sweeping movement, "this room, this city, this continent. To talk of love seems frivolous —after what you have suffered and all the darkness in front of us. . . ."

"But surely," he argued, "you have all the more right to personal happiness because you have suffered and the world is a grim place. Helen," he spoke her name, slowly, with relish, as if he tasted it on his tongue for the first time, "this is not an age for conventions and formalities. I—I find it difficult to speak my thoughts to you because I do not know the weight of words. But words are a poor substitute for feelings at any time. And we are wasting time on words when . . ."

He kissed her again. But she was passive, a vessel for his passion not flesh and blood he could kindle into a fever. He let her go and rose.

"I think I'd better go," he said. "But you must think about what I have said—about us. I'll be here to-morrow at noon and we'll go out where we can find a little solitude and peace, no houses, no ruined buildings. You will come, won't you?"

She nodded but she did not plead with him to stay. He was a little uneasy as he walked along the darkened corridor. Perhaps he ought to have waited—or perhaps he ought to have stayed. He was not certain. She must be a virgin, he decided; or perhaps unused to making love. If he knew a little more of her—only a little more.

A few months ago it would have been easy. There were Heinrich's famous files, the Library of Blackmail—no doubt he could have found out everything about her, her family, her past, her likes and dislikes. It was amazing how complete those files had been—but they were either buried at the bottom of a salt-mine or burned, scattered, useless.

He shrugged. He had always been at his best when there were great obstacles to surmount, impossible odds to beat. And it was worth taking trouble, worth while biding his time. His half-formulated plans began to fall into a pattern as he made his way back to the Astoria. Fritz Huber would be very useful—for the first and last time in his useless life. Perhaps the plan he had evolved was a little crude and melodramatic—but with the limited means at his disposal and time pressing, he could not afford to elaborate it, to invent something subtler. And in spite of her obvious intelligence and international background, she was naïve, naïve and romantic. It should work. It had to work.

Fritz was not at all enthusiastic when he explained to him what he wanted. Horst had to speak to him rather sharply before he came to heel—and even then he muttered sullenly that he would be a fool to meet trouble half-way.

"You want to get out of Germany, don't you?" asked von Falkenau.

"Yes, sure, but——"

"Have you any hope of getting away if I don't help you?"

"No, but *Herr Ge—Herr* Reznicek, there are so many things that can go wrong. . . ."

"You leave the worrying to me. And you'll do exactly as you are told. Repeat your instructions."

The S.S. man stood to attention. This was something familiar, something his rather narrow mind could grasp and react to. Often before he had been given orders and had to repeat them over and over again until it all became part of his brain, an almost hypnotic command.

"I am to go to the Ranstaedter Steinweg where the *Goldene Laute* garage is. I am to use the password and recognition sign and get one of their hidden cars—a Mercedes, if possible. I am to drive it out on the road to Taucha. When I am two kilometres from Taucha, I am to slow down."

"Right," nodded Horst. "Now what about the rest? And don't forget to paste the UNRRA sign I am going to give you on the windshield."

"Yes, *Herr Ge*—yes, sir." Fritz was still standing at attention, a little frown on his unshaven face as he was trying to remember the rest. "Two kilometres from Taucha I am to leave the car and proceed on foot towards the town. When I see you and a lady, I am to pretend to attack you with a knife. You will then disarm me and I am to flee."

He relaxed suddenly and asked:

"But what if I don't get away? And what if——"

"You will get away. You forgot part of your orders. You are to wait with your pretended attack until you see that we are quite alone. Is that clear?"

"Yes, sir. I am sorry I forgot. But I will remember."

"All right, then. You can leave the rest to me. Report

at the house in the Frankfurterstrasse after dark to-morrow. I'll be there with the papers and we can start immediately."

Fritz Huber saluted, turned on his heel, hesitated and swung round again:

"But if anything should go wrong—if I——"

"Get out!" snapped Horst von Falkenau. "Get out, before I change my mind and pick someone else to do the job."

Like a whipped dog, the S.S. man retreated. When he was gone, Horst lit a cigarette and went over the whole thing step by step. Someone might think, he thought, that he was staging the whole *Attentat* because of the hoary convention that if you saved a maiden's life she was bound to marry you. But that was ridiculous; things like that happened only in the novels of Frau Courths Mahler. No, what he wanted was to jolt this cool and self-possessed Miss Fleming, to jolt her out of her complacency and discover how she would behave in a crisis. That would give him all the pointers he needed. If, as a by-product, he could win her gratitude and sympathy by the whole staged scene, that was a secondary consideration. But he had to know more about her before he went further, before he risked his carefully built-up plot by—but there was plenty of time for that. Even if Captain Whitney returned, it was now too late for him to do anything. Yes, he told himself, it was now too late. Those two might have been lovers but now something had come between them—something he would uncover, something that had separated them. Perhaps he was catching Helen on the rebound but what the hell did it matter as long as he caught her.

XVII

EVERYTHING HAPPENED STRICTLY according to plan—like one of Rommel's retreats. There was one distressing moment, but even the smoothest, best-organised plots have their little snags and uneven passages. And Helen had not noticed anything.

They had walked out on the road towards Taucha. The weather was crisp and clear; her pale face flushed in the fresh, cold air. She was wearing her uniform which he would have found frumpish on any other woman but which suited her admirably. Skilfully he made her talk about herself, her family, her travels and experiences. Much of what she said he did not fully understand; there were references to places and persons, institutions and ideas with which he was totally unfamiliar, but his nimble wit built bridges wherever they were necessary and he received a good overall idea of her mind and emotions. Rich—all these girls were rich—pampered and with a will of her own, she was so unlike the other women he had met. But that made it only more attractive and tempting to follow his plan, to put it to a test. She had lost her father and her young brother through a rocket bomb and she hated Germans—good and bad, Jewish and Gentile, Nazi or Communist—she hated them and was a little ashamed of this hatred. This did not disconcert Horst von Falkenau. It only helped him. This hate blinded her to a certain extent; it made her more in tune with his own adopted role of a Czech patriot; it confused her clear thinking. Horst quite agreed in his mind that she was right in her hate, entitled to it, fully justified; hate was a clear-cut emotion, better than lukewarm disapproval or uncertain indifference.

But he was truly bewildered by her allusions to the dispute or quarrel she had had with Captain Whitney because the American did not share her views about the treatment of Germans, the future of Germany. These Anglo-Saxons were certainly amazing people; a grown-up man and a grown-up woman arguing about something neither of them could influence or do anything about! Letting their personal relationship be affected by abstract considerations of international politics and questions of racial theory! It was something so alien, so inconceivably futile to him that he did not quite believe her, though she was patently sincere about it. There must have been some other reason for their quarrel; something more tangible, more human—but though he efficiently steered the conversation back to the subject which she had soon given up, he could not discover anything more.

And then he saw Fritz Huber walking towards them on the deserted icy road. He was wearing a thin overcoat which was too short for him; his hat was pulled down over his forehead and now and then he peered around suspiciously.

Evidently he wanted to make sure that there was no one else about. Helen glanced up and saw him but continued speaking:

". . . there must be some way. If I knew that there was a third world war coming, I would kill myself. I just could not face it. Perhaps because I was born on Armistice Day . . . something must have conditioned my whole body, my nerves, my brain—I——"

Fritz had reached them and Helen stepped a little to one side to let him pass. The S.S. man stopped and pulled a knife from his inside coat-pocket. He fumbled a little, the blade caught at the lining. Horst called: "Look out!" and the next moment had closed in with his assailant. He had instructed Fritz to put up a good fight and they swayed to and fro while Helen watched them, horrified at the suddenness of the attack. Then she started to tug at Fritz's uplifted arm which held the knife as if preparing to stab. This was not at all according to plan and Horst shook her off, shouting to her to stand aside. She obeyed and a moment later the knife fell from the S.S. man's hand. Horst pretended to try and hold him but Fritz slipped from his grasp and started to run back, along the road he had come.

It was then that von Falkenau fired. The distance was only five or six yards and he was an excellent marksman. He fired to kill, not to wound, but for safety's sake he pumped three bullets into the shabby, uncouth figure. The first made Fritz stop, throw up his arms, spin round and fall. The second bullet went wide but the third smashed the hand with which he was clutching his chest just above his heart.

Horst was conscious of Helen's presence close to him but she did not speak. He started to run towards the crumpling figure. As he bent over Fritz, the dying man opened his eyes and spoke. It was a short, obscene word, expressive of infinite loathing and contempt. Then he saw a filmy, opaque glaze slip over the pupils of the narrow, deep-set eyes and a tiny bubble of bloody froth appear on the lips.

He opened the overcoat and slipped his hand under the grey pullover beneath it. There was no need for that—the S.S. man was dead. He straightened and found Helen's eyes fixed on him. She asked in a whisper:

"Is he dead?"

He nodded.

"Did you—did you have to kill him?"

"What else could I do?" he shrugged. "Such vermin must be destroyed."

"But who was he? Did you know him?"

He looked at her. She was pale but composed, without a trace of hysteria. He took her arm.

"We'd better go back to the city and report this."

"You—you aren't going to leave him here?"

"Now, Helen," he said. "Pull yourself together. There is no need to guard a dead body."

He made her turn away. Reluctantly and in silence she walked at his side.

About a mile and a quarter farther on they came upon the car—a somewhat battered Mercedes.

"This must be his car," he said.

"How do you know?"

He tried the handle on the left side, near the driver's seat. It was not locked. The ignition key was where he had told Fritz to put it—in the tiny compartment above the speedometer. He slipped it into his pocket and then showed it to Helen who stood by listlessly.

"Here you are. No one else would leave a car like this, unattended. Get in, we'll drive back."

"But what if it isn't his car. . . ."

"Now Helen, don't be difficult. I know what I am doing. If it isn't his, I'll leave the car at headquarters and whoever wants can claim it. Come along now."

They drove along in silence until he felt something warm and wet along his left arm. He stopped and explored his sleeve. There was a gash there, shallow but long. Fritz must have done it . . . by mistake, he decided. But it didn't matter now. Fritz was dead.

Helen looked at him and saw the slowly surging blood.

"You are hurt," she cried, "he . . ."

"It's really nothing. But we'd better put something around it or it will mess up my suit."

He took a large white handkerchief from his inside pocket and slipped his arm from the coat.

"You'd better get out," she said, "I can't properly bandage you sitting down."

They stood near the car; the road was empty and the light was lead-coloured because of the low clouds. She took a little cotton-wool from the shoulder-bag she was carrying and made a compact, safe bandage. "You must show it to a doctor," she said, "as soon as we get back."

"It's nothing," he said again.

He shivered a little and reached through the open door of the car for his coat.

"Did you know him . . . who he was?"

"No, but I can guess," he smiled. "Either one of the Vlassov men or just an S.S. thug. We'll find out—sooner or later."

He put the coat around his shoulder. But she made no move to get back into the car.

"And if he had killed you . . ."

"He didn't really have a chance. I had a two months' course of unarmed combat and was pretty good at it. I was only worried that you might get involved."

"But was it you or—me—whom he——"

"I don't know, Helen. It's best to forget about it. It's best to . . ."

She swayed suddenly and would have fallen if he had not caught her. But her fainting fit only lasted a moment. She opened her eyes and he bent down and kissed them.

"I am a fool," she said softly, "I ought to be used to death and violence. It's my tummy that betrays me every time."

But he was kissing her hungrily now, her throat, her lips, her hair. At first she made a half-hearted attempt to push him away. It started to rain, a few sleety drops but they did not notice it. A raindrop ran down her face and he caught it with his lips before it reached her chin. She laughed. He made her sit in the car and stood in front of her.

"Just keep quiet for a moment," he told her. "Very quiet. I want to look at you."

"Whatever for, Karel?" she asked, wide-eyed.

"Just for a moment," he pleaded. "It is such a wonderful contrast. I want to forget about the man on the road and the rain and the cold. It is not a very romantic setting, I am afraid. Moonlight and roses and soft music, that is the conventional way, I believe. Helen, will you marry me?"

He had not paused between the last two sentences nor had the tone of his voice changed. And she did not speak, just stared at him. Horst was quite certain he had done the right thing. But now he was a little uneasy whether he had not done it too early. But no, he had to put it to a test, he had to provoke a crisis; and he had never failed before. Though with this girl of unexpected moods, who offered him coffee after he had kissed her for the first time, who was not shaken by death and violence as other women would be . . .

He waited, uneasily.

And then she spoke and he knew it was all right.

"Oh, Karel," she said, "I—why don't you get in from the rain? You will be soaking wet in a moment."

"But the question—you did not answer the question. . . ."

"I will, darling, I will. It is the most beautiful thing that ever happened to me. It . . ."

He wanted no more and silenced her in the most effective manner he knew. They drove back to Leipzig with Helen at the wheel, her hair brushing his face; and it was a wonderful, fascinating thought that soon he would know her as a man should know a woman—the only way he believed in, the way of the body.

XVIII

FRITZ HUBER, A FORMER MEMBER of the *Spezialdienst* was identified by a *Gruppenfuehrer* of the S.S., awaiting trial in the Leipzig gaol. Horst settled everything without Helen being called as a witness; the knife was found and no one appeared to doubt his word that he had acted in self-defence. Because he made his deposition in her absence, he could tell the military police that Huber had worked as a waiter at the Astoria and that he had noticed his suspicious behaviour but as he had had no proof of the man's intentions he could do nothing. He signed the necessary documents, and was free to go.

Next he drove in the Mercedes to the colonel who had been so sceptical about his ability of finding a car. The colonel was duly impressed by Horst's acquisition and made no difficulty about assigning it to his use. He only asked that when Horst had finished with it, he should turn it over to the nearest transport centre for further disposal. "You

—you wouldn't like a smaller car?" he asked a little wistfully. "I mean, in fair exchange?"

Von Falkenau declined the offer with thanks. No, the Mercedes would do perfectly well—it was a make of car he had driven before and it was particularly suitable for long distance journeys.

It was late in the afternoon when he came once again into the hall of the Kaiserhof. Helen had gone out and he settled down to wait for her in the cavernous lobby.

He was well satisfied with all he had achieved. A day or two and he would have the safest camouflage anybody could wish; and he would have a woman, too. In a fortnight they could be in Spain where he would collect the money he had deposited five years ago—the money and certain other things which would be very useful—and then he could settle down to work. He trusted his ability to keep his two lives apart nor had he the slightest doubt that Helen would refrain from prying into his secrets if he handled her in the right way. He supposed that she might want to return to London and perhaps display her husband—but he could dodge that for the time being. And later—but there was time, time for everything. Perhaps, on second thoughts, they might take a little longer to get to Madrid—after all, he had had a strenuous period of activity and deserved a little relaxation.

He glanced up and found himself looking at Captain Peter Whitney who had just come through the swinging doors, unshaven, mud-spattered and evidently in a very bad temper. Horst smiled; here were the makings of a nice dramatic climax in which he would enjoy his part. Should he wait till Helen came back? He decided against it. After all, she had not told him anything about her relationship to the American and he was not supposed to know anything about it except their quarrel over an idea—a ridiculous, childish thing which had nothing to do fundamentally with reality.

He rose and walked up to the desk; Whitney was just asking for his key and enquiring about any messages.

"Good afternoon, Captain Whitney," Horst said.

The American swung round. There was no recognition at first in his eyes and Horst helped him:

"My name is Karel Reznicek. You were kind enough to give me a lift when my car caught fire."

"Oh yes, sure, Mr. Renzicek. "The American's politeness was rather perfunctory. "You're staying in this hotel?"

"No, I am at the Astoria. You've been away, I believe?"

"Yes, for a couple of days, to Nuremberg. Chased all the way just for a——"

He stopped, suspicion kindling in his glance:

"Say, the last time we met you spoke no English."

"Oh, that!" Horst laughed it off. "I must confess to a little innocent deception. But you see, while you inspected my papers, I had no opportunity of checking up on your identity. Please, accept my apologies. . . ."

But the American was not quite satisfied.

"How did you find out about my trip?"

"I called in your absence," explained von Falkenau glibly but not too glibly. "I had something important to tell you but as you weren't here, I saw Miss Fleming."

"Something important? Well, if you don't mind—I am rather tired now. What about coming back later in the day and having a drink with Helen and me? Then you can tell me whatever your news is."

"I'd much rather speak to you now," Horst said. "Could I come up to your room, please?"

"Listen, Mr. Reznicek. I've had the hell of a time, what with bad roads and driving in pitch-dark. I haven't slept much these last few nights. You're sure it can't wait an hour or so?"

Von Falkenau shrugged. "As you like. But Miss Fleming thought that I should talk to you at the first opportunity."

"She did?" He frowned. His boyish face looked haggard and absurdly earnest. "Well, if you don't mind assisting at my ablutions. I must have a bath if it bursts all the plumbing in this joint."

They did not speak as they walked upstairs. Whitney's room was at the other end of the corridor from Helen's, a fact Horst noted with amused approval.

Inside the room Whitney sighed and peeled off his mud-spattered overcoat, letting it drop on the threadbare carpet with his gauntlet gloves and his cap. The brief-case—pigskin, with his initials and a Yale lock—he put on top of the wardrobe.

He yawned and stretched his arms.

"Excuse me," he said. "I'll take off these filthy clothes and jump into the tub. Old Konrad downstairs told me I'd better grab a bath while the water is hot. I'll leave the door open and we can talk."

He disappeared into the bathroom and returned a minute later clad in a singlet. The bath water was running and steam started to curl round the door.

"Now what is it?" he asked. "I hope you don't think me rude, but I want to get a few hours' sleep. I'll be very busy all day to-morrow."

Horst told him the same story he had told Helen, a little more carefully detailed, adding the bit about Fritz Huber and the adventure on the Taucha road. Half-way through the recital the American rose, went into the bathroom and shut off the water.

When he had finished, Whitney said:

"That's very interesting and I am most grateful to you. I am sure you meant the best—but I can't look at such things seriously. I have always been able to take care of myself . . . and as for those papers which you say those two men mentioned . . ."

His eyes moved a fraction towards the brief-case on the bureau.

". . . I have no papers of value to anybody. I am a very junior officer and no one would dream of trusting me with important documents. So your two Russians or whoever they were, must have made a mistake. Are you sure you heard my name?"

Horst made a gesture which expressed his conviction that he could not have been mistaken.

"Well, thank you again. I'll look into the matter with the proper authorities. Are you staying long in Leipzig?"

"Not for very long."

"I can reach you at the Astoria, can't I?"

"For the next day or two, certainly."

"Well, I'll get in touch with you as soon as I have looked into this whole affair. But as I said, I don't expect it will come to anything."

He disappeared in the bathroom and Horst could hear him stepping into the tub. He hesitated; he needed a conversational gambit to speak about Helen. A bald announcement would mean spoiling everything; yet somehow he felt that he had to tell the American about their engagement before Whitney saw the girl. He made a step towards the door when Peter called out, raising his voice above the sound of running water:

"Reznicek?"

"Yes?"

"Oh, you are still here. I am glad. I just wanted to tell you that while I was up at headquarters, I had a look at your record."

"You did?"

There could be no danger, he reassured himself, none at all. Still, the American's voice was difficult to analyse. Did it hold some menace? But then, he would have known. No, Captain Whitney was not a good actor. And all the tracks had been covered carefully enough.

He moved to the door of the bathroom. The American was sitting in the tub, sunk in the water up to his chin. His arms were brown, lean and strong as he reached out for the soap and began to rub his shoulders meditatively.

"Sure," he grinned and scratched the top of his head with a soapy forefinger. "Just routine, you know. And I must hand it to you—you are apparently quite a guy. Yes sir, quite a guy."

The Americanism disconcerted him a little. What did it exactly mean? He hoped it was complimentary. It must be—or Whitney would not be grinning. It was a friendly, appreciative grin. He smiled back.

"I am afraid I don't understand."

"That job you did in Posen—first class," elaborated the captain. "Why man, you must have borne a charmed life. Still on the same G–2 work, I suppose?"

This was more familiar ground.

"More or less," he replied cautiously.

"That's right, Reznicek," Whitney laughed. "Don't trust your own grandmother. And as for those phoney Russians—don't think I fail to appreciate your warning. I'll keep you posted. And if I was a little abrupt just now—well, I had a hell of a journey and you know how it gets you down sometimes."

"Yes, I know."

He stood there for a moment, leaning against the door-jamb, inspecting the other man reflectively. The American was no fool, he could tell that much; but his ideas and conceptions were so utterly different from his, he moved on a different plane and his reactions were bound to be different, too. He was not a bit afraid of him; instinctively he felt that he could play on the very differences in prejudices and traditions that separated them.

"Forgive me," Horst said suddenly, having found the bridge which he had been trying to build, "I know you must be very tired. But if you can spare a few more minutes . . ."

"Sure, sure. Go ahead."

"It's really a private matter."

"I am honoured by your confidence."

Was he laughing at him? He could not tell for Whitney's face was covered with soap and his eyes closed.

"I need your help," he continued. "I wouldn't have mentioned it except that you told me you have taken the trouble to find out a little about the things I have done and endured. It was nothing much," he added in quick depreciation, "any of my countrymen would have done the same—many have done far more. But I feel that you know something about me and won't misunderstand. It is about Miss Fleming."

The American opened his eyes and closed them again, yelling that the soap had got into them. Blindly he stretched out his hand for the towel; Horst handed it to him and he started to rub his face.

"What?" he asked. "About whom?"

"Miss Fleming—Helen," replied von Falkenau.

Whitney sat up in the tub and absent-mindedly soaped his chest and his armpits.

"What about her?" he repeated. "I didn't know——"

"I don't quite know how to put it," continued Horst with pretended diffidence. "It is a matter of the heart."

"What?" roared the American. He tried to rise but slipped and only saved himself at the last moment by clutching at the edge of the tub. He sat down in undignified haste. Then he smiled.

"For a moment you almost had me worried," he said. "You mean, you have fallen in love with her? Well, Helen is quite a girl. Quite a girl, if I may say so."

There was reminiscent warmth in his voice and Horst wondered whether these two had, after all, been lovers. It did not make him jealous or angry; it was rather in the spirit of scientific curiosity that he tried to guess the answer. He knew enough to realise that it would be a grave mistake to ask Whitney point-blank—even to hint . . .

"Yes, isn't she a wonderful person?" continued the American. "So alive, so . . ." He waved his hand as if the gesture supplied the missing adjective. "Heck, she makes me feel like a small boy and at the same time . . ."

Horst felt that it was time to cut this conversation short. And he felt a sly pleasure at the anticipation of the American's reactions.

"It is true," he said. "I have fallen in love with her." Then he added quietly: "We are engaged to be married and that is why I need your help."

Whitney sat stock-still in the soapy water. The expression on his face was a mixture of dismay and unbelief—and it was utterly ludicrous.

"Do you mind saying that again?"

"I said that we are engaged to be married and that is why I wanted to ask your help," repeated Horst patiently.

"But dang it man, you have only met her—what was it?—less than four days ago! You can't mean to say . . ."

"It has happened before, has it not, that people fell in love very quickly?" enquired Horst.

With quick, nervous gestures Whitney finished his ablutions. He stepped from the bath and wrapped himself in a coarse white towel.

"Don't think me ungracious," he said while he began to rub his chest and back. "But you must admit it was rather unexpected. You—you are sure?"

"But of course I am," laughed von Falkenau. "It is not a thing a man can make a mistake about, is it?"

"No, I suppose not . . . still, Helen is not the sort of girl . . . and in any case . . ."

He sat down, his hair all awry, starting to dry his toes with great care, wiping each one separately and massaging his foot.

Horst kept silent; he knew that this was not the time to crow or display his triumph.

"Did she—did she say anything about me?" asked Whitney after a long pause. He slipped off the towel and put on some light blue pyjamas, covering them with a brown camel-hair dressing-gown. He brushed back his hair with his fingers and lit a cigarette. He remembered a second later to offer one to Horst as well.

"About you? Nothing in particular—except that you had

a little dispute about Germans and Germany," smiled Horst. "A very important subject, of course."

The American blew some smoke through one nostril.

"Look here, Karel," he began, "I like everything to be frank and above-board. If you are going to marry Helen, you ought to know——"

"Please," Horst held up his hand, "I don't want to know anything she would not tell me by herself."

"Don't be absurd, man. Probably she did not tell you because she considered me so unimportant in her life . . . so insignificant, so . . ." He squashed his cigarette savagely on the glass-topped table. "What I mean to say is, she and I were sort of engaged. At least I always understood that she would not mind marrying me once this damned war was quite over. I met her in London, you see, and she was badly cut up, jittery, because her old man and her kid brother had been killed by rockets. Then we were both sent to this accursed country and from the moment we crossed the frontier, I just couldn't do right. Whatever I said, it put her back up, as we say in the States; whenever I opened my mouth, I put my foot in. But I never thought . . . I never dreamt . . ."

He leant forward, his hands on his knees, and asked in a tone of naïve curiosity:

"Say, how did you do it?"

But before the other man could answer, there was a knock at the door and Helen's voice, fresh and a little breathless, called out:

"Peter, I just heard you were back. Can I come in? Are you decent?"

"Come in, come in," the American replied.

The door opened and she stood facing them, her eyes rounded in surprise, her very mouth a red, glistening O. For about three seconds none of them spoke. Her first glance was for Horst and he was reassured, absurdly relieved that her eyes said nothing had changed, everything was all right. Then she looked at Peter. Von Falkenau was sitting sideways so that he could see them both. In the glance the American and the girl exchanged there was something he could not fathom, something from which he was excluded. As if she were pleading for time to explain, for understanding and help; and as if Whitney had promised her all she asked.

Then the American spoke, breaking the spell:

"Come in, Helen. Come right in. We were just going to have a drink. Karel here has been telling me the good news and we were going to celebrate."

She moved closer and he asked, in a less boisterous voice: "I suppose it's true—about Karel and you?"

"Yes," she said slowly, keeping her eyes upon his face. "Oh, Peter, I am sorry. It is true and it is wonderful—but I am sorry. You do understand, don't you?"

The American was fumbling with a bottle he had produced from a cowhide bag. He clinked glasses and when he answered his back was turned to them:

"Understand? But my dear girl, I am delighted. You are sane, white and twenty-one and this is a free country." He laughed and as he turned round with the glasses, he added: "That's rich, isn't it? A free country, I said . . . a free country. . . ."

XIX

IN THE NEXT TWO DAYS HORST discovered that it was easier to find a ton of coffee, a lorryload of coal or an American soldier without campaign ribbons than for an English girl and a Czech—genuine or the imitation article—to get married in occupied Germany. And if it had not been for Peter Whitney, he and Helen Fleming would never have achieved this wonderful and unique feat. Or at least not for weeks and weeks.

Yes, Peter—Horst got into the habit of calling him by his first name though it was not easy—certainly proved a marvellous help. Surprising, too, if you took everything into consideration. After all he had been in love with Helen, still was, however well he camouflaged the fact behind that mixture of nonchalance and rather silly jocularity. . . . But here he was, running around, interviewing colonels, huddling with army padres, quoting precedents, sending telegrams to various mysterious places, making arrangements and plotting to overcome difficulties which cropped up anew every hour. As if he really enjoyed it. Or as if he were a glutton for punishment. "A glutton for punishment," Helen used this expression when they—Horst and she—walked alone one afternoon through the shivering, black city, right out to the battered *Völkerschlacht Denkmal* where a hundred and fifty Nazi fanatics had planned to hold out for three months and gave in after thirty hours.

"I am worried about him," she said. "I hope you don't mind, dear," she added, putting her gloved hand upon his arm. "He seems to be obsessed. As if he wanted to . . ."

"But I think he is only a good friend," Horst had replied. "He wishes you to be happy and he thinks you can be happy if we get married. Is it not so?"

She turned to him. "Yes, yes, ever and ever: yes. You needn't remind me. But Peter—he has changed. Very much so, in the last two days. Ever since I came into his room just after you had told him. You had told him gently, hadn't you? I mean, we can't avoid hurting those we cannot love—but there are ways . . ."

It was then that she had used the strange expression and Horst had said, a little stiffly:

"Please, forgive me . . . my English is not so perfect. What does it mean?"

"Oh, Freud has probably another word for it," she smiled. "It means that he likes to torture himself, that he feels he must make himself unhappy to make us happy—as you said. But it can't be helped. All happiness is selfish—even when it's shared, don't you think so?"

And he agreed, because for once she had something with which both his personalities, Karel Reznicek and Horst von Falkenau, could agree perfectly.

In the end Peter had succeeded in getting the necessary permits and dispensations. They were married in a small army chapel by a Roman Catholic padre. Karel Reznicek was a Catholic and Helen was Church of England but she had wanted the Roman ceremony.

"It is somehow more permanent and more beautiful," she said. "It binds you for ever and ever. Just as we want it."

He had agreed with a polite show of enthusiasm; he did not mind either way. There was a civil ceremony to follow the church wedding and then they all drove back to the Kaiserhof. Peter had given away the bride; he even provided the ring. Two American sergeants, wearing a sheepish grin all the time, were the witnesses. Helen wore her uniform and Karel his formal black clothes, a little the worse for wear.

Peter had also provided the wedding breakfast—which was really a lunch for it was late by the time they came back from the ceremony. There were no guests apart from the two sergeants, the padre and Peter himself. The newly-married couple were to start for Cologne late in the afternoon though they planned to break the journey somewhere on the road.

There was plenty to eat and a lot to drink. The padre left soon after lunch and the two sergeants also faded away. The three of them were left alone over the coffee cups—Helen's little hoard had again provided this rare treat—and the drinks. Helen spoke but little, she seemed to be absent-minded. The tiny furrow between her brows kept reappearing and she tried vainly to rub it away. Horst kept glancing at her and wished that she would speak to him. It was an awkward situation; suddenly she seemed a stranger far away; as if they had not been properly introduced.

The only gay person seemed to be Peter Whitney. He had been drinking steadily but except for a certain brightness in his eyes and a somewhat feverish loquacity alcohol seemed at first to have no effect on him. He was pressing Horst to drink; but von Falkenau did not care for alcohol beyond a certain quantity and refused the generous tots of whisky which the American poured out for him. Helen had not tasted any of it, she had only drunk a little wine with the meal.

"C'me on," Whitney insisted, "be a good sport. You don't get married every day in your life."

"No, thank you, Peter," Horst said a little stiffly. "It's rather late and I'll have to drive some distance to-day."

"So what?" grinned the American. "You—you will be on your honeymoon. Heaps of time. A lifetime of bliss." He started to sing. It was a song about a lady named Sweet Genevieve, cloying and sentimental. He sang softly and rather well. Helen sat there, rubbing the little frown that would not go away. Horst rose.

"I think we ought to be going."

"Give me ten minutes," Helen said suddenly and smiled. The smile made everything all right. "I want to change and make sure I have put the right things in my small bag."

She got up and Peter also struggled to his feet, a little unsteadily. He held on to the edge of the table.

"Farewell, fair lady," he said with a gesture that started to be sweeping and cavalierly but ended rather clumsily as he upset a wine-glass. "May all your days be merry and bright . . . and may all your Christmases be white."

"Peter, you need a breath of fresh air," the girl said. "You are not at all romantic when you are tight."

"Who is tight?" protested Whitney. "I resent that. I resent that considerably and with gusto. Try me. Try me on anything. Just try me." He lifted his arms slowly, as if there were great weights attached to them. "See!" he said triumphantly. "Perfectly steady. Respiration: normal. Blood pressure: splendid. Try me." He spoke slowly, deliberately, emphasising each syllable: "Pro-cras-ti-na-tion. Hyd-ro-ce-pha-lic. Trans-sub-stan-ti-a-tion." He appeared to like the last word because he repeated it two or three times. Then he sat down, rather abruptly. He waved his hand again. "Good-bye, my lovely. Like a vision, softly, coming into the darkness of the night. And gone again. O-ho, gone again. Just a fleeting visit from a better world."

Helen laid her hand on his shoulder for a moment.

"I'll meet you down at the car in fifteen minutes," she whispered to Horst and then she was gone.

As the door closed, the American swung round.

"Have a drink," he said. "Have two drinks. Take the bottle. I don't need it. I can be perfectly miserable without it."

Horst moved closer to him.

"Wouldn't you like to lie down?" he asked. "You know, you have had a little too much."

He touched Whitney's arm but Peter jerked it away

"Take your hands off me," he shouted suddenly. "Don't you dare. I am perfectly O.K."

He drank and poured out another jigger of whisky.

"I am sorry," he mumbled. "Bad manners. Must be good sport. Good loser. Good sport. Good loser. I apologise."

He narrowed his eyes and looked at Horst.

"A Czech," he said and laughed suddenly. "Just imagine. Helen marrying a Czech. Schwanda the piper. The Good Soldier Schwejk. Skoda munitions. A wonderful country. A wonderful people. Long live President Benes!" He got up again and lifted his glass. "I said three cheers for President Benes! He is a jolly good fellow! So are you! So are we all! All jolly good fellows."

He sat down and dragged Horst to the chair next to him. He bent close to his ear and Horst could feel his warm breath, spiced with whisky.

"Every bone in your body," he was saying fiercely. "You understand? I break every body in your bone—I mean, the other way round—if you don't treat her right. You got to treat her right. I'll be watching you. All the time."

A sly, secretive look came over his face.

"You don't believe me? You don't think I speak the truth? The gospel truth. I have my little secrets. Buck Ryan and Superman ain't a patch on little Peter Whitney. At this very moment . . ."

He checked himself. Horst was rather bored and not a little shocked. To him Peter Whitney was an officer and a gentleman. Of course these Yankees . . . but even so. He wanted to get away but he was afraid that the American would follow him down to the car and possibly make a scene. He poured out a drink and Peter took it gratefully, gulping it down as if he were very thirsty.

"Yes, my friend," he continued with his monologue. "Do you know that I am an important man? Do you know I was hauled all the way to Nuremberg—what a ghastly place it is now—and given a most confidential task? High-ly con-fi-den-tial!" he repeated, breaking the two words into syllables. "Do you know what I have in my brief-case—this very moment?"

"No, I don't," said Horst curtly. "And you'd better not tell me."

"Look at the coward!" shouted Peter Whitney. "Look at the tactful little Czech. Who the hell are you to tell me what I am supposed to say—and what I am not? You . . ."

He caught hold of Horst's coat and shook the lapel to emphasise every word:

"I got a list in there of all the Kraut bigwigs who are still at large . . . and what we know of them . . . and where we hope to catch them. Every single mother's son of them. Every . . ."

He raised himself with some effort hanging on to Horst.

"Perhaps you don't believe me? Perhaps you think I am a liar? I'll show you—I'll . . ."

He fumbled in his pocket and pulled out a thin gold chain to which three keys were attached. He shambled across the room and pulled out a drawer.

He had some difficulty in finding the right key and inserting it in the lock of the brief-case but at last he succeeded.

"Here you are," he cried triumphantly and swept a bundle of papers upon the untidy table. "Everything's here. Only one copy. Very important. I am a very important man. I am . . ."

The papers slipped from his fingers and the brief-case thudded on the floor. He would have fallen if Horst had not caught him.

"Dizzy," he murmured, "everything dizzy—just rest my eyes. Just rest my eyes for little minute—just——"

Von Falkenau dragged him to the sofa and straightened his limbs. Peter Whitney was dead drunk now and almost in a coma. Horst put up his legs and placed a pillow under his head. Then he returned to the table and collected the papers, bending now for the brief-case. He was just about to slip the sheaf of documents back into the case when his glance fell upon the top sheet—and his own name.

He hesitated. But he would have been less than human if he had resisted the temptation. His hand moved almost without conscious volition and then he was reading the closely-typed lines:

"Horst von Falkenau, 45, *Gauleiter* of ——. General of the S.S. Decorations ——. Personal description ——. On the war criminal list of ——."

It was the usual stuff and his lips curled in a sneer—there was a good deal they did not know. But then his glance went down the sheet and he stopped, standing quite still. In red ink a few lines were added:

"A body, badly burned, supposed to be that of Horst von Falkenau was found at ——. Certain circumstances however indicate that it was not H. v. F. See dental chart procured from Dr. Thaler, Bielefeld, Kurgasse 18. Compare also partial fingerprint record in possession of Gestapo archives found at Salzlangan. Dactiloscopical evidence unreliable because only fragment of skin remained on body. Investigation advised."

For a moment he felt panic but it was less than a fleeting impulse. He was safe now, he told himself, safer than if he were alone—and he thought of Helen almost with gratitude. He never expected that they would have gone into this whole matter so carefully and thoroughly. After all he had not been one of the "Top Ten"; his fame or notoriety was

European but not world-wide. He remembered now with some annoyance Dr. Thaler, a tall, handsome, fresh-faced man whom Heinrich had recommended and who had stopped one or two of his teeth. And of course, Kemmerich's teeth were deplorable.

Swiftly, methodically he went through the rest of the papers. He removed the sheet relating to himself and then he found a sort of general list, an index to the rest of the documents. These two he put into his inner coat pocket, then he gathered the rest, smoothed them out, put around them the rubber band which Peter Whitney had removed and replaced them in the brief-case. Back it went into the drawer after he had locked it. Thoughtfully he twirled the thin gold chain with the three keys around his thumb. The American was still dead to the world. Horst rolled him over on his right side and insinuated the keys back into his trouser pocket. He stood there for a second, staring reflectively at the unconscious man. Then he shrugged. Captain Peter Whitney would have a whale of a hangover when he woke up but that was not his, Horst's, headache. As a matter of fact he hoped that he would never meet the American again—not in this world, anyhow. And the next world could take care of itself.

Softly he closed the door behind him and ran lightly down the stairs. Helen was waiting for him at the bottom, smiling a little tremulously, and he took her arm.

XX

THE CAR STOPPED; HORST PUT on the handbrake and switched off the engine.

"*Liebchen,*" he said, "this is an awful confession to make, but I am afraid I have lost the way."

She turned towards him and smiled but he could see that she was tired.

"I must have taken the wrong turning after Fulda," he continued. "We are much too much to the south. I suppose you would not mind if we missed Cologne after all?"

"No, not a bit. Only it's a little late—if we could find a place . . ."

He put his hand on hers. Her fingers were cold, inert; she did not return his pressure.

"I know," he went on, "it's rotten luck. Perhaps we should have stayed in Leipzig the first night. . . . But somehow I wanted to get away."

He was carrying it off very well, he thought. Helen had been silent and very quiet throughout the long drive and had not noticed that he had deliberately taken the road to the south. Horst did not think that Peter Whitney would wake for several hours and even then it was unlikely that he would go through his brief-case and even if he did that . . . But still, it was better to take no chances. He touched his chest near the spot where the two thin sheets of paper nestled in his pocket. It would be awkward if the American . . . The best he could do, at the first quiet moment, was to memorise the contents of the second sheet and then burn both of them. Only one copy, Whitney had said—yes, it seemed to be foolproof.

"What about driving to the next village or town?" he said brightly. "There is bound to be something—even if it's a private house. . . ."

"Yes, that would be the best," she answered. Then she added, surprisingly: "Oh, Karel, I am really a very stupid woman."

"Regrets?" he asked with a half-smile.

"No, no regrets at all," she said quickly and though he measured her voice and watched the inflexion, he could find no insincerity in it. "Only—for some reason or other, probably nerves—I feel suddenly afraid."

"Afraid? Of what? Of me?"

"I suppose," she laughed, a little nervously, "because it was so sudden. . . . It is the most idiotic feeling but somehow I started to think of my mother. As if I were a schoolgirl who needed to be told the facts of life . . . and as if Mummy would ever do anything as grown-up or maternal. But—you understand, don't you?"

"Of course, dear," he said quickly. He did not understand her at all. But he put *that* problem resolutely out of his mind. There were other things to think about. They were married, it was all legal, sealed and delivered and . . .

He switched on the engine. If he kept to the south,

this secondary road would take them into Urzell. It was a pleasant little place so far as he could remember it and quite possibly it might be unoccupied by any troops—it was so unimportant and out of the way. Once, a very long time ago, he had spent a week with a girl in Urzell. He could not remember her name nor her face—but her hair was long and heavy and fair; the sort of hair which she used to comb for hours, drawing electric sparks from it and he liked to watch her. What was her . . . no, it was not worth the effort trying to remember her name. She used to write him letters to Dresden when he was there at the *Schauspielhaus* and she wrote on cheap, scented stationery—which was one good reason why he never answered the letters. . . .

. . . Half an hour later they drove along the long, moonlit street he remembered quite clearly. The overhanging gables, the whitewashed houses, the little benches set at the side of each door—all this was familiar. But the street was empty, not a soul about. He glanced again at the houses; they all seemed to be undamaged, the roofs sleekly gleaming, the windows unbroken though blind, lightless.

He stopped the car in front of the small inn called *Zum Posthorn*.

"I'll see whether I can rouse someone," he told Helen. She nodded and he walked up to the heavy oaken door and started to hammer on it with the end of his torch. It took several minutes before the door opened and a tousled head appeared in the narrow crack.

"What do you want?" a sleepy, quavering voice said.

"Food and a bedroom for two," replied Horst in German.

"We can't take in anybody without permission," replied the voice plaintively.

"I am a member of the Allied Control Commission," said Horst and his tone was clipped, firm. "My wife and I have been on the road for twelve hours. Open at once. . . ."

The door creaked open, reluctantly, and disclosed a tall, thin old man clad in a threadbare dressing-gown under which showed his long nightshirt, embroidered at the neck. He was actually wearing a nightcap—a venerable piece of clothing Horst had not seen for thirty years. He held a candle in his hand and his bare feet were thrust into leather slippers.

"*Jawohl, Herr General*," he said, choosing for safety's sake the highest rank he could think of. "But we have no electric light and no——"

"You have a stove?"

"Yes, that we have."

"And wood?"

"A few logs . . ."

"Good. And I am sure you will have some food. Eggs. Milk. Anything. I'll bring in the luggage."

He returned to the car and found that Helen had dozed off. He tilted up her chin with a gentle forefinger and she opened her eyes.

"It's all right," he said. "We'll get something to eat and a warm room. Probably feather beds, if you don't mind."

"No, I don't mind. I am so tired, I could sleep on a plank." She staggered as she got out of the car and he had to steady her.

Inside there was a large flagged hall in which the shadows danced; only two flickering candles illuminated it. The old man had disappeared but a lad of about thirteen had taken his place. He relieved Horst of the suit-cases and led the way upstairs.

The room was large and very cold; but the old man was already kneeling in front of the tiled stove, stuffing its maw with thick slabs of wood and kindling. He touched a match to the paper and the flame shot up as if eager to consume all.

"We have no running water," the old man said, rising stiffly from his knees. "But Klaus here will fetch some from the well. Where would you like to have your meal, sir?"

"Up here, I think," replied Horst. "Does it suit you, my dear?" he asked Helen. She nodded wearily. "You might try to find us some wine," he added.

The old man looked dubious but von Falkenau slipped a folded note into his hand which made his eyes light up with happy greed. He bowed and scraped as he backed out of the room.

Helen sat down in one of the brown, carved chairs. She looked pale and worn. Horst opened his bag and took out a flask.

"Here," he said, "drink some of this. It will warm you up."

She took a sip. It was brandy, strong and rather crude. It made her choke but it also brought back some colour to her cheeks. She smiled.

"I ought to say something, oughtn't I?" she giggled. "But all I can think of are the stock phrases. 'Alone at last!' and 'Oh what a blissful night!' I wish we had special words for special occasions, don't you?"

He was rummaging in the bag, his back to her. He turned now:

"What did you say?" he asked.

"Oh, nothing. I was just being silly."

He explored the room, drawing aside some bright cretonne curtains. Behind them there was an alcove and in the alcove a tremendous four-poster with bedding piled up high on it. He slipped his hand under the double eiderdown.

"Not even damp," he said. "And the mattresses seem to be all right. There is nothing I hate so much as a lumpy mattress."

"Oh Karel," she said and started to laugh. "Oh, Karel, you are priceless. . . ."

He frowned, turning away his face. He did not understand her.

"You'd better take off your coat and boots," he said. "What about your dressing-gown? Look, I'll go down and see about our supper. The boy ought to be here with the water any moment. Tidy up—I'll be back in ten minutes."

She nodded and he retired, closing the door softly behind him. Downstairs the hall was still as dim and deserted; on the dusty desk a big, leather-bound register lay open, a pen with ink-encrusted nib marking the page.

There was no one about though he heard some subdued rattling of crockery through a half-open door on the left. He hesitated for a moment, then, idly and without any real curiosity, he glanced at the register. The inn *Zum Posthorn* did not seem to have many visitors. The last one had checked out two days ago and the one before him . . .

His finger suddenly stopped half-way up the page. He stared at it and noticed that the nail needed cleaning; an undisciplined, incongruous thought that made him annoyed.

Two men had signed the register together—their names were bracketed. Both had come from Leipzig and were bound for Stuttgart. There was nothing unusual about that. What was unusual and maddening was the name the first man had signed in bold, flowing script.

Frederick Rickman, U.S. Army.

Frederick Rickman. Frederick Rick . . . Something repeated the name in his brain as if he had turned into a cracked gramophone record. Frederick Rickman was the fictitious American whose papers had been stolen from the safe in the Frankfurterstrasse. Frederick Rickman was his enemy, the thief who took the money and documents which would have meant final and absolute safety. Frederick Rickman, of all people, had been staying here in this small inn. Naturally he had to sign the register with the name on his faked papers. Only four days ago he had been here.

A blind, inarticulate rage possessed Horst; he felt that his collar had grown tight and with trembling fingers he tried to loosen it. If "Frederick Rickman," whoever he was, could have stood in front of him, he would have shot him down and damned the consequences. He felt that he had never hated anyone so much in his life as the faceless, anonymous figure who had robbed him of what was his, reserved for him, almost his birthright. He took up the pen and jabbed it into the ruled page, leaving a ragged tear along the side; then the pen-holder broke and he threw it aside.

With an almost physical effort he lifted himself from the trough of fury. He turned round and stared at the old man in the shabby dressing-gown who had shuffled up without Horst noticing him.

"What do you want?"

The old man winced. "I—I just came to say, *Herr General*, your supper is ready. And I found a bottle of Rüdesheimer." He added in an obsequious tone: "Would you sign the register, please?"

"What?" Horst was still dazed, occupied with his own thoughts. "Oh yes . . . the wine . . . the register. . . ."

He actually had scrawled the letters *Ho*—— before he realised what he was doing. Savagely he dipped the pen which had broken into half, in the inkstand and superimposed the first two letters of his adopted name. "*Karel Reznicek and wife. . . .*"

This would never do. He had made one or two small slips before. No one had noticed anything and only he himself knew how he had failed. But from now on he would be less and less alone; he must remain on his guard twenty-four hours a day. He could deal with this old fool easily enough, he knew: but Helen was an entirely different matter.

He turned to the innkeeper:

"What's your name, by the way?"

"Andreas Foerster, at your service."

"I was looking at your register and noticed the name of a

friend. I have lost sight of him for some time and would be glad to meet him again."

Don't talk too much, he warned himself, don't be garrulous, that's always suspicious. You are giving a sham performance. More nonchalance, less patronising superiority.

"Yes, *mein Herr*?" The old man did not quite understand him.

"His name is Frederick Rickman. Of course it isn't impossible that it may be a different man altogether. Do you remember him?"

"Not very well," Foerster answered. "I was in bed with lumbago most of the day he and his friend stayed. But I saw him when he left."

"Could you describe him?"

It was hopeless; the old man was the typical vague witness. He said Rickman had been tall and rather plump; but he could not give the colour of his hair or eyes, any special marks or features. After five minutes Horst gave him up in disgust.

"Do you happen to remember what was their destination?"

"I can't say I do," the innkeeper scratched his head. Then his face brightened. "Of course, it's there in the book." He read it out laboriously: "Stuttgart, Hotel Marquardt . . . That's it, Hotel Marquardt. And a very fine hotel it is . . ."

He looked expectantly at Horst but he was in no mood of tipping the old fool again. At this moment the boy came into the hall, carrying a tray. Horst followed him up the stairs.

XXI

IT WAS WELL AFTER LUNCH before they started next day.

"We'd better make for Stuttgart," Horst had said as they sat after breakfast in the pleasantly warm room. The big tiled stove had kept the heat and young Klaus had rekindled the fire when he had brought their breakfast tray. A touching domestic scene, von Falkenau thought sardonically as he looked at Helen across the table. She was wearing her blue dressing-gown, her naked feet were thrust into feathery mules; her brown hair was tousled and its strands caught the sun coming through the deep-set window. A sense of possession and security took hold of him, however much he tried to sneer at her and himself in his thoughts.

"Yes, Karel," she said meekly. "Stuttgart."

"I don't like main roads— there will be far too much military traffic," he continued. "But we can cut across the Spessart and the eastern part of the Odenwald . . . perhaps the best place to hit the Stuttgart road is at Michelstadt. Even that isn't an *Autobahn*. What do you think?"

"Yes, that will be fine."

"You weren't listening," he accused her and took her hand. Her fingers curled up and pressed his; then she turned his hand palm upwards and traced the three deep lines across it.

"If I were a gipsy, I would tell your fortune now—and my own, too," she said. "Karel—do you think it will last?"

He pretended to be dense. "What are you talking about?"

Last night it had been simple and rather wonderful. There had been no need to play any part. Karel Reznicek had disappeared and Horst von Falkenau lost his identity. There was no cause for pretension, for the guards and barriers being watched second after second; no need for planning and caution. It was the basic equation of all human relationships: a man and a woman. He could not have put into words what he had expected from the night. He knew that she was different from all the other women he had slept with, and yet fundamentally, beneath the trappings of convention, nationality, upbringing, traditions—the whole ridiculous mass of shields and reservations—she must be the same, he thought.

What she gave him was perfect contentment and relaxation. He took her, as naturally and gently, as if he had handled a young animal, a half-blind puppy or a soft, seemingly boneless kitten. And she did not play the part of the blushing bride; nor did she try to be the harlot in order to cloak her fears. The fact that she had been a virgin did not seem to be important; as she became a woman, it was as if she had never been outside the threshold, waiting for fulfilment.

He thought that he was foolproof against any weakness; but though he consciously struggled, it was all swept away. He yielded to the impulse of tenderness, of protective love. For the first time in his life he felt that here was something, something he wanted to keep. Perhaps in a day, a week, a month he would think differently and hate himself for this momentary weakness. But now it seemed impossible that he should ever reach such a state. For one wild moment he thought that he would tell her everything; nothing could separate them now, not even the load he carried, the shadows that trailed him. It lasted only a moment and then he forgot again everything outside the warm shell of the room, the firelight flickering on the walls, coming from the opened iron door of the stove, the warm white body close to him.

"What are you talking about?" he asked and hoped that she would not reply. It was better not to put it into words.

And she understood him. "You know. You know better than I do. And there is no need to answer. Your eyes . . ."

Suddenly for no reason at all she felt proud and gay. Proud because of the joy and pleasure she had given this man; gay because the doubt and restlessness, the strangeness and loneliness had vanished. He was closer to her now than any human being ever was. Last night there had been the initial shock and violation of what she felt to be her privacy, her integrity. It had been more of a mental than a physical shock; but it had not lasted long. Its place was taken by a feeling that all her life, all her twenty-seven years, she had waited for this, that she had grown towards this, fumbled her way blindly until suddenly she realised: this was the end of the road, this was the goal. . . .

"If we find something nice on the way, we'll stop," he continued. "There is no hurry. If we make Paris in three or four days—what's the difference? I haven't had a holiday for six years—almost seven. We deserve one, don't we?"

She nodded and thought that she ought to have a friend, a confidante, an old-fashioned duenna to whom she could talk about him. You could not very well discuss a man with himself; and yet she had so many things to discuss, analyse, put into words. She decided to write a letter—to her mother, to one of her colleagues in the Paris UNRRA office, to Peter . . . no, not to Peter. It was the first time she had remembered the American since they left him at the Kaiserhof, and he was dim and unimportant as if he had never played a part in her life. Yes, a letter, a long, chatty letter—even if she never mailed it.

Horst got up, folded the map, gathered the breakfast things on the tray and put the tray outside the door.

"We have plenty of time," he said.

As he bent over her, she began to tremble. It was stupid and she wished she could control herself. The shiver of anticipation ran down her spine and she closed her eyes, waiting for him, falling into the deep and dark abyss, falling and yet safe because they were falling together.

XXII

THEY HAD DINNER AT SODEN IN the Sulzbachtal where they found a French divisional headquarters installed. Horst produced his papers and the colonel in charge welcomed a gallant Czech ally with effusive protestations of admiration and friendship. When von Falkenau hinted discreetly that he and his wife had been recently married, the Frenchman became all smiling courtesy and solicitude. *Hélas*, he could not offer them a night's lodging, for the houses of the little watering-place nestling in the wooded valley were packed with his troops and with some French workers awaiting repatriation, but he promised that he would give them a dinner that would have made Brillat-Savarin lick his lips in delighted appreciation.

It was all so easy and pleasant; they had an aperitif on the veranda of the hotel which served as headquarters. Helen and the colonel chatted amicably and vivaciously about Paris; Horst was content to lean back and listen. One or two junior officers drifted in, attracted by a feminine presence like homing bees to the hive; in a few minutes Helen was the centre of a laughing, chattering group. *Monsieur le mari* was a little neglected—but then, it served him right, withdrawing such a beautiful and charming woman from circulation, the selfish beast. That was what the glances of the young officers expressed and even the colonel, his brown face intent as he listened to one of Helen's stories, seemed to agree with them.

They lingered over the dinner which was really excellent, with plenty of Rhenish wine and two bottles of champagne. There were toasts to which Horst replied in his careful but idiomatic French. The colonel was sure that they would find accommodation just across the Main in Klingenberg;

he had stayed at the hotel a few days ago and found it in good repair but almost completely empty. If M. Reznicek had any difficulty he should only mention the colonel's name; that would be quite sufficient an introduction as he had the hotel-keeper under his thumb.

It was dark when they said good-bye to the friendly French; but they had less than ten miles to drive and the road was easy to follow. It climbed the side of the valley and then ran through the woods towards the river. The stone bridge was down, the colonel had told Horst, but there was a pontoon bridge.

About a mile from the river the road narrowed and became twisting, with nasty double bends and potholes that shook even the well-sprung Mercedes. Horst drove carefully but absent-mindedly. Helen was talking about the officers, their unquenchable gaiety and high spirits; how one of them had travelled all the way from Lake Tchad to the Rhine and yet longed for the last lap of the journey that would take him back to Paris. He listened to her with one ear; she had just made some funny remark and he turned to her when she cried:

"Look out, Karel! Look out!"

Sharply outlined in the headlights of the car a stag stood in the middle of the road. It seemed quite undisturbed by their approach or perhaps it was blinded by the lights. Too late Horst wrenched the wheel aside; too late the stag bounded, now alarmed at the closeness of the four-wheeled monster. The last thing he felt was Helen's hand pressing his arm. Then something rose and hit him sharply on the head. He lost consciousness.

When he recovered it, he was lying on his back in the grass on the roadside. Helen was bending over him, bathing his temples with eau-de-Cologne with which she had saturated her handkerchief. It stung his abrased skin and he sat up suddenly. The incautious movement sent a stab of pain through his head.

"Lie down," she said and gently forced him back. He noticed that she had folded his overcoat and placed it under his head. He closed his eyes.

"What happened?" he asked.

"You almost hit the stag—and finished up by hitting the roof with your head. But you stopped the car before we ran into the ditch."

"You—you are all right?"

"Of course, dear. Luckily the window was open on my side or I would have dived through the glass. Does your poor head hurt?"

He was all right so long as he kept his eyes closed. It was ridiculous that a slight blow on the head should incapacitate him. He felt it gingerly. There was a sizable lump there but no blood. He opened his eyes again. Helen's face was above him, dim and tender. He could not resist touching her cheek.

"We should be getting on," he said faintly.

"Yes, in a moment. Just rest. There's heaps of time."

"How long . . . how long was I out?"

"Only about ten minutes. You looked so uncomfortable in the car, I dragged you out. I was afraid that . . ."

He lifted her hand and pressed it to his lips.

"No, no, Helen. I have a very hard skull. Very hard."

His hand crept to his coat-pocket, as if to reassure himself that the sheets of paper were still there. To-morrow, at the latest, he would memorise them and then burn the lot. To-morrow . . . He closed his eyes again for the pain had returned. It must have been a slight concussion, he reasoned.

"Helen," he murmured, "I'll just rest a few minutes and then we can go on. I'll be all right."

"I can drive," she said. "You ought to see a doctor."

"No," he said stubbornly. "It's nothing. Just a bump on my head. A cold compress and a night in bed . . . I'll be fit as a fiddle. . . ."

She squatted down at his side, holding his hand. Now, in the darkness, the stabbing pain was more bearable. He breathed softly, carefully, as if the motion of his lungs might jolt him back into agony. He counted his pulse-beats slowly, between each surge of pain which still ebbed and rose regularly.

He must have dozed off, for when he opened his eyes next, though it was difficult to focus them at first, the pain had become a dull throbbing. Helen had been watching him, her eyes upon his face. She smiled.

"Feeling better?" she asked.

"Yes, much better." Gingerly he sat up. "Quite well, I think," he added. "I can drive now."

"No, dear, you might feel groggy quite suddenly. Let me do it."

"Nonsense," he said gruffly. "I——"

But when he tried to get to his feet, he suddenly agreed with her. The trees spun round and he had to clutch her shoulder to steady himself. She bore up well under his weight and helped him to the car. He was panting heavily by the time he sagged down on the seat.

"I'll be all right in a moment," he mumbled, keeping his eyes closed. The darkness was filled with purple shooting stars and yellow Catherine wheels. Slowly the dizziness melted away. "I am sorry to be such a nuisance," he said. "You can drive on now."

Silently she let in the clutch and the car jerked forwards. The jolt brought back the pain but he gritted his teeth.

"We'll be there in no time," Helen said. "And you can go straight to bed. Poor Karel."

He felt a little irritated by her compassion. But it was only natural. The next moment she put into words his silent thought:

"You know we women like nothing better than to get a helpless male in our hands and nurse him."

"I am afraid I am a very bad patient," he smiled. "That's one dark secret I did not tell you. I like to be left alone."

"Oh, I won't make a fuss. Only—even a slight concussion might be dangerous. That's why you need rest and a doctor."

He did not answer; he was quite certain that he would be all right by the morning. In a few minutes they reached the pontoon bridge and were challenged by a French sentry. Horst produced their papers—the colonel had given him an extra pass—and Helen drove slowly, carefully, across the swaying, broad contraption. Ten minutes later she stopped in front of the hotel.

Again the French colonel's name worked wonders; they were given a spacious, pleasant room overlooking the river. Horst felt a little better; he refused Helen's offer to help him undress. But it was quite an effort to get off his clothes and when he stretched himself under the cold sheets, he started to shiver. Helen had disappeared and he was grateful for that; he could fight the nausea alone.

But she returned in a few minutes, carrying an earthenware hot-water bottle which she pushed under the bedclothes, fussing and persuading him to tell her whether it

was all right; then she made him drink a glass of mulled wine.

"Now go to sleep," she said. "I put a luminal tablet in the wine—it should give you plenty of rest."

He wanted to protest that he had never used drugs; but gradually the shivering stopped and warmth stole over his body. Drowsily he turned towards the wall. It was good for once not to feel responsibility, not to be tense. His head still ached but it was a distant, rhythmic, almost pleasant pain. He opened his eyes and saw Helen moving about the room; she was wearing her dressing-gown and doing things at the built-in wash-stand. She seemed to belong to the room, to his life. Yes, he decided with a sigh as he closed his eyes and surrendered himself to sleep, he had chosen well and acted wisely when he married Helen Fleming.

XXIII

Everything was grey, with infinite variations and shadings of the same greyness. Darker overhead as if there was more substance to it; gradually lightening as it neared the ground until it became the gossamer-grey of a moth's wing. All colour had been drained from this world except grey and at first it was restful and pleasant. No longer had the eye to contend with clamouring purple and rampant blue; the full-throated yellow and the ostentatious green had vanished alike. He had no sense of space or shape. Everything melted and merged into this neutral tint. Its very drabness seemed to give security as if it camouflaged all that might mean betrayal.

Perhaps it was some cavern in which he stood, some vast underground chamber stretching into the infinite with hundreds of tunnels, passages, shafts and galleries opening from it. He could not see these but he knew they were there. He felt perfectly confident that he could pick his way through this dingy maze, this dun-coloured underground world. He needed no Ariadne's thread, no guide, no blazed marks; the compass was inside him, its needle swinging always into the right direction, unerringly, with supreme confidence.

But still he hesitated. He was confident of his strength and his ability but he did not quite know what task had been set, what labours had been chosen for him. He stood there, on the floor of the sombre cave, waiting for the word. Someone, surely, would tell him what he had to do. It was no use setting out, no use beginning the fight unless he knew the goal and the enemy.

Someone, he felt sure, would speak in a moment, lull his uneasy doubts which began to whirl around him as if shaped out of the cinereous fog. The voice—he could almost hear it now—would echo from the vaulted, invisible ceiling, reverberate in the funnels and chambers of rock. Still, it would be clear and easy to follow. Until it came, until the words were spoken, he had nothing to do and nothing to fear. Relaxed, he could wait in this slate-grey world, disembodied and yet poised for instant action.

He waited. But there was only silence and the ages passed, now fleeting, now dragging leaden feet. Impatience and irritation welled up in him. He was ready and willing; why did not the voice call him? Perhaps if he reminded it of his existence, perhaps if he moved and spoke, it would come. He was not a bootblack or a lackey to be kept hanging around because of some whim or deliberate malice. He . . .

Air flooded his lungs as he opened his mouth and called out. His voice shattered the silence, the greyness swirled as if a myriad bats had taken flight from their nests, the spirals and whirling columns of tawny, intangible colour danced around him as if they would never settle. He stood his ground. He wished he could remember the name he cried, the word he spoke, but it seemed to be lost in the grizzled air, the grey storm.

No matter: the answer would come. Question and answer, black and white, right and left, good and evil, night and day—there was a duality in all things. A voice calling out a query could not be left without reply; not in his world where everything was orderly and carefully planned. He felt no uneasiness as the swirling draperies of fog gradually came to rest and once again he was standing firm in the mouse-coloured space.

But the silence remained unbroken and suddenly he knew that it would be no use challenging it again. All at once the greyness, restful and protective, held a menace. There was something or someone hidden in it, opaque as the dingy tint itself; crouching, preparing to pounce. He could feel its physical presence as if it were the scent of an animal. For a moment he was well satisfied with this discovery. If there was danger, he could defy it; if his enemy was about to attack,

he could defend himself. Anything would be better than this vague feeling of uneasiness, this pallid silence, this tension without any apparent cause.

Still he waited, but though the crouching foe was somewhere around him, nothing happened. He was left with this feeling of hidden hostility that would perhaps never reveal itself. The thought crept on him that it would never happen; that for the rest of his life he would stand here, isolated and forlorn, waiting for an attack that never came, a voice that never called. It filled him with revolt and bitterness that quickly turned into rage. His hands clenched, he felt his nails digging into his palm and he knew, without a mirror, that his face was distorted in a fury that was unreasonable because there could not be any valid reason for it. They could not treat him like this, he thought and did not pause to consider who "they" were. They could not ignore him or just pay him enough attention to keep him in this state of uncertainty. He had proved to a full measure what he could do. Let them crush him, let them release all the demons of this grey hell; it did not matter as long as they took notice of his existence.

He plunged forward and rushed against the nearest wall of rock. He lifted his hands and began to pound the grey, slate-like substance. He had expected sharp pain, blood, splintering bones; but the wall was soft and pliable as if its substance were rubber. His knuckles made a deep impression on it; but a moment later it had sprung back and there was no trace of his blows.

The panic which swamped him was stronger than any force he had ever encountered. His arms flaying, perspiration streaming down his body, he repeated the assault. Fear forced him into furious activity; he knew that if he stopped for a moment now, everything would be lost. He heard himself utter inarticulate, choking cries and as the soft, yielding wall was smoothed out again and again, he stumbled and fell against it and woke.

Horst von Falkenau lay still and stared into the darkness. He heard Helen's quiet breathing. He was exhausted as if he had gone through a boxing match of many rounds. But in a few moments he was reassured and calm again. It must have been the slight accident, he told himself, while his eyes gradually discerned the outlines of bed and chair, cupboard and table. He could not remember having ever dreamt before in his life; at least he had never been able to recall his dreams and even now the outlines of the one he had just had began to fade until he was left with a vague impression of something unpleasant that was already half-forgotten. His headache had gone and apart from the weakness and the clinging, cold sweat that covered his body, he felt almost normal.

He shook his head. This would never do, he told himself; quite confident that it would never occur again. If there was anything he prided himself upon, it was the steadiness of his nerve, the non-existence of what that old Jew had called the "subconscious." Semitic claptrap, no doubt. One of these days he might even read a book about it; but now he'd better go to sleep again and recover his full strength. Nothing could harm him; certainly nothing that was inside him, in his brain or—he almost had spoken the word aloud—in his so-called soul.

XXIV

THE GENERAL WAS THIN AND only five-feet-four. He lived on liver pills and files—at least that was what his aides used to say. Wiry and irascible, he had the deserved reputation of a compact little devil who worked eighteen hours a day and expected his subordinates to do the same. Blasphemy punctuated his sentences; obscenity flavoured them with a special spice. No one could ever explain the mystery why everybody liked and admired him. He was a dour Connecticut Yankee who took nothing for granted; a bachelor with a grudge against mankind and the sole relaxation of writing hymns when the spirit came upon him. But the hymns he never showed anybody in the army; at least he did not make his troops sing them.

His main grudge against humanity and the War Department was that they had not given him a fighting job. He held one just after Pearl Harbour but malaria laid him by the heels for six months and when he bullied Washington into letting him return to active duty, they put him into Intelligence. He had the necessary qualifications, being a good linguist, a superb psychologist and a born policeman

—three qualities which are seldom combined in one man. Nor was his task without an element of danger and romantic excitement. Yet General Steele looked upon it as a pen-pushing, Paul Pryish sort of occupation.

He was in a worse temper than ever because for once he had every reason to be angry. The young officer who stood stiffly at attention had to use all his strength not to quail before the storm that broke upon him.

"Don't remember! Don't remember!" the general repeated with infinite scorn. "Damn it, Whitney, are you a half-wit?"

He paused in his pacing, thrust his wizened face right up to Peter's chest—he did not reach higher—and repeated:

"Are you a half-wit? Yes or no? Answer me!"

"No, sir."

"My best man, I told Washington. The brightest or at least the only one who doesn't think that we are playing Dick Tracy or Superman in G-2! For Christ's sake, speak up? Can't you remember anything?"

"I only know, sir, that the papers were locked in my brief-case and that the key did not leave my pocket for a moment."

"Did you go to bed in your trousers?"

"No, sir. But I had the key strapped to my wrist."

"Mysteries! Sure enough, the man is asking me to solve riddles! Do you want a bucket of water to sober you up?"

"I am quite sober, sir."

"But you were drunk, weren't you, Whitney?" The small man's forefinger stabbed at his lowest coat-button. "You were roaring, stinking drunk in the Kaiserhof, weren't you? The dispatch-rider found you . . ."

"Yes, I was drunk, sir."

"An officer! A man of brains! A youngster with legal training and experience! Drunk!"

Peter kept silent. There was nothing he could say. All the evidence was against him and he could hope for no mercy. The General had broken men for far less. Desperately he tried to remember once more what had happened. The wedding . . . and then the three of them . . . and nothing more. What had happened when he had had that last drink—at least he thought it was the last—he could not recall. As if an iron curtain had descended which divided the two moments. One second he remembered staring at Karel's face—pleasant enough but it seemed to wobble and dissolve in that alcoholic memory—and the next there was darkness until the dispatch-rider shook him into consciousness the next morning. As he sat up, his first thought was for the keys—and when he found them, nestling between the small change in his pocket, he was filled with almost delirious happiness. He could not have explained why he was worried about them—except that every morning when he woke, his first unconscious gesture was to touch the narrow bracelet to which he always fastened them—but there they were, all correct and present . . . and he could have kissed them in his joy.

The dispatch-rider had looked curiously at him. He had sat up and explored the roof of his mouth with his tongue. This was not the usual hangover but the grandfather of all "mornings after." He wished he had some hot black coffee handy. But there were only empty bottles and glasses on the table and the room looked a shambles. He signed, with slightly trembling fingers, the receipt of the message. The General wanted him again, at once. A fine thing when he had only returned three days ago! But there was nothing he could do about it.

It was later in the afternoon when a bath had restored him to something like semi-normality that he thought of the papers in the brief-case. He might refresh his memory before he faced the old devil, he thought, and spilled the contents of the leather case on to the table. Half-way through the pile he noticed that they were not in their accustomed order. He had not looked at them since he had come back to Leipzig but he had a trained memory and he remembered how he had grouped them in the Nuremberg office. In a small red-leather note-book he had made a check-list of them, using code abbreviations no one could understand, and he started to compare it with the papers. Fifteen minutes later he knew that two of them were missing—the general summary and one individual sheet. His check-list did not show whose name had been on that personal sheet; for the list was simply numbered and could be re-checked against the summary. Now that was gone he could only determine the number of the missing document but not to whom it referred.

Frantic now, he went through the empty brief-case, then the drawer in which he had kept it and finally through the whole room. This was pure madness for he knew the missing papers could not be there—if they had been removed from the brief-case, whoever did it must have taken them away. But who could it have been? The key was with him all through the days and nights and . . .

Helen? But why should she do it? Anyhow, she never had the opportunity, she never was in this room alone—nor did she know what papers he had in his brief-case. Then who else? The staff of the hotel? But how did they get hold of the key? And he knew that hotel staffs at houses where Allied officers were staying had been checked rigorously. Then . . .

Karel? It was impossible. He had made it his business to investigate the Czech and there could be no doubt about his *bona fides*. True, they had been together in this room until he had passed out. What happened afterwards? However hard he cudgelled his brains, he could not remember. He was almost certain that Helen and Karel had left before he drank that last glass . . . he had nothing to accuse them of, nothing to confront them with. . . .

He was almost frantic with worry by the time he reached Nuremberg. It was no use postponing the ordeal—he told General Steele that somehow or other he had lost these important documents and that he was now prepared to face the music.

That, of course, made Old Leatherguts—another nickname of General Steele—explode with wrath.

"Face the music! Face the music!" he repeated. "What do you think this is, a Hollywood supercolossal? Come to your senses, man! Think! Think!"

As a matter of fact when he faced the General, Peter Whitney felt himself participating in an unreal scene—something out of "The Four Feathers" or "The Lives of a Bengal Lancer." The brilliant young officer, he sneered at himself, who gallantly takes the blame and, disgraced, redeems his honour by a brilliant deed of heroism. At the end of all there was the heroine in pink organdie, the old family mansion with the Virginia creepers and the final dissolve as the lovers melted in a kiss . . . But life was not Hollywood. He was in a devil of a mess and with no prospect of getting out of it . . . No prospect . . . no prospect. . . .

He was jerked back by General Steele's rasping voice:

"The only other copy of that summary is in Washington. I am sending a radio message at once to have it returned—by air."

"There—there is another copy?" Peter stammered.

"Do you think because you are an idiot, everybody else must be one?" shouted the General. "Of course there has to be a court martial," he added. "You have every chance of being dishonourably discharged—with perhaps a year or so in prison. A fine career, Captain Whitney!"

"But, sir, if there is another copy——"

"Don't start snivelling. Do you think I can hush this up? Do you think the War Department will think it is a charming fancy of mine to waste a few thousand gallons of gasoline just to fetch a sheet of paper from the District of Columbia? I have to tell them the truth. The matter is out of my hands. Completely out of my hands."

"Yes, sir."

"Don't yes-sir me, you drunkard! Don't you realise what this means? Satan knows, they hate me enough, those pen-pushers in the Pentagon. A slip like this and . . ."

"I am sorry, sir."

"As if that would make the slightest difference. I can take care of myself, don't worry. But what about you? What are you going to do? How are you going to face your people at home? Do you think any law firm would have anything to do with you?"

"I'll be all right, sir."

"Don't try to console me as if I were a maiden lady who lost her umbrella. Let's go over it again. Now . . ."

It was no use. They went over it again, three times, and the General only desisted because it was time for his pills and hot barley-water. Having refreshed himself, he dismissed Whitney.

"I am not putting you under arrest until I hear from Washington," he said. "But, of course, you'll stay close to headquarters. And . . . Whitney?"

"Yes, sir?"

Old Leatherguts drew himself up and said:

"I wouldn't do anything stupid. The coward's way out and all that—though it's a damned silly expression. You take hold of yourself and try to remember. That's all I ask for."

Try to remember! It was no good asking that. Peter began to think that something must have been put into that last double whisky—a devilish drug, brewed by Dr. Fu Manchu or some similar fictional Borgia which gave him partial amnesia. Or had he been hypnotised? He wandered out of the General's room in which not so long ago the crazy sadist, Streicher, had given pep-talks to his underlings, and sat down in the courtyard. He was hidden by some hideous columns from which the swastikas had been chipped off. No, the "coward's way out" was not for him. He liked the Old Man's sauce, assuming that he would think of anything as cockeyed as suicide. If he only knew what had happened . . . if he only knew. . . .

The aide-de-camp looked at young Captain Whitney with a pitying smile.

"What? Disturb him when he is in conference? I don't want to find myself in some God-forsaken hole supervising Kraut prisoners," he said. "No, you be a good boy and wait."

So he had to wait and this was sheer agony. But at last the conference had ended and he was once more admitted to the august presence of General Steele.

"Well," Old Leatherguts greeted him, "what is it? Did you get that brain of yours to work? Do you remember?"

"No, sir. But I——"

"Get out, man. I can't waste my time on fools like you. Of all the gosh-darned, ornery, low-down . . ."

Captain Whitney took a deep breath and committed *lèse-majesté*. He actually interrupted the General.

"Sir, I think I know who could help me to remember."

"What?"

"I have told you about Miss Fleming . . . that is, she is Mrs. Reznicek now, and her husband. They were with me just before . . ."

"Before you got stinking drunk. I know. Go on."

"They left while I was asleep. I know their route. If I could catch up with them, I am sure they would be able to give me some clue, some indication of what had happened. They may have noticed something . . . someone lurking around . . . or anything suspicious. Of course they could not know that I had lo—mislaid the papers. But if I could talk to them, I am sure . . ."

The General who had been doing his hungry tiger act, stopped and gave him a searching look.

"Captain Whitney, are you trying to take me for a ride?"

"No, sir. Honest, I could locate them—in a few days—a week at the most. They were stopping at Cologne and then going on to Paris. Karel Reznicek was bound to get in touch with the Czech military mission. In a car or a plane I could . . ."

The General folded his short arms and teetered on his heels while he weighed Peter's proposal.

"Uhmhm . . . by rights I ought to lock you up. Instead of which you have the colossal effrontery to ask for a Paris leave. I must say you are the most insolent bungler I have ever seen."

"Yes, sir."

"Don't act so meek as if peanut butter wouldn't melt in your mouth. If you think you can go A.W.O.L., you are greatly mistaken. I'll catch you if I have to travel all the way to Tokyo to do it."

"I am not running away, sir, I give you my solemn word of honour. . . ."

"Pah, don't use your copybook words with me. If I let you go—*if* I said—it will only be because I think you are too much of a fool to pull a fast one on me. A week, you said?"

"Yes, sir," replied Peter, having great difficulty to keep his face straight. The old devil was going to play ball. He would get his chance—and he would be a prize idiot if he could not take the full advantage of it. But he knew he was not out of the wood yet.

The General sat down behind his desk. He looked small and forlorn behind its vast expanse but his leathery face was taut and menacing in expression.

"Listen Peter," he said slowly "I am taking an awful chance. I am giving you a fortnight to wind this up. In a fortnight from now you'll report here whether you have cleared up this business or not. At midnight a fortnight from to-day your time is up. I can't let you have a plane; that means answering awkward questions. But you can take a jeep and a driver."

"I'd rather go alone, sir, if you don't mind."

"Oh no, you won't. You are taking a driver—one of our ex-cops. He'll keep an eye upon you. God help you if you don't stick to the bargain. I am getting old and sentimental, that's why I am doing it. But these silly moods of mine don't last long. Go and draw a month's pay," he scribbled something on a sheet of paper, "some K-rations and get yourself enough gas coupons for a couple of thousand miles. That's all."

Peter knew better than to try and thank the General. He just said: "Yes, sir. Certainly, sir." He marched out of the room and when he got into the hall, he danced a little jig to show how happy he was. Helen and Karel would help him, he was sure. There had to be an explanation to this stupid mystery. He had a fortnight and a fighting chance. That was all he had wanted.

XXV

HELEN AND THE FRENCH ARMY doctor who called him "*mon vieux*" and told jokes that were reminiscent of very old copies of *La Vie Parisienne*, kept Horst in bed for three days. At first he stormed at his wife that he needed no doctor but she was tactful and persuasive. He realised that he would benefit from the rest if not from the medical attention; he had been on the go for a good many days, living to a certain extent on his nerves and perhaps this drowsy idling was a good tonic for the journey ahead. Up to now he had had amazing luck and everything had gone smoothly. He was too good a tactician not to realise that it could not last for ever. He was quite confident of his ability to tackle any emergency—but there was Helen who represented camouflage and safety but at the same time was a responsibility when he had a part to play demanding all his artistry. So he endured her cosseting and attention; yes, she had been quite truthful when she had said that every woman loved to nurse a man who was thus helpless, at her mercy. The doctor said that he could find no trace of a concussion, his reactions were all normal; but a blow on the head was always a tricky matter. He should rest and sleep as much as he could; he prescribed a mild sedative and then departed after congratulating Horst upon his charming and intelligent wife.

But on the fourth day von Falkenau began to be fidgety and impatient. After all, he had a certain task to carry out. Stuttgart first and then Strasbourg; Paris, if necessary, but if he could devise some way by which they could avoid the French capital and strike south-west, it would be much better. Paris was big but Paris was a centre for many Allied activities—among others, Intelligence. It would be safer to keep away from the big cities; his papers and his acting would stand up much better to the scrutiny of provincial officials, innocent subalterns or simple village policemen than . . . But that was something he could decide later. Fortunately in Helen's eyes he had built up his work as something confidential and irregular; so long as the part was well acted, he could make her believe anything he wanted. At least he thought so.

He slept late on that fourth day and when he woke he saw Helen sitting at the small table, her short hair tousled, her face intent; she was writing.

"Is it an autobiography?" he asked lazily. "Or has spring stirred you to poetry?"

She turned quickly:

"Oh, Karel, you are awake! Now I am sure you want breakfast. I'll go down and tell them. It's no use ringing, they simply won't answer the bell."

"I don't want breakfast," he said. "I want you, young woman. But first: no evasions. What were you writing?"

"A letter."

"To Peter Whitney, I suppose?"

"No, Mr. Nosey Parker. To my mother. I am a very errant daughter but even so I think she ought to know I am married."

"By all means tell her," he said indifferently. "But don't make it too long."

While she continued to scribble he lay on his back and watched the ceiling. What would happen, he thought, if he found the man with the ring—the man who had stolen the papers of Frederick Rickman? Now he was not angry, he could weigh the possibilities dispassionately. The papers were not much use to him—unless he could persuade Helen that for some reason or other he had to change his identity. But that might take a lot of explaining and an even more careful watch over every detail. No, he decided without the slightest emotion, he would have to kill the pseudo-Frederick Rickman and his companion, too, if necessary; but the papers could not be of any use to him. Of course if they had money on them, that was a different matter.

Helen finished the letter, sighed, put it into an envelope and sealed it.

"You really don't want any breakfast?"

Horst looked at his wrist-watch: "No, but I wouldn't mind having some lunch. And after that I am going to get up, have a bath and a shave—and off we go, *Liebchen*."

"I'll see about the lunch at once. But as for going—the doctor said . . ."

"No, no, my sweet. I am strong as a lion. The doctor is an old fool. And you must not forget, that this is not our proper honeymoon. We will have that next year, in the Tatra. I really must get on with my work."

She came over to his bed and sat down close to him.

"Karel," she said, while he started to play with a strand of her hair and then slipped his fingers down to her small ear, "may I ask a question?"

"But of course."

"Don't tell me if you can't or don't want to . . . but what is your work?"

He took her into his arms and whispered in a mock-dramatic voice:

"I am a gunman. I track down people and kill them."

She remained passive and there was a tiny edge to her voice when she spoke again:

"I meant it seriously. Don't laugh at me, please. I feel a bit like Bluebeard's wife. Are there any skeletons in your closets?"

"Alas, I have no closets. Listen, Helen. My secrets are not my own. I am not being pompous or melodramatic. But though the fighting in Europe is over, there is still much to do. Call me a special agent—a cross between a diplomat and a detective. I—I may even have to change my identity at one time or another. You trust me, don't you?"

"I married you."

There was no pathos in the three words; a simple statement of faith, it reassured him and chased away the slight uneasiness he had felt at her original question.

"Be patient a little," he said slowly. "It won't last long. And then we'll spend our evenings in a nice, quiet way. I'll tell you an interminable serial story and you can listen and admire your husband's valour."

"You are silly," she laughed and as he bent her head back,

searching for her lips, protested: "Don't, Karel. You want your lunch. I must . . ."

"I am not hungry," he murmured. "Food is an evil necessity. It won't harm you either if you miss a meal. You are getting plump, you know."

She laughed, closing her eyes. The curtains were drawn and outside rain lashed the windows. Again the sense of being enclosed in a shell of safety came upon him; her closeness, the scent of her hair, his own rested and stirring body all contributed to it. Yes, she was someone to keep. He almost made himself believe that he could keep her.

Afterwards she went to sleep like a tired child, curled up against his side. He watched her for a while and gently drew his arm from under her head. He, too, began to feel drowsy. They could start later in the evening, he thought, or to-morrow morning; it would make no great difference. He was sure, somehow, that he would overtake those two men —and if he did not, there were others who could deal with them once he was in Spain. Spring should be pleasant in San Sebastian. And later they could go up to Madrid or . . .

. . . The wet snow which had started to melt in the afternoon squelched underfoot. He was second in the Indian file and every step was a special effort. They had been on the move for three days now but Franz had said that they could take a long rest after this job had been finished. It was the most important of all. Kowalski was a rich man and an important one; a mill-owner who had stolen all his wealth from the Germans and would now die for it. They would show them who was the master in Silesia which those murderers and thugs in Versailles had given to Poland on a platter. They would show them . . . they would . . .

Weariness crept up his feet, encased in old army boots, under the leather leggings and the riding breeches until it reached his midriff. His arms felt frozen and stiff; he had to give his leather jacket to Paul, the youngest, who was coughing badly. But Kowalski was sitting in his mansion, swilling champagne and growing fat on German blood and marrow, the swine. . . .

For six hours they had been walking, skipping through the woods, avoiding the main roads, crossing the ravines, slithering across the railway lines where they could not help coming out into the open. Franz was the leader; dark-haired, twenty-two, and his face the colour of clay. He had been a U-boat commander—he still wore his Iron Cross first class under his shirt—but that was in the other world, the one before the November day which had ended everything. Franz was the leader but he, Horst von Falkenau, was the second-in-command and the real brains of the outfit. He liked Franz to think that he gave the orders; but the orders were suggested by him, a stripling of nineteen, who had only fought for two years and even that in the infantry. . . .

He was no longer conscious of the long, weary tramp, the melting snow, the sharp stones jutting out of it. Everything had grown more than life-size. He knew what was going to happen but at the same time he felt a sense of expectation as if he were reading a serial, avid for the next instalment because it was broken off at the most thrilling point. The seven men who marched over the ridge, around the slag-heaps and made their way towards the big house on the hill, were part of some pageant; their movements, their subdued voices, all directed by some off-stage power they could not resist. He was spectator and actor in the same person; though he could not see his own face, it was an indistinct blur, he had no doubt about his identity, his participation in the events that would unroll, yard by yard, like the painted canvas of a song-vendor on an old-time fair.

They were at the house now; with Paul he made off to the left where the dogs were kept. Big, ugly brutes, Alsatians the spy they had sent ahead three days ago had reported. They were trained to attack prowlers on sight. Snow began to filter down from the dark skies again; he felt the flakes as they landed on his hand and the wet kiss tickled his skin.

The three dogs came on them in a compact, almost silent group, as if their fury would not waste itself on snarling or barking. Paul slipped and almost fell but Horst steadied him and the next moment he felt the fetid breath of one of the dogs upon his face as it reared up on its hind legs, snapping at his throat. He had some difficulty in freeing his knife and cursed himself for not having it ready, but before the sharp canine teeth could fasten in his flesh, he had slipped it from the sheath just in time. Even so the teeth of the brute grazed his arm as it fell back with a smothered yelp, its throat slit. Paul was having trouble with the other two but together now they dispatched them. The younger boy was sobbing and trembling and Horst smacked his face hard to bring him back to his senses. He was impatient to join the others who were having all the fun and did not wait for Paul to recover completely, but set out silently to make the circuit of the house.

He felt the biting cold, the burning spot on his skin where the dog had nipped him; his feet were wet and his nose was running. But at the same time, with all the physical discomfort sharply impressed upon his senses, he saw already the scene in the big flagged hall with the refectory table upturned and the people lined up in front of it. He saw it and saw beyond it, too, their journey back into the forest, the braggadocio and the loud-mouthed talk slowly dying down until Franz began to sing the old marching song. . . . It was as if he saw three pictures superimposed on each other like a film which had been exposed three times. A little blurred but clear enough. But there was no emotion in him, only an emptiness and an urgency to get it over.

It was exactly as he had seen it: Franz and the others in their shabby and fantastic clothes standing with their backs to the nail-studded immense oak door and in front of them the six people: Kowalski, his wife, his son and the three servants. He wondered that there were only three until he remembered that the others slept in the cottages behind the house and that Kurt was taking care of them in case of need.

But Kowalski was not fat; he was a tall old man with a thatch of white hair, a brown face and a white moustache. He looked just like one of the Roman Senators he remembered from the history book, sitting stiff and proud while the Vandals prowled through the Forum. Only he was standing, not sitting. His wife was a faded small woman and his son, dark-haired, dark-eyed, with twitching lips as if he could hardly restrain himself from jumping at the invaders.

He had no personal feelings about Kowalski; it was a Vehme *job like the others the* Freicorps *expected you to do—you killed and burned, wrecked and then went away; a plumber did his job with leaking pipes, a carpenter planed some shelves—it was exactly the same. Rather dull and unpleasant, but you had no choice. You did not expect retribution because you had no sense of guilt; though Paul and some of the younger ones often gnashed their teeth and moaned in their sleep as if they were going through all of it again.*

"You beasts," Kowalski was saying in a high, strained voice, and Horst noticed that he had a strong Polish accent, "you beasts. It won't last long and you'll hang—every one of you."

Franz nodded and the rifles spoke. The echoes shattered

the air, reverberating from the high rafters, sweeping along the panelled walls as if they would never end. Kowalski slowly slid down in front of the upturned table; one hand grasping the edge of the polished top, was sharply outlined with trembling fingers. The nails were clean and square-cut, but the hand was old with grey hairs and uneven skin. Horst watched the hand, waiting for it to release its grasp and slide down. But it took an endless time and he shifted his eyes.

The woman had fallen on her back and the young man on top of her as if he wanted to shield her even in death. He could not see her face but her dressing-gown had opened and showed her yellow skin. It was an obscene and disturbing sight, though under the dressing-gown she was wearing a high-collared nightdress. Just that triangle of skin between neck and breasts, wrinkled and yellow and dead. The son had fallen across her body, his face upturned, his nostrils black, and on his face an expression of scorn and awe. The three servants were also dead but he did not bother to look at them.

It could not have lasted more than a few seconds but he felt that this brief interval would never end. He found himself wishing passionately that someone would move or shout. The echo had died away now and the silence was complete. Suddenly panic seized him that he would be left alone with the bodies, that the others would steal away. It was not the guilt of the deed; it was only the sense that he would have to face them alone, already stiff, sprawling in the undignified attitudes of death that made him uneasy. Perhaps they would rise and demand to be killed over and over again—and what if he had spent all his ammunition?

Then back in the darkness and the cold; again he was second in the Indian file. Behind them the house was dark and desolate. Their orders were not to burn it for they were a long way from headquarters and the blaze would raise the alarm too early. Twenty-five miles or more in the snow, and at the prospect of the long tramp his heart sank. It was not fair, he thought; they ought to provide transport. The killing was a nuisance —but this long walk. Frostbite and chilblains, rheumatism and even pneumonia—the Cause was not worth all this. You could not expect heroes to walk fifty miles like footsloggers. They did the dirty work and the Chief sat in the farmhouse and gave orders. It was not fair. He was going to do something about it. He would tell the Chief what he thought of him. One day, perhaps, he might press the trigger by mistake and no one would notice it in the woods. Sometimes the Chief came with them—if it was a specially spectacular job or someone he knew personally and hated. Then, in the forest, among the trees—an accident. And he, Horst von Falkenau, an officer and a gentleman even if they had torn his epaulettes from his shoulders when he came back from Flanders, even if the Kaiser had fled and the Sozis *were playing at starting a Republic . . . he might become Chief instead. There was Franz, but Franz was not ambitious; he just wanted to kill because he could not break himself of the habit.*

But the twenty-five miles still stretched in front of him, endless and disheartening. The squelching snow, Paul's snuffling, the roots jutting out from the snowdrifts and tripping up the unwary—it was hateful. This was not what he had joined the Freicorps *for. He would do something about it. He would . . .*

. . . Horst von Falkenau opened his eyes. He felt a stranger, lost in some world of others' making. Why was he lying here in bed and who was this strange woman at his side? She was breathing softly and she was lovely—but this was no time for women or for bed. He must tell the Chief . . . he must remember to impress upon him the vital importance of . . .

Helen stirred and opened her eyes. As she lay on her side, for one moment their glances met. There was blank, puzzled lack of recognition in Horst's, while hers were shining with sleep and contentment, the soft warm glow in a woman's eyes who has—at least for the moment—nothing to ask of Fate. But her look dimmed; almost dismayed, she asked:

"What is it? What has happened? Is anything wrong?"

The eyes and the voice brought him back from the distance. The effort was tremendous but he just managed to find the tone of nonchalance and affection that was needed.

"It's nothing, my sweet. I've only just woken myself. I thought I had had a dream—a very silly one."

She sat up, the flimsy nightgown slipping from her rounded shoulders.

"How exciting!" she clapped. "You never told me that you used to have dreams—I mean, dreams to remember. I always make a vow while I dream to keep it in my mind—but I never can. It slips away. And I *do* love dreams. Tell me, what was it about?"

"Nothing . . . really . . . I can't remember."

This was getting tougher. It was not the dream that disturbed him. Those years were so distant and all trace of them had been wiped out except in his own mind—and even there, he thought, they were safely under lock and key. Lost or just locked away, together with those childhood memories, the first shameful and starving days at the *Kammerspiele*, the intrigues and disappointments of his rather brief but not unglorious acting career. What came afterwards . . . no, he could control that, at any time.

What made him uneasy was the mere fact of dreaming. He could not remember having ever dreamt before—except that first night in Klingenberg but that was immediately after the stupid accident and did not count. Surely it did not count . . . surely there were ways and means to prevent them coming? He was quite confident that there were and that he would be able to use them. He could beat anything outside and inside him—he had done it before, again and again—why should it all change suddenly?

Dreams could not change nor influence reality and all his life he had been a realist. Perhaps his nerves were a little overstrained. Well, he would take better care of his body and his mind could take care of itself.

Lazily he stretched. The darkness had disappeared; all this was familiar and homely. He traced the tender curve of Helen's arm and said:

"If I am not mistaken, you promised me some lunch—about three hours ago. . . ."

XXVI

STRASBOURG WAS LIKE A madhouse and it took them three hours before they found a room in a third-rate hotel on the Place de la Gare. Horst was furious and Helen meekly amused at her lord and master's storming that did not seem to produce the right results this time. His temper was still short when they unpacked in the shabby, soiled room, and wisely she kept silent. She had met enough Continentals and knew a sufficient amount about men to realise the virtues of keeping one's mouth shut.

But after dinner he seemed to be more cheerful. He had drunk more wine than usual but it had no special effect on him except that he talked more than normally—about Czechoslovakia, about the news in the paper he had picked up from an empty chair and about Paris.

"Would you mind very much if we had to turn south?" he asked. "I have to get my instructions here—as a matter of fact I have an appointment in fifteen minutes—and it is not impossible that I'll be sent to Bordeaux."

"No, I wouldn't mind," she replied slowly, "except that sooner or later I have to report in Paris. You know, I only made temporary arrangements for leave and . . ."

"But of course you will resign. I mean—I don't want a wife in uniform. You have a perfect reason now, a husband to look after."

This was quite a surprise. She had not thought that he would be so possessive . . . and somewhat old-fashioned too.

"I don't think I can do that," she answered, picking her words carefully. "You see, I undertook to serve two years and only six months have passed. I have to apply for release in the normal way and . . ."

He lifted his hands in a gesture of comic despair.

"Red tape! Nothing but red tape! Terrible! I'll settle everything if you leave it to me. If I have to go south, we'll telegraph from Bordeaux to your chief in London. Then I'll take you to Spain and we'll be lazy for a month or so. . . ."

"But Spain, Karel . . . I mean . . . you never mentioned it before. . . ."

"The war is over. People have once again the right to live private lives. They will look after the Germans without you."

That hurt her. "Of course I know my work is not important," she began, but he cut her short.

"Work and you—that's a contradiction in terms. If I were an Indian prince, I would build you a string of palaces and you would have nothing to do except to sit in them and stay beautiful."

She laughed. He was so absurd and lovable; and every hour she discovered new things about him. But she would not give in—yet.

"We'll talk about it—when you get your orders. Let's finish the wine and forget that we are grown-ups."

He nodded as if he thought the whole issue unimportant. They drank, toasting each other. Then he glanced at his watch.

"I must go now, darling. Promise me, you'll stay indoors. There is all sort of riff-raff about and after dark it is not safe out in the streets. I may be a little late—but I'll hurry, I promise."

"All right," she smiled. "I'll write another letter. Mother must be frantic by this time—I only sent her a brief note."

She watched him as he walked across the square, tall and handsome, no longer a stranger but the closest kin, the dearest in the world. What if his ideas about women's careers were different from hers? She smiled again, a quick, secretive smile and turned towards the hotel hall.

As soon as he had left her, Horst put her out of his mind. He wanted two things—more money and some tablets of that stuff Hermann's boys used to take on the long raids to keep awake. No doctor would give a prescription for them . . . but there were other ways. He wondered whether the *cache* of stuff was still there in the woods near Blamont. It had been one of his duties to provide the place for it in the disused mine—and then he forgot about it for it could concern him no longer. He never dreamt that he would think of all those cases again—enough drugs to keep a dozen hospitals going, enough poison to put the whole of Europe to quick and final sleep. And some of that sulpho derivative preparation—he remembered the final list which he had checked with the pompous and fat *Oberst* of the Medical Corps. . . . It would be easy to make a detour. . . .

His mind worked clearly and swiftly as he made his way towards the hotel on the Place Kléber. The Maison Rouge, it was, a somewhat old-fashioned but excellent house. He hoped the French had not taken it over for an officers' mess. But even then, Gaston was certain to hang on. Trust Gaston —he had survived greater calamities. And Gaston would know where the Strasbourg station of the underground was— it stretched all across Europe, it had been organised—when? Just after Stalingrad. There was foresight for you, if you please.

He reached the hotel and was a little relieved to discover that it was still open to the general public. Two French policemen stood at the entrance but they did not challenge him. A well-dressed civilian, circulating freely in the military zone, must obviously be all right—and Horst smiled at the bottomless stupidity of all these prople. Or perhaps it was due to his well-laid plans that it had all gone without a hitch . . . except for the empty safe in the Frankfurterstrasse. But he must not think of that, he must not get angry. Anger was the petty vice of fools.

The hotel hall was crowded with officers in uniform; and one or two women of the usual type. He marched up to the desk and said: "Excuse me . . . but could I see Gaston?"

The man behind the desk stared at him with narrowed eyes and Horst thought that this journey of his seemed to be from one reception clerk to the other. Like signposts, they marked the stages of his trip.

But the man just stared at him and he grew irritated.

"Does he no longer work here?"

"*Monsieur* hasn't heard?" the clerk asked.

"No, I've only just arrived in Strasbourg . . . why, what has happened?"

"Gaston was killed in a raid, three days before the liberation of our city. It is a great pity, *monsieur*, that he could not live to see it—he was such an ardent patriot."

Horst did not care two hoots whether Gaston had been able to fool the reception clerk of the Maison Rouge with his fake patriotism. This was getting serious, he thought. The next place where he could get money was Paris—and Paris was a spot he would rather avoid. He still had a comfortable sum in his pocket but prices had rocketed and he had to be prepared for every emergency. So . . .

"I am sorry to hear about Gaston," he said curtly. "Did he leave any family? I might be able to help. . . ."

"Oh but, *monsieur*, Gaston was a confirmed bachelor. He always used to say that as long as other men had wives . . ." smirked the clerk. "I never heard him mention his family. I believe he was an orphan."

Horst decided that he was not interested in Gaston's private circumstances. Though he had little hope of any results, he wanted to make sure of his other quarry.

"Do you mind if I look at your register?" He changed the subject abruptly. "It is just possible that a friend of mine whom I missed in Stuttgart may have stayed here—or possibly may be still at your hotel."

The clerk hesitated and Horst slipped a coin across the desk.

"But of course, *monsieur*," and the man swung round the heavy book fixed to a revolving wooden block.

"Thank you." He ran his finger down the column of names. Most of them were French. But his finger stopped suddenly. It was almost incredible luck—or perhaps just his usual good fortune. *Frederick Rickman* . . . The date was that of three days ago.

Again he turned to the clerk:

"I am in luck," he said. "My friend . . . is M. Rickman still staying here?"

The clerk nodded. "Yes, *monsieur*. But he is out."

"Oh, what a pity! When did he say he would be back?"

"About eleven o'clock," the man behind the desk replied. "I believe he is expecting a telephone call. He told me to have it put through to his room."

"What number is that?"

"Four-hundred-and-nine. *Monsieur* will come back?"

"Yes, but I don't want you to tell him anything. He is an old comrade of mine and I would like to surprise him. Is it understood?"

This time it was a banknote that passed between them. The reception clerk winked: "Naturally, *monsieur*. I understand. A little private joke, *hein*?"

"A very private joke," smiled Horst.

He turned away and the next moment found himself vigorously embraced by a young French airman.

"Edouard!" the Frenchman roared. "What a delightful surprise! Edouard of all people! And in Strasbourg of all places!"

Horst freed himself abruptly but the Frenchman clutched at him again. He was a handsome, brown-faced youngster with a small dark moustache *à la* Adolphe Menjou and a double row of ribbons on his tunic. He was also roaring drunk.

"I am afraid you are mistaken," von Falkenau said frigidly. "I am not Edouard."

The Frenchman clung to him with limpet-like tenacity.

"Of course you are Edouard, even if you don't know it!" he insisted with the crooked logic of the gloriously drunk. "And you cannot do this to me . . . not to Jules, your old pal! Edouard, please. . ."

Horst thought that this was the worst possible place to

call attention to himself. He took the arm of the staggering airman and drew him away, behind a thick imitation marble column.

"Listen, you fool," he whispered fiercely. "I am not Edouard. You are drunk. Go to bed before you do something silly."

He turned to go but found the young man still hanging on to him.

"You are always scolding me, Edouard," he wailed, and tears stood in his bright brown eyes. "You are always telling me I am drunk. But I am not. I am just happy."

"Well then, be happy without me. I must go."

To his surprise the airman nodded. "I know. And you want the auto." He stumbled and almost fell. He was leaning against Horst and the ex-*Gauleiter* felt the fumes of brandy assaulting him in strong waves. It was miraculous that this young fellow could still stand up. He was apparently in the final stage of drunkenness, the last flicker of aimless effort, before collapse and unconsciousness. "But it's no use . . ." the drunk continued. "I—I got the—key—and the garage is locked. The at—the atten—the attendant," he brought out triumphantly, "has left. You can't go unless you take me. Little me. Little Jules the bright star of the skies. . . ."

He started to sing in a cracked voice:

"*Sur le pont d'Avignon* . . ."

Horst clapped his hand over his mouth and whispered:

"Ssh, Jules! You don't want to wake the others. Of course I'll take you. I wouldn't desert a pal."

The plan had come to him in a flash. It still had a vagueness, an element of uncertainty about it that he disliked; but this was an occasion for improvised measures. The real genius in strategy, Clausewitz had said, was the man who could turn the chance elements to his own advantage at the shortest notice. If Clausewitz had not said it, he ought to have, thought Horst with a wry smile, remembering how little use the wisdom of the General Staff's High Priest had been against the intuition of the Bohemian corporal.

Hules bubbled over with bibulous gratitude:

"That'sh wonderful, Edouard . . . that'sh a real friend . . . C'me on . . . we musht hurry. . . ."

As he half-carried the young airman through the front door, Horst glanced at his watch. It was just half-past ten.

Outside the cold air seemed to revive Jules for a moment. Purposefully he made for a narrow alley which led alongside the main hotel building towards the rear. But this new animation did not last long. He staggered and would have fallen if Horst had not caught him. Reception clerks and drunks, he thought again . . . signposts of my journey. For a moment he remembered Peter Whitney, but already the American was something immaterial and dim, a figure from a story-book who could not possibly matter.

"Keys and locks," the young airman muttered. "Locks and keys. What are they for, I ask you? What need is there to lock up things? Why don't we trust each other, Edouard?"

He threw out his arms in a wide, eloquent gesture and really fell over. They were in the alley now, dark and narrow and dank; Horst began to feel an increasing irritation. Perhaps he could find some other way to work this . . . perhaps. . . . But as he knelt down, rolling Jules over on his back, he decided that if the garage was the place he wanted, it would be better to stick to his original plan.

Jules had temporarily given up the ghost—he was dead to the world. Horst hoisted him on to his shoulder and carried him towards the end of the alley which showed, a little lighter, against the dark space of the high walls. Once they passed under a beam connecting these walls and Jules's head must have knocked against it for he suddenly recovered consciousness and began to sing again about the dancers on the bridge at Avignon.

Horst set him down on his feet. The young airman reached up dazedly and fingered his head.

"What'sh the matter?" he demanded. "You wanna fight?"

"It's Edouard," Horst reassured him. "Where is that garage? A little drive will do you good."

Jules pointed vaguely and von Falkenau switched on his torch. There was a steel door in front of them, a few yards ahead. "The key?" demanded von Falkenau. But Jules did not reply. Jules was well and truly lost in the paradise of the drunk. Horst had to go through his pockets to find the garage key. It was one of those lock-up places, not the regular hotel garage; within were two cars—both French army vehicles—a bench, a concrete floor, and in the back a pile of rusty tools, oily rags and other rubbish. Horst opened the door of the car nearer to the door and dumped Jules in the driver's seat. His torch wavered briefly over the bleak, dusty interior. He retreated softly to the door and locked it from the outside.

The clerk looked up with alacriity as he reappeared at the desk. "I am afraid I won't be able to keep my surprise appointment with Mr. Rickman to-night," Horst said. "Perhaps I'll look him up to-morrow. Or I'll ring him. But I still want you to keep quiet—a surprise is a surprise even twenty-four hours later."

The man behind the desk nodded. He did not understand the whole thing but this tall, handsome civilian had tipped him royally and he, for one, did not concern himself with matters that were outside his ordinary duties. These were bewildering times and one had to be grateful to be alive at all. As for M. Rickman—he was a surly brute and never had a civil word for anybody. The clerk turned to the pigeon-holes behind him and by the time he looked round again, his visitor had disappeared.

The corridor of the fourth floor was deserted. A single bulb burned at the turn, a few yards from 409. Horst reached up a gloved hand and removed it. The black-out curtains were still in position at the window which was just opposite the room of M. Rickman. He pulled them and stepped behind them, leaving a slight crack. As he waited, he felt a fierce pleasure of anticipation which blotted out everything—Helen, the long journey behind and ahead of him, the slight weariness he felt under his burning eyelids. This was like old times and he knew exactly what to do.

Heavy, blundering steps along the carpetless passage. A voice swearing in German at the darkness—the stupid idiot, Horst thought, a wonder he had lasted so long. Then the fumbling at the door. Von Falkenau stepped forward.

"Go on, right to the middle of the room," he said. The gun he held jabbed into something soft and bulky. The man stiffened under it but did not call out.

Horst followed him over the threshold and closed the door behind himself. He found the light-switch.

"Turn round," he commanded.

The tall, heavily-built man swung round and his mouth opened in a comic expression of surprise. His heavy-jowled, mottled face tried to crease into an ingratiating smile but it was not very successful.

"Why, there must be some mistake . . ." he said in a squeaking, high-pitched voice which contrasted strangely with his bulk. "Who are you? What do you want?"

"Put up your hands," Horst said quietly. "Don't move."

He ran his fingers over the man's body and removed a gun. He threw it on the small table on his left.

"But I tell you——"

"Keep quiet." On the pudgy left hand of the fat man there was the ring—the ring with the snake. With scientific curiosity Horst studied him. In his mind he put back the moustache under the swollen, purple nose; cropped the long, greasy hair until it again had a military cut; stripped off the gold-rimmed glasses. Yes, his memory had been right. "Who told you, *Gruppenfuehrer* Obmann," he continued in the same even tone, "about the safe in the Frankfurterstrasse?"

"You must be mad," the other man protested. "My name is Rickman and I am an American citizen. I'll raise the alarm and——"

"No, you won't raise the alarm, Obmann. And it is no use bluffing me. You know, I can kill you in at least six different ways—quick and slow, nasty and nice. It all depends on you."

The tongue of the cornered man darted out. He was still bluffing but afraid:

"I don't understand your gibberish. There must be some mistake. If you are from the police, identify yourself."

Horst had met Obmann perhaps three times in his life. The *Gruppenfuehrer* was one of Heinrich's less bright boys; but for the more brutal jobs he was efficient enough. A much-travelled man who left a trail of torture in his wake. Horst was a little surprised that Obmann had had the guts and intelligence to remain at large so long—but fear sharpens the wits of the dullest hippopotamus. It gave him particular satisfaction that Obmann had not recognised him.

"Come on," he urged the man who called himself Rickman. "I haven't time to waste and you haven't much left."

"But—what do you want to know? If it's money——"

"It's money as well. But that comes later. Who told you about the safe in the Frankfurterstrasse?"

"I don't see what business of yours it is . . . but if you already know . . . it was Kemmerich."

So Kemmerich had planned to double-cross him! The

swine. Kemmerich whom he had raised from a fifth-rate pimp, "working" the district behind the Alexanderplatz, to his personal aide! Kemmerich who had regularly received his cut of all the rackets and "capital levies" in the *Gau*! Kemmerich who . . . The ingratitude of man was really unspeakable. Horst did not pause to think that he, in turn, had double-crossed Kemmerich; that he had killed him because he needed a corpse for his get-away. Kemmerich could not have known that in advance—his treachery must have been prepared beforehand and . . .

The other man must have noticed the tightening of Horst's face. The flicker of fear became panic in his eyes.

"It was all his idea," he blurted out. "And I was waiting for him but he did not come."

"Who was the other man with you?"

"Heinz Braun—but they caught him in Stuttgart because he got drunk."

"Go on."

"There is nothing more to say," Obmann continued in desperate haste. He began to feel that he was pleading for his life. "But I swear I didn't know—I—but—who . . ."

He paused and stared at Horst.

"Why, you are——"

The gun, pressed against his belly, stopped him. His breath whistled thinly as he drew back, as if the fraction of an inch by which he removed his body from the cold touch, would mean a margin of safety.

"No names, my friend," Horst whispered. "It is enough that I know yours."

"But *Herr Ge* . . . I mean, you know me. I have a place in the Plan. I can be useful."

"Give me the money."

"I only took half. Braun had the rest and——"

"The money."

Obmann sighed. Regretfully he reached into his inner pocket. He brought out his hand armed with a knuckle-duster decorated in addition with five-inch nails. But Horst warded off his blow with ease. Under his grip the fat man's arm became lifeless. He stripped the ugly weapon from the swollen fingers. Then he lifted his leg and kicked Obmann in the groin. The obese *Gruppenfuehrer* doubled up with a yelp of pain. Before he could straighten out, Horst kicked him again.

"The money," he repeated.

This time a bundle of notes was forthcoming without any opposition. Horst thrust it into his coat-pocket.

"I want the rest. I am sure you have kept back some."

"But I need a few hundred if——"

"Give me the rest."

Another, smaller wad came out.

"You won't want it," Horst said dryly. "Come on now."

The fat man did not budge. His bulk shook slightly and his voice was hoarse:

"But I have given you everything. What more do you want?"

"Come on." Horst prodded him with the gun. "If you let out a sound, I'll shoot. I have a silencer—a little plop won't disturb anyone."

As they passed along the corridor, they heard distant singing. Some young officers were making merry. They did not meet a soul, marching down the passage to the back stairs which Horst had reconnoitred. Once Obmann made a movement as if to bolt but his captor kicked him again and after that he seemed to have lost all fighting spirit. They came out into the courtyard from which a narrow passage led to the alley. It was pitch dark here and Horst kept his gun pressed to Obmann's back, holding it there while he opened the garage door.

"Inside," he said.

The *Gruppenfuehrer* hesitated. Horst pushed him across the threshold. He closed the door behind himself and switched on the light. "Go right to the back," he ordered his prisoner.

Jules was still sleeping blissfully in the driver's seat, snoring lustily.

"Please, consider what you are doing, "the fat man began in the tone of someone appealing to reason. "I never knew that the money and the papers were so important. I swear to God that if I had known . . . and we are in the same boat. I would do anything for you, really anything. Just now, upstairs, I lost my head—but I wouldn't be a traitor—for anything in the world. Please, *Herr General*—please pause to think . . ."

"Take off your overcoat," Horst said curtly.

Obmann obeyed slowly. Von Falkenau made him take off his jacket and his waistcoat as well.

"Turn towards the wall," he commanded.

"But please . . ."

"Raise your arms and turn towards the wall. . . ."

"For pity's sake, *Herr Ge* . . ."

Horst came closer and Obmann hastily did as he was told. Keeping him covered, the other man switched on the engine of the car nearer to him. The steady purr of the motor filled the enclosed space and the car itself vibrated strongly. There was no sound or movement from Jules.

"I have dreamt of this, Obmann, for quite some time," Horst said softly. "Stand still and don't try to turn your head. It is no use. You have to die."

He had his gun pressed against the man's back, in the middle of the lumbar section of the spine.

"You will take a long time to die but you won't be able to do anything about it," he continued in the same even tone. "And I am sure you will go straight to hell."

He pressed the trigger. The recoil was considerable and he staggered, steadying himself against the purring, trembling car. The echo, too, sounded like thunder but actually the engine almost completely absorbed the noise. The Frenchman stirred but did not open his eyes. Obmann slumped down, shot through the spine and paralysed from the hips downwards. An animal-like sound came from his open mouth. Horst twisted the fat man's tie into a narrow strip of fabric and gagged him. Then he slipped from the garage after he had switched off the engine.

Inside the dying man was struggling for breath. With an immense effort of his torso he threw himself forward so that his head came to rest close to the footboard of the first car. The young aviator opened his eyes and stared down into the fat, upturned, distorted face, bisected by the twisted gag. He shook his head as if to scare away the vision. It would not go away. He reached out his hand to touch the matted hair but withdrew his fingers before he came in contact with it. He slid into the far seat and closed his eyes again. He slept while Franz Obmann died—by inches, with all the blood and pain pent up in his body. The solitary bulb swung slowly overhead and there was no more sound except Jules's snoring.

XXVII

THE BLACK MERCEDES SPED through the famous vineyards of Burgundy, past Dijon and Vougeot, Corgoloin and Beaune, Champforgeuil and Sennecey-le-Grand. It roared across the plain of Bresse and the wide valley of the Saône. They lunched in the shadow of the lovely Eglise de Brou and in the afternoon came to Bellegarde in the foothills of the Jura.

It would have been a pleasant drive—but Helen was a little puzzled and uneasy. Her husband had been taciturn and pre-occupied ever since he had come back, shortly before midnight, from receiving his "marching orders" in Strasbourg. She had waited up for him and he had kissed her good night; but for a long time she heard him tossing and turning and when she woke in the morning, he was already dressed.

Now, in Bellegarde, he amazed her with a suggestion she could not understand.

"Helen, my dear," he said, "you drive on to Annecy alone. I have some business here and I'll join you in the evening."

"But . . ."

"Please, Helen, I have no time to explain."

He softened the harshness of his words with a quick, absent-minded smile. But she felt that he was drawing away from her, impatient for her to go and that alarmed her more than anything. Moreover, she was a forthright sort of person who disliked mysteries and did not take kindly to being treated as a child.

"Karel," she said and held on to his sleeve as he stood outside the car, "do tell me if something is wrong. I am your wife and I have a right to know."

"There is nothing wrong. You are imagining things. I thought you were a sensible woman. Just drive ahead and I'll see you to-night. The rooms are reserved at the Grand Beau Rivage." He patted her hand reassuringly. "I swear to you that I am not up to any mischief. Or do you think I have an assignation with a beautiful blonde spy?"

The joke fell flat for she had heard only part of what he had said. She repeated blankly:

"The rooms?"

He hastened to explain: "I have been sleeping so badly and I may be a little late. I thought if I took two rooms for the night I would avoid disturbing you."

"But that's absurd. . . ."

"Please, Helen, do trust me. Everything is all right, normal and pleasant. But if you persist . . ."

It almost sounded like a threat. It almost sounded as if he hated her. Blinded with tears she let out the clutch and the car shot forward. She had driven a couple of miles before she noticed that he had left his overcoat on the back seat. The weather was far from warm. She hesitated whether she should turn back. But no—he was in a strange mood. Perhaps something was worrying him; perhaps all he had gone through and endured had caused a belated shock—she had read of delayed nervous effects caused by strain. . . . Tenderness welled up in her. She drove on, slowly, puzzled and almost unhappy.

As the car disappeared round the bend, Horst von Falkenau sighed with relief. He sat down on the roadside and pulled a map from his pocket. He did not want to stay on the highway but neither did he want to make a detour. Yes—his finger followed the contours of the map—there was a short cut. It meant plenty of hard climbing but that was what he wanted. He had to test his theory. He had to strain his body, tire out his muscles, arrive at a state of almost complete physical exhaustion. He could not do it sitting in the car—nor could he expect Helen to share a vigorous course of physical training; she would think that he had gone mad. But he was sane, saner than ever in his life. He knew that something had started, way deep in him that was just barely to be perceived; yet it was dangerous and he had to do something about it. He had picked up those pills in the woods near Blamont—but he was not sure about their effect. In any case, he hated drugs. They were unmanly, habit-forming and somehow obscene. No, this was the better way. . . .

He found the secondary road a few hundred yards to the right and started his march. Three hundred paces at a hard trot, three hundred at the pace of quick march and then three hundred of ordinary walking. He smiled—how long it had been since he had tried this! The "toughening up" in the army . . . why, it lay almost thirty years back. How he had hated it and yet how he had loved the years of fighting, of anonymity, of escape from every kind of responsibility . . . escape from Aunt Agatha and the life in Marienbad. . . .

Last night had been the worst so far. He had kept awake almost till dawn and had then thought that his sleep would be deep enough to save him from dreams. But it did not. It seemed that he had hardly closed his eyes when it began. . . .

. . . *The long table in the panelled dining-room. The candles and above them Aunt Agatha's dead-white face, the hair severely upswept from the waxen forehead. The cameo brooch at the neck of her black dress. Her long, narrow, beringed hands hovering above the plate.*

"You must eat your vegetables, Horst. It is a question of self-discipline. There is no bad food or good food. Everything served in my house is wholesome."

"Yes, Aunt Agatha."

"Marie told me to-day that she saw you playing with one of those Czech boys again and that you were laughing. Is it true?"

"Yes, but he spoke to me first."

"How often do I have to tell you that you are German and that you must have nothing to do with those horrid ragamuffins? You are a German, not an Austrian or a Polack, remember that!"

"Yes, Aunt Agatha."

It was no use, he could not shut his ears. Her nasal voice continued inexorably:

"Your father fought at Gravelotte. Your grandfather was the leader of the Conservative Party at Frankfurt. Your great-grandfather commanded his own regiment at Jena and Leipzig. You have seen his name on the Denkmal *last summer, remember? You are a weak child, Horst, but you carry a great tradition."*

"Yes, Aunt Agatha."

And afterwards in the mausoleum-like drawing-room with its family portraits, the high-backed uncomfortable chairs, he was allowed to look at an illustrated copy of Scheffel's Ekkehard. *He turned the stiff pages slowly, loathing the feel of the gilt, hard edges. Aunt Agatha was reading the* Preussische Staatszeitung; *she never touched the local or the Viennese papers. She was an exile in the Empire of the Habsburgs, an exile from Prussia and Mark Brandenburg. Since her only brother and his wife had been drowned in a sailing accident, she had devoted her life to charity and the correct upbringing of her nephew. He was only five when he came to her, a wilful, moody, unsatisfactory child; but she was determined to do her duty. The duty of Agatha von Falkenau was to make life as uncomfortable and unyielding for everybody as she could. A former* Stiftsdame, *she still hankered secretly after the secure and narrowly confined life of the nunnery-like institution; but she would not shirk her responsibilities and did not believe in boarding schools.*

If he could only have laughed at her; but there was no chink in her armour of whalebone and black jet. And fear crept upon him, day and night, whenever he saw her or thought of her. She never beat him but her words were tiny lashes, lacerating his mind and body. And when she was seriously displeased with him, there was the small room on the ground floor, bare and dark. She locked him in until he apologised. At first it took hours, half a day even, before he could bring himself to humiliation and self-abasement. But the small room gradually broke his spirit. He did not know what was the terror it held; it looked ordinary enough when the door was opened and the sunlight streamed in. But how many hours he had sat there on the single stool, staring at the faded newspaper and watching the single gaslight, trembling lest it go out. That was his supreme fear: that one day, one moment the light would start to flicker and then die and he would be left alone in the dark. The dark was peopled in his imagination by a dozen Aunt Agathas, blackclad, the thin, long hands ending in sharp, rending claws, their faces like that of the witch in the fairy-tales of the Grimm brothers. If the gaslight failed, the ghostly, vampire-like Aunt Agathas would start to fly around above his head, quicker and quicker, their long black dresses flapping like bats' wings until they swooped down upon him and . . .

His imagination always stopped at this moment but not his dreams. The soft, cold shapes were around him, closer and closer they pressed and he sobbed, trying to wake up, to open his eyes. But it was no use trying to escape, no use trying to remember that it was not real. That was why after a year or so he apologised at once, meekly and abjectly. But Aunt Agatha did not believe in rapid repentance. Even so there was the measure of time he had to spend in the small room, When he grew a little bigger, at ten or eleven, he started to think of digging a tunnel, of breaking through the walls. But it was no consolation to plot such an escape even though he had managed to get a chisel and a crowbar. On the other side, in the bleak and formal garden. Aunt Agatha would wait for him and shoo him back into captivity . . .

. . . She had her first stroke when he was sixteen but she clung on to life with reptile-like tenacity. She had her wheel-chair equipped with a bell and the bell punctuated his days with its persistent clangour; it even rang in his sleep and often he started up, with clenched fists, sweating, pursued by the fiendish sound. It seemed that her crippled state gave her mind a sharper edge, a greater ingenuity in taunting and bullying him. He often played with the idea of killing her but his adolescent imagination took it for certain that physical death would not end this thing between them. She hated him because she had hated his mother: a pretty, feather-brained woman who was perhaps one or two degrees lower in the rigid social hierarchy Agatha von Falkenau believed to be the only reality in a gradually disintegrating world.

The second stroke came a few days before he enlisted. Her right side was paralysed and she could no longer use even the wheel-chair. She lay in her big, bier-like bed but her influence, her presence was in every room, following him into the street, the school, the playground. The decision to break away had come suddenly. This was the third year of the war and already recruiting offices were less particular about the recruits' age and physical condition—and he was, at not quite seventeen, a tall broad-shouldered youngster, in perfect health, with unimpaired vitality. All the way from the barracks he ran home. The two old women servants stared at him aghast as he burst into the hall, clad in Feldgrau, *his eyes shining. He paid no attention to them but hurried upstairs and, without pausing to knock, rushed into his aunt's room. She was lying on her back, staring at the ceiling, her lips pursed, the creases in her face dark and cavernous. He stopped just inside the door, panting a little. With some difficulty she turned her head and looked at him.*

"What's this masquerade?" she asked in her thin, precise voice. The stroke had not affected her nasal, prim enunciation.

"I am going away, Aunt Agatha," he crowed, unable to keep the triumph out of his voice.

"You are mad." Her eyes slid down his figure. "Completely mad. You should be ashamed of yourself. Take those things off at once. A Falkenau—dressed up as a private! What foolery is this? And a private in an Austrian regiment! Your grandfather would have whipped you! Your father . . ."

He stepped to the bed and looked down at her. Inwardly shaking, he forced insolence and defiance into his voice:

"You witch!" he said contemptuously. "You blood-sucking, inhuman, black-hearted witch! I am rid of you now. You can do me no more harm. I have stood it for twelve years. But now I am free."

Her mouth opened in dazed surprise.

"How dare you . . ." she began in a hoarse whisper. But he continued.

"There is nothing you can say or do that will hold me back. It isn't the way I wanted to go but any way is good as long as it takes me away from you. I hope you'll die—I hope you'll die soon. I don't care if I get killed. I don't care where they send me. But you can't do anything about it. You can't . . . you can't. . . ."

With a painful, gigantic effort the old woman half-raised herself. Her left hand moved spasmodically; a little froth appeared at the corner of the thin, wasted lips. Her voice was now an inarticulate croak. He watched her, feasting his eyes on her helplessness. A cramp shook her; her teeth chattered and she cried out though the words could not be distinguished. He turned on his heels and marched from the room, slamming the door. He hoped the shock had killed her. He hoped . . .

. . . All this had come to him last night, in the dim hotel room at Strasbourg. Not in a connected series of pictures but as something he knew and remembered; the knowledge of the memory was a flickering background to the disjointed scenes, sounds and feelings that filled the hours of the dawn. He re-lived his youth again, telescoped into minutes—but there was no sweet sense of triumph over the witch, the incubus of those years. In his dream Aunt Agatha was alive and now he was flogging his body, straining his sinews, seeking relief in weariness and exhaustion to kill her again. It seemed the most important thing in the world to do this; while he topped the next hill and made rapidly for the ravine ahead, he spoke the words aloud: "*I hope you'll die . . . I hope you'll die soon. . . .*"

XXVIII

SERGEANT IRA EADS CAME FROM the Bronx and was a sceptic. He only believed what he saw and heard—and even that reluctantly. When Old Leatherguts called him into his office and told him that he was to accompany Captain Whitney on a confidential mission, he immediately suspected the catch. And sure enough, there were strings attached to the assignment; he was to keep his eyes on the young man and see that they got back in a fortnight's time. Also, he was to be prepared for some rough stuff—and of course, keep his mouth shut. Now Ira was the sort of man who talked a good deal but never said anything that was useful to the people listening to him. He was thirty-eight, a small, wiry man with reddish hair and the face of a benevolent Brer Fox; he looked upon life as one huge hoax which never fooled him for a moment. He was also a first-class driver and an excellent marksman. He had to be, to have survived eight years on the toughest beat in the Bronx.

By the time they reached Strasbourg, Peter Whitney knew the sergeant's preferences in chewing-gum, Hollywood stars, baseball teams, comic strips and women. But he still had no idea how much Eads knew of the purpose of their mission or of his superior officer's nasty predicament. As they swung round the square and came to halt in front of the tall, gabled building in which the American Military Mission was housed, he turned to the sergeant:

"Sergeant, do you know why we are here?"

"No, but I can guess."

"Well, spit it out."

"The Old Man sent you to look for something—or someone. And you're in trouble. But I don't believe you really know who you are looking for."

"Thank you, sergeant. That's most helpful. Now grab yourself a bite to eat in the mess while I see the adjutant."

"I ain't hungry. If you don't mind, I'll stick around with you."

Peter shrugged. It might have been worse—at least there was a little laughter hidden in Sergeant Eads' narrow, grey eyes. And he certainly needed someone who would be a corrective to his own volatile, over-optimistic nature. Now that he had reached Strasbourg he was not really quite sure what he was looking for. Perhaps it would have been better to go straight on to Paris. He had friends there in G-2 and Karel and Helen were certain to spend a few days in the French capital.

General Steele's name made things easy in the adjutant's office. Peter was introduced to a keen-eyed, grey-haired Kentuckian, in charge of Intelligence.

"Sure," the major nodded, "we have a good check on all hotels. Let's ring them one by one and see what happens."

At the sixth try they were lucky. Yes, Monsieur Reznicek and his wife had stayed at the Carlton. They left yesterday morning by car. Destination? Paris.

"They have a Mercedes," the intelligence major said. "Here is the number. Do you want us to send out a general call?"

"No, that isn't necessary. I am going on to Paris. But first I'd like to have a bath and a bite to eat. Which is the best place for it?"

"The Maison Rouge. We keep half a dozen rooms for visitors like you. One night's the limit, though. Here you are."

He scribbled a chit and Peter, followed by Sergeant Ira who had kept silent all the time but was thinking plenty, drove over to the big hotel.

They found it in an uproar. French policemen, Sûreté detectives, military intelligence officers crowded the lobby. The clerk behind the desk seemed almost out of his mind with worry and Peter had to grab his coat and shake him before he gained his attention.

"What's the commotion about?" he asked.

The man behind the desk stared at him:

"*Monsieur le capitaine* hasn't heard?"

"No, how could I? I have only just arrived."

"A murder, most mysterious and horrible, *monsieur*. And in the lock-up garage right next to the hotel."

"That's interesting. Who is the victim?"

"One of our guests. Oh, it is most distressing. An American gentleman by the name of Rickman."

"Civilian?"

"Yes, *monsieur*. But"—he bent closer, whispering confidentially—"they say his papers were forged. Someone told me that he might turn out to be a pretty important person."

Peter was only half-interested.

"Really? And who may that be?"

The clerk bent even closer. He was all self-importance as he murmured:

"Hermann Goering."

Whitney could not help laughing. "But that's absurd. Goering was caught long ago. He is in safe custody."

"I am not so sure, *monsieur*," the clerk shook his head. "Hitler had his doubles, *n'est-ce pas*? Why shouldn't Goering have them? Perhaps it isn't the real Hermann they have caught. Perhaps he was trying to escape. . . ."

"Sounds much too much like a Hollywood spy story," smiled Peter. "And what about the murderer? Any clues?"

"They found him in the garage. He was dead drunk."

"What?"

"Yes, *monsieur*. A young French officer of the Air Force. Such a nice boy, too."

"But . . . dead drunk? And he stayed there? It sounds screwy."

"It is most mysterious, *mon capitaine*. Especially as they did not find the gun. This man, this Rickman was shot through the spine and was gagged. And Lieutenant Jules Dubois had no revolver. Of course, he may have thrown it away. They are questioning him now. Naturally, if it turns out to be Goering—he'll get a decoration. But he may get the guillotine, who knows?"

It was not his fight, but Peter could not help being interested. While he soaked in a hot bath and listened to Sergeant Ira's disparaging remarks about the French generally and French coffee particularly, his mind puzzled over the disjointed and fragmentary facts the clerk downstairs had given him. "Dead drunk," the words stuck in his brain—for the obvious reason that his present troubles had begun with the same condition. It was really a waste of time and he had no business to interfere with what was obviously a French police affair—but he decided when he got out of the bath and sat down to a scanty meal, to ask a few questions. He informed the sergeant of his intentions but Eads made no remark.

The French colonel, in charge of the investigation, flanked by a *juge d'instruction* and an Air Force officer, was harassed but polite. Yes, on the face of it the victim was an American citizen of Danish origin. He had not been definitely identified; that is, there were certain suspicious circumstances . . . To see the corpse? Well, if the *capitaine* had such morbid tastes. . . . But he was pretty firm about young Dubois. He was just sobering up—it seems he has had a veritable poisoning of alcohol, very regrettable. He did not remember anything. No, *monsieur le capitaine* must excuse it, there was no precedent for interviewing a murder suspect in such circumstances.

So Peter thanked him for his courtesy and drove to the *morgue* which was a few blocks away. A military policeman took them down into the basement which smelled of disinfectant and was more dingy than horrible.

Frederick Rickman was not a whit prettier in death than in life. He was a perfect stranger to Whitney who felt no regrets that he had never met him. He was just about to drop the grey sheet over the gross features when Sergeant Ira spoke.

"I know this guy," he said.

Peter jumped.

"Don't startle me," he cried. "Where did you meet him?"

"I never did. But I've seen his picture. Put a moustache on his face and crop his hair—you can't mistake him. He is on our list—or was."

"What list? What moustache? Sergeant, don't play Information, please, with me. This is not the sixty-four dollar question."

"Can I tell you outside?" Eads pleaded. "This place is giving me the jitters. I wish I hadn't eaten those baked beans."

Peter led him into the corridor and urged him to speak up.

"Look, captain," the sergeant said, "it's dead easy. These guys really know nothing about proper disguise. Why, I believe they would be frightened stiff if you mentioned the words plastic surgeon in their presence. For all their beautiful rackets, they're not a patch on our Dillingers. Mercy me, the tough guys in the Bronx would think nothing of buying themselves a new face every Thanksgiving or mebbe Fourth of July. I spotted the man right away. Me, I have a photographic memory."

"O.K., you are great, sergeant. Dick Tracy isn't a patch on you. Who is he?"

"Why, he is——"

"Go on!"

"Shucks, I have forgotten the name. But he was on the list, with his ugly mug and all. But it will come to me in a moment—just don't you rush me!"

His pointed ears twitched a little, his good-natured fox-face was puckered with concentration.

"I got it!" and hit his right palm a resounding blow with his left fist. "Franz Obmann, *Gruppenfuehrer,* former Kommandant of Buchenwald, second-in-command at Maidanek, S.S. *Spezialdienst* and on Heinrich Himmler's staff from——"

"Never mind the biography! Are you sure?"

"As I have never been in my life."

"Good. Come on!"

They rushed back to the Maison Rouge. The French colonel listened to them wearily and spread cynical hands.

"But what proof have you, *monsieur*? Just because your *sous-officier* thinks that . . ."

"Just look at the left thigh of the corpse," Sergeant Ira spoke up manfully. "You ought to find a scar—a long one—running cross-wise. The files said he got it in Hamburg, in the early street fighting days."

The colonel looked brighter. "*Bon.* If your theory is borne out by fact. . . ."

It was. Especially when the colonel reassured himself that neither Eads nor Peter had seen anything of the corpse except its face. He thawed completely and confessed his troubles to Peter.

"This is a most confusing case, Captain Whitney. Here is this young boy, Dubois. He was celebrating because he had just heard that his parents and sister were safe—they were found in Austria. He celebrated too well and cannot remember much. He does not know how he got into that garage. He swears he has never seen Rickman—or shall we say, Obmann?—never in his life. He talks vaguely of another man who was with him at one time during the night . . . but he cannot describe him. Then there is the question of the gun. . . ."

"Another man?" the young American lifted the pertinent detail from the colonel's flow of words.

"Yes. Strangely enough, the reception clerk—a rogue if I ever saw one—also said that someone had asked for Rickman earlier in the evening. A tall, fair-haired man who spoke French well but with a slight accent."

"Well, colonel," Peter said, "if I were you I would release

Lieutenant Dubois. He could not have committed the crime. And if he killed this Obmann, he must have done so in self-defence. After all, the man was a notorious Nazi, evidently on the run."

"Do you really think so?"

"Sure I do. And if I could have another talk with that clerk . . ."

The harassed little man was produced and Peter, using much tact and patience, extracted from him the pertinent facts. The man who had asked for M. Rickman . . . the clerk's description was sketchy, he was a bad witness, but certain details had stuck in his mind. These details were infuriatingly, vaguely familiar. They described someone Peter knew but could not identify. And so he and his faithful Ira departed from Strasbourg, making for Paris—and the young captain was puzzled and unhappy. He was no whit nearer his goal . . . and he began to suspect that after all, his trip might prove a wild-goose chase. . . .

XXIX

DURING THE THREE DAYS THEY spent in Annecy—still bearing the scars of the long-drawn-out battle between the Maquis and the Germans that devastated so much of the Haute Savoie—Helen became more and more mystified and worried. In the last ten years her life had been entirely cosmopolitan. She had known many nations, races, creeds; she realised that human beings of a different nationality from her own could not be judged by English standards. Their psychology, their upbringing, their "conditioning" was so utterly different. She also realised, humbly, her own limitations in understanding them, following their mental processes. But there were certain fundamental verities, certain rules and facts which applied to all normal men and women.

Now she began to ask herself whether her husband was a normal, sane man or not. It was a question she would still silence with a little effort; a question to which there were many reassuring answers some of which satisfied her.

But the vague uneasiness remained and his behaviour gave her new cause for anxiety almost every hour.

That first night he had arrived very late. She sat up, waiting for him, in her room, having left the connecting door open. His steps as he came in, were heavy, he almost shuffled instead of walking, and she heard him throwing himself on the bed without pausing to take off his clothes. When she went in, she found him sprawling on his back, dusty and sweat-plastered, breathing heavily. He managed a smile but avoided her questions. She helped him to undress, forced a glass of hot milk on him and then went back to her own room. For a long time she could not go to sleep. Once or twice she got up and tiptoed to the door, but he had closed it and she could not discover whether he was asleep or not.

He never told her what business had kept him in Bellegarde and how he got to Annecy. The appearance of his shoes and clothes seemed to show that he had walked—but that was absurd, the distance was too great and he had never shown any inclination for mountaineering or hiking. But his behaviour grew odder and odder as the three days passed. He seemed to have conceived a sudden great passion for physical exercise, for aimless exertion. Every morning he rose early and went for a swim in the lake—which was icy-cold, even the reeds being covered with hoar-frost. Afterwards he had a brisk run. By the time Helen had got up and come down to breakfast, he had spent three hours in the open air. He should have been glowing with good health but as a matter of fact Helen noticed for the first time that there were tiny wrinkles under his eyes and that the eyes themselves lacked lustre. Only his hair, close-fitting, sleek, almost white gold, retained its vitality. She had learned not to speak much during breakfast for he was moody and, though always polite and tender, the conversation often petered out into brooding taciturnity on his part and embarrassed silence on hers.

After breakfast they went for a walk, taking their lunch in a rucksack. Helen was a healthy girl who had always played golf and tennis; but after the first day she let him go alone. She simply could not keep up with him. He always chose the steepest, most uncomfortable paths and though he helped her over the awkward spots, he did not slacken his pace. It was as if something was driving him, mercilessly and continuously. He did not pause to admire the view or to get his second breath. He almost *ran* uphill, a feat Helen was unable to imitate after the first or second attempt. Even during the brief rest while they had their meal, he seemed unwilling to sit down. And when they got back after tea-time, he had a bath and went out again—explaining that his muscles were getting stiff and that the only cure was to have more exercise.

She stayed at home during the second and third days and he did not urge her to come along. When he got back, later than usual, he seemed to be in a better mood; they talked and laughed almost like in the first days of their meeting. But the nights frightened her again. He had been a curiously gentle lover, almost child-like, and her tenderness, her jubilant affection had increased a hundredfold during the first nights they were together. But now even this changed. Sometimes he hurt her and she gritted her teeth or cried out softly; always he apologised, always he was contrite and ashamed, but soon he forgot.

The last night he had fallen asleep in her arms and for a while she had watched his face: lean, brown and smooth. But as she watched him, a tiny muscle started to twitch just above the left cheekbone. She put her fingertips over it and felt the sleep-warmed flesh; but the twitching did not stop. Something went on, under the smooth skin, behind the shield of bone and muscle. Something in which she had no part, which she could not fathom. It seemed to her that nothing was more important in the world than to smooth away the tiny twitching, the sole outward sign that there was turmoil and strife beneath that face. But as her fingertips gently caressed the skin, he suddenly freed himself from her arms and rolled over to the edge of the bed. As she had bent close to him, his arms, flailing through the air, passed within an inch of her face . . . and two of his fingers slapped her cheek. It was a gentle touch, not a blow, but it frightened her. She drew back, leaving as much space between him and herself as the narrow bed would allow; she closed her eyes and began to cry, quietly, desperately. She scolded herself for a fool—he must have been dreaming or it was an unconscious, unintentional gesture . . . but she could not forget it and cried herself to sleep.

. . . This time the dream was brief and sharp like a series of

snapshots, quickly unrolled. But it was all there, with the colours of the dead, dry grass, the dusty yellow of the courtyard, the drab grey of the huts and the steely blue of the freshly-erected barbed wire. The sun focused into a yellow patch upon the muzzle of the machine-gun in the nearest watch-tower.

They came up shuffling, in their striped uniforms, their heads shaven, their eyes deep-set. He flicked his whip against his gaitered leg, to feel the sleek hardness and reassure himself of his inviolable superiority. The guards were in a line with him and the prisoners came on, men and women, their faces empty, the skin dried to the bones, the wrinkles deep-cut ditches in the soil of the spare flesh.

There was the line where they were to stop, come to attention and await his inspection. There was the line but they did not stop. They came on, their broken hands hanging inert at the side of their thin shanks, their feet shuffling in the clay-mixed dust. At first he thought they were blind and he called out a harsh command, echoed by the Kommandant who stood at his side and whose features he could not remember. But nothing happened, across the narrowing space the blurred, immense mass moved on, shuffling and silent, passively hostile, menacingly helpless. He roared at the guards to fire and his ears were filled with the detonations, the rat-tat-tat of the sub-machine-guns. He saw the bullets strike, he saw them tearing through the thin figures as if through air. They bled and the blood made strange patterns, now mixing with the stripes, now criss-crossing them.

But still they came on, closer and closer. He could see their faces now, the ashen, transparent faces of the walking dead. Again he gave the order to fire and again the volleys rang out. But even as he saw a bullet plough a furrow across a man's face, a woman's breast, he knew that nothing could stop them. There was no other way except to turn and run. But he could not run. Never before, dreaming or waking, had this feeling of helplessness, this utter paralysis come over him. They were only a few yards off now and though he suddenly felt convinced that he could move and run, his brain told him that he was a Great Man and had to remember his pride in the midst of panic. The guards had vanished, the Kommandant alone stood at his side and he heard his voice. It was fat Obmann's voice, speaking in a grotesque lisp:

"I have a place in the Plan. I can be useful," he was saying. "Useful, useful, useful," he repeated like a parrot. "Useful, useful, useful. . . ."

The mass of men and women was now close enough; he could sense their breath, the odour of the unwashed bodies, lacerated by hunger, disease, the whip. He half-turned and swung out to hit at least one of them, to reassure himself of their tangible reality. His hand touched something soft and warm which was more horrible than if he had touched air or dead, wet bones. He backed away with a violent gesture and started to fall. It was an endless fall with the certainty that he would be maimed, broken for ever, at the end of it; and the anticipation of a sickening contact with the earth was worse than . . .

XXX

THEY STARTED EARLY NEXT morning. In brilliant sunshine they drove along the western shore of Lake Annecy, past Saint-Jorioz and Duingt with their prehistoric lake dwellings, through Faverges and Albertville, following the valley of the Arly and later the Arc and the Isère.

Sitting in the warm security of the car, Helen watched her husband's calm profile and scolded herself for the weakness and fears of last night. He had told her his story but it could not have been a complete tale: how could she know that he had really suffered, what ghosts haunted his dreams? It was something that could not be dragged brutally into the open; put into words it would lose its reality. Again she felt ashamed, just as in the Leipzig hotel-room after he had first spoken, soberly and with restraint, of his adventures. Who was she to resent any secrets he might be keeping from her—probably to spare her anguish and the need for sympathy that could make no difference to the past? The wisest, best course was to ignore it, to wait patiently until the misery and sorrow should dissolve, should find some outlet in his soul. Her mere presence ought to help; she was woman enough to believe that.

"What about lunch?" she asked as brightly as she could.

He removed his eyes for a brief spell from the road and gave her a smile:

"Saint-Jean-de-Maurienne, I think," he said and reached for the map. "Just see how far it is from Albertville. We must have the car checked over—there is a rattle somewhere I don't like. And after lunch I'll show you the cathedral—please, don't say you have seen it before, I want to be the first to tell you all about its beauties. . . . And we'll stop for the night at Briançon. Or we can go on to Barcelonnette. It's only sixty-odd miles farther on—but of course, it means a lot of climbing."

"No, let's not go very far to-day. It's such lovely weather. Unless of course . . ."

"Unless what?"

His voice had changed—just a little, but she could sense it. Tense again and somehow expectant as if she were the only person who could give him the right clue.

"Nothing important, darling," she replied. "You did not tell me very much about your conferences at Strasbourg and Bellegarde. I have still one week of my furlough—but I'll have to get in touch with Paris if I want to prolong it."

"Of course you'll have to prolong it. We are going down to Nice—not Bordeaux as I originally thought, they changed my orders—and then probably on to San Sebastian."

"But Karel . . ."

"Now, I don't want to hear any objections from you. That would be rank mutiny. And I assure you that Spain is very nice in the spring. There'll be things in the shops and when I have finished my business, we'll fly to London and you can introduce me to your family. I promise to behave and not to disgrace you."

"Oh, Karel," she laughed, "you are impossible. Do you think that my people have never seen a foreigner before? True, there was never one in the family—but it's time we made a beginning, anyhow."

"No regrets?" He turned suddenly towards her with a fierce intensity in his voice. "Are you sure . . . no regrets?"

"What?" she mocked at him with pursed lips. "Married a week and already doubting your wife's affections? Fie on you, sir, to think so poorly of women!"

He swerved to avoid a military lorry and when he spoke again, his tone held relief and laughter:

"No . . . it's rather that I think poorly of myself. I have been moody and strange these last days, haven't I?"

At first she meant to deny it, but she knew that honesty was the best policy even if it led to complications.

"A little, darling. I thought you were tired."

He stopped the car and put his arm around her shoulder. "I am really looking forward to our stay in Spain," he said. "It will be my first vacation in six years."

"I am sure you deserve it, poor dear," she sighed. "Only ... I hate loose ends. I'll have to go to Paris, I think, before we cross into Spain."

"Why?" He was fondling her hands, having pulled off her gloves. "You can write or wire. . . ."

"But Karel, I am just as much under orders as you are. . . ."

"Nonsense. You are just playing at being a woman of affairs. Anyone as beautiful as you ought to be content to . . ."

"You said that before. But beauty, my friend, is only skin deep and doesn't last for ever. I want to be useful—to you, to myself, to the world."

"Let the world be," he said, and she sensed that he was withdrawing again into that strange, distant shell of his. "It can only hurt you. You and I—we are quite sufficient."

He kissed her and for a few moments she felt that he was quite right—that it was futile to bother about the world, about humanity. The big words were meaningless in any case; the earth and mankind were only real in terms of individuals or limited loyalties. You could not really feel a citizen of the globe—only of a country or, even more usual, of a city or village.

But her mood did not last long. All her adult life she had dealt in realities, in tangible facts; and she was one of those who wanted to know where she was going—at least as far as that was possible in human life.

"And after Spain?" she asked. "You know, Karel, we've never really talked of what we will do when your work has ended—I mean, when you will no longer be under orders, military or diplomatic or whatever your department is. . . ."

"I don't know," he replied. "Perhaps we'll go back to Prague and I'll open my law office again. I am not sure. Europe, for many years to come, will be an uncomfortable and dismal place. Czechoslovakia was comparatively lucky —but even there the problems are vast and complex. We don't yet know quite clearly how the Soviet Union is going to influence our lives . . . after all, we are the most highly industrialised country near to Russia . . . and of course, political events may change one's plans. . . ."

"You mean, you don't like the Russians?" she asked, eager to gauge his opinions, to find out more about his preferences and dislikes.

"I lived for two years in Moscow," he replied cautiously. "I admire them greatly. But it is one thing to appreciate a person and quite another to adopt his way of life."

He had put that neatly, he told himself; the real Karel Reznicek could not have done better. But this was dangerous ground—for he still thought of the Russians as bloodthirsty barbarians, sub-human creatures whose mental processes were as different from a civilised man's as a Dahomeyan Negro's. They were all mad, anyhow. He trusted his acting talent to cover his real opinions but he preferred not to strain it unduly.

"Perhaps I'll become a diplomat," he joked. "How would you like to be an ambassador's wife? Parties, big sleek cars, diamond tiaras and . . ."

"Oh, Karel, stop it," she laughed. "I wouldn't like it a bit."

"No . . . I thought you wouldn't. Sometimes, you know, I wonder whether it wouldn't be best to turn our backs on Europe. It will be a long weary waiting for things to return to normal—and another war may come before that. I couldn't stand another war. I know I couldn't."

"Oh, but there won't be another war while we are alive," she cried in quick optimism. "There just can't be. People have suffered too much not to have learned the lesson."

"Maybe," he said and started the engine again. Bornery, Chamousset, Epierre. At Aiguebelle they began the climb. The engine settled down to a deep-throated purr and they were both silent.

There is some fear in him, Helen thought, something he is too proud to confess. If I could worm it out of him . . . it would be better for both of us. But it takes time. She felt reassured, though, because he had talked freely and she had a share in his plans. Perhaps, she decided, he needs just as much adjustment to this mad marriage of ours as I do. But nothing can happen . . . nothing must happen to spoil it.

But while she sank gradually into a semi-conscious, comfortable state, Horst was again fighting his battle.

He was still uncertain whether his rather crude method of flogging his body in order to keep his mind quiet had worked or not. For a couple of nights it had been all right;

though he had not slept well, he had got some rest—and no dreams. But last night there had been that damnable experience of re-living something he had thought buried safely and for ever. The whole idea that there was something in him he could not control was monstrous and he refused to accept it. He had overcome all the difficulties, won all the battles he had chosen to fight. Here he was, driving free and of his own will through the French Jura, with a lovely woman at his side, plenty of money in his pockets and a set of papers that would take him across the Spanish frontier. But what had happened to the others? Himmler, dead on a barrack floor, after carrying that phial of poison for days in his mouth . . . Ribbentrop, caught naked in a fifth-rate boarding house . . . Streicher, arrested skulking behind a woman's skirts, having to grow a beard in a futile attempt at disguise. . . . Seyss Inquardt and Quisling, Rosenberg and Ley, Sepp Dietrich and Frank—none of them had escaped. True, they were much too conspicuous, much too important while he had preferred to be second rank, the power behind the throne. But even so—he only had to count his blessings to reassure himself. And whatever was in him, he could overcome—it was unthinkable that his own brain should turn against him.

A line came into his mind, half-remembered. Its rhythm mingled with the rhythm of the engine. He could not disentangle it.

"*Though fleet, we shall find him . . .*"

Where did the line come from? He had always prided himself on his memory. He was about to give up the attempt in disgust; after all, what did it matter? But with a sudden leap a second a third line added themselves:

"*Though fleet, we shall find him,*
Though strong, we shall bind him,
Who planted a snare for his friend . . ."

That was all, and however hard he tried, he could not remember the rest. It was not a German poem, he felt certain—but where had he read it? Or had he heard it recited?

All through lunch he was silent again and Helen teased

him that he was making up to the waitress who was fat and on the wrong side of forty. But he replied to her banter absent-mindedly and she, too, fell silent. They inspected the cathedral and he remembered enough of his manners and his part to be an adequate guide. But while she was lost in admiration and appreciative delight, he could feel no glow, no enthusiasm. Again the lines tantalised him.

"Though fleet, we shall find him . . ."

It was not till late in the evening, in their hotel at Briançon, that the solution came to him. And then he did not like it all. He could remember now the whole strophe:

"From primal ages hoary,
This lot, our pride and glory,
Appointed was to us;
To Hades' gloomy portal,
To chase the guilty mortal,
But from Olympians, reigning
In lucid seats, abstaining;
Their nectared feasts we taste not,
Their sun-white robes invest not
The maids of Erebus.

"But, with scourge and with ban,
We prostrate the man,
Who with smooth-woven wile,
And a fair-faced smile,
Hath planted a snare for his friend;
Though fleet, we shall find him,
Though strong, we shall bind him,
Who planted a snare for his friend."

It was silly, of course; silly yet dangerous to go back to the distant twenties when he had played his part on the stage and not in real life. It was that crazy fool Martin who decided that what the people of Munich needed in all their misery and near-starvation were the tragedies of Aeschylus. There were only a dozen performances of the trilogy—and Horst had been most unwilling to take the part of Orestes. He thought it was a weak and dull task for any actor—that nincompoop who murdered his mother and then whined that it was Apollo who put him up to it. . . . Now that he had placed the Furies' chorus, his own lines came back to him:

> "*. . . The blame—what blame may be—*
> *I share with Loxias, who fore-augured griefs*
> *To goad my heart if, by my fault, such guilt*
> *Should go unpunished. I have spoken. Thou*
> *What I have done, if justly or unjustly,*
> *Decide. Thy doom, howe'er it fall, contents me.*"

How silly, his lips curled in a silent sneer, how unspeakably silly the whole idea of "The Eumenides." One character passing the blame to the other, Orestes to Apollo, Apollo to Athena, Athena to Zeus—and all the time the Furies shrilly protesting that they had to have their prey or the whole universe would collapse. And old Aeschylus, with his tongue in his cheek, making up to the swollen-headed elders of Athens, slyly planting propaganda in the Argive mind that they should be faithful to the alliance with his city . . . "*Thy doom, howe'er it fall, contents me. . . .*" That was the cowardly pleading of weaklings. It was a nuisance, remembering that old junk . . . and he had been rotten as Orestes because all the time he had violently disagreed with the lines he had to speak. But now that he remembered it, there was no need to ascribe any particular significance to this piece of rubbish spewed out from the depths of his brain. None at all. And with great vivacity he started to explain to Helen the beauties of the Porte d'Embrun.

XXXI

A MOMENT AGO HE HAD BEEN safe and pleasantly drowsy; the warm sheets surrounded him with an armour of contentment. A moment ago he had heard Helen's soft breathing and his half-closed eyes had followed the soft curve of her arms and shoulders. A moment ago he had been certain of his identity and his strength.

But now something or someone took him by the scruff of his neck, clamped his head into a metal vice so that he could only look in front, fixing his eyes upon a certain narrow strip of ground. It was hot. He felt the heat rising from the cracks of the parched soil, whirling in sluggish spirals in the dry runnels like mountain mist. He blinked his eyes but the sun slowly and relentlessly moved across his horizon, so slowly that there was no appreciable change in its position, nothing to show the passing of the time.

"Let me go," he said aloud. "Don't be a fool. Let me go. I won't run away. I can take it."

But there was no answer and he knew that it was no use to struggle. This land, this spot was accursed; nothing would grow and no man could live here. The heat burned the soles of his feet and he felt perspiration trickling down his neck, his shirt clinging to his back, his whole body feeling clammy. But he could endure it. He was not going to break down and plead for mercy.

They came over the ridge, the small bedraggled procession. In his brain a slow, solemn music accompanied the straggling procession; for a moment, in sheer delight of release, he identified it as the opening theme of Tchaikovsky's Fifth Symphony. But there was nothing rhythmic or musical about the people approaching the centre of the arid plateau. The guards on both sides, their guns at the ready; and in the middle the seven men and three women. He could not distinguish their faces nor were they important enough to be observed closely. They were partisans and they had been sentenced to death. This was a good place to die, nothing human about it, no contrast between the violent end and the smiling face of Nature. The thirsty soil would absorb the juices of their bodies—like water poured on a patch of parched earth, they would disappear in no time. He had no personal stake in what was happening; nothing but this unseen, mysterious force that clamped his head in an iron vice and fixed his gaze. Could he close his eyes? He tried and immediately molten lead poured upon his lids: the sun which, strangely enough, he could endure with open eyes but not when he sought refuge in blindness. As he looked again, the hot rays seemed to dissolve the landscape, even the soil disappeared and only the middle horizon remained, with the small group crawling closer and closer.

The gallows rose from the ground like the Demon King in a pantomime's transformation scene. Gaunt and grey, they broke up the scene into fragments. Six of them were quite erect and formed perfect parallels—but four were crooked and disturbed the balance, the symmetry. He felt angry with those who had erected them; slipshod work, what if the weight of the bodies made them overbalance and topple? But he again reminded himself that it was none of his business; he was no active participant, only an eye-witness, a detached observer.

Black trousers, torn and dirty shirts—the men ascended one by one the narrow platform. The three women wore voluminous skirts, embroidered blouses, their hair was bound in kerchiefs. For a moment he had the curious conceit that they would perform a national dance; but there was no fiddler, no guzlica*-player present and the only dance they would dance was the* kolo *of death. All over this country of mountains and forests, of sunbaked plains and barren cliffs, the* kolo *of death went on day and night. It served them right, the stubborn fools. That leader of theirs, calling himself a marshal, graduating from bricklaying to anarchist plots, a man who refused to give battle when all military canons prescribed it and slunk back from the mountains when he was, by all rights, annihilated! Well, there was plenty of rope in Jugoslavia or if there was not, it could be imported. . . .*

The ten candidates for death stood there, lined up like actors in front of the curtain of the brazen sky. The S.S. men busied themselves with the ropes. There was no ceremonial. One man opened his mouth, but before he could speak he was kicked into paralysed silence. The executioners stepped back and pulled away the dais. Instantly the ten figures turned into grotesque manikins, puppets dancing at the end of a rope. He watched but there was no satisfaction. They died too quickly or . . . no, not all of them. There was a woman, clawing at the rope, trying to lift herself, to remove the relentless pressure upon her throat. There was a man swinging back and forth, in a broken rhythm, and his eyes were still alive.

Then the shots rang out, behind and around them. The S.S. men took cover and returned the sporadic firing. But he stood there, the vice still holding his head; feeling that at any moment a bullet might strike him, that at any moment lead, hotter than the sun, hotter than the sweating earth, would plunge into his flesh. The anticipation, as always, was worse than the actual blow. He watched, dully, the last of the bodies settling down to an inert swinging; but suddenly he could not stand any more of it. Hoarsely he cried out and wrenched at his head with hands that had acquired a will of their own. And all the time he heard the music, swelling in his head until it filled the whole space, the whole universe; the brass and the tympani, the drums and the fiddles. . . . When he tore himself free, it was too late. As he swung round, the partisans were upon him and he went down in a chaos of flailing arms, flashing teeth and manes of coarse black hair. But the music stopped and there was silence; silence with a sibilant, futile little breeze that died as soon as it sprang up but touched with cool fingers his forehead for a moment, like the fingers of a ghost. . . .

. . . This time his awakening was gradual; he shed sleep as a snake sloughs off its skin. His dazed brain took a long time to grasp a few physical facts: that he was alive, that he was lying in bed, and that another human being was breathing a few inches from his body. He shook himself and opened his eyes.

Barefoot he padded over the wooden floor to the wash-stand. The water in which he immersed his head was ice-cold but it did not sober him up. His skull ached, he could feel the waves of pain radiating from a central point. He started to rub his forehead, his temples, his face. The rough towel's touch was warm and gave momentary relief where it passed over his skin. But as he straightened, he felt dizzy and had to lean against the wall for a moment. He glanced at Helen; but she was asleep and her still face made him forget his misery for a second.

He crept back to bed and lay on his back, staring at the beams of the ceiling. He had to reason this out, he told himself. There was nothing that did not yield to the cold, clear penetrating power of his brain. It was his brain that had given him all the advantages over the men of instinct, the men of stupid brawn. It could not forsake him now when he had come so far.

The dreams . . . How many did he have? Four or five . . . he could not quite keep track of them. But it was something that had never happened to him before; something that had a beginning and therefore must have an end, too. It was not a mysterious affliction sent by some dark divinity—he did not believe in God nor Devil, in any case. It was some trouble that had a perfectly natural cause—if he could only find it.

He cast back his mind over the last few days—over the period that had passed since they left Leipzig. There was nothing wrong then. He felt strong and secure; he gloried in his genius that had combined a foolproof method of getting away with winning the woman he wanted more than anyone in his life before. The first dream—when did it come? It was in that little town on the Main—Kronenfeld . . . Klingenfeld . . . no, Klingenberg, just after the accident with that stupid animal. Of course, he had received quite a blow on his head; he was weak and in a bad physical condition though there was certainly no need of that stupid fussing by Helen and the little French doctor . . . Yes, that was when it began.

He turned over and let his arm hang over the edge of the bed. There was a small rug there and mechanically he started to scratch at a loose strand in the cheap fabric.

It was impossible, he told himself, that a perfectly normal man should be free of dreams—of nightmares, if you wanted to use a vague and far too melodramatic word—free of uncanny shapes and sounds, colours and sequences one day and fight a losing battle with them the next. It was impossible unless there was a reason. That blow . . . the doctor spoke of mild concussion but that simply could not be the reason. He could still think clearly, he could still make immediate decisions. More important and more conclusive: he could still play his part, the part of Karel Reznicek, without a false tone, without the slightest hesitation. Helen had noticed something—how could she help it?—but it had only increased her compassion and love. She did not, she could not suspect him. True, sometimes there was a little strain, he felt a bit tired with the whole pretence of being a noble Czech patriot. Especially because he did not like Czechs. But that was a personal taste; it could not interfere with his task. If Obmann had not beaten him to the safe in the Frankfurterstrasse—but no, the man was dead, the world well rid of him; and why should it have been easier to act the part of a Danish-American than that of a Czech?

He had tried some remedies. In his young days he could always wake at a given hour, however early, if he told himself a few times before going to sleep: I must be up at six. Or: I must not oversleep. It worked every time. He had done the same thing about these dreams or whatever they were. He had repeated (not because he believed in the silly nonsense of that French professor, but because he had tested its efficacy in a different matter)—he had repeated to himself that he must not dream, that his sleep should be deep and undisturbed. Whatever there was in him, subconscious or just a nameless evil imp, received the command. But whoever or whatever it was, proved insubordinate. Until now he always had had time to recuperate between these broken, restless nights—there was a pause of a few days, there was relief and new strength. But what if they came every night? What if . . .

That idea of tiring his body, of driving himself physically to the limits of endurance had not worked either. It had only made him impatient with his own body and had caused Helen real anxiety. No, whatever this thing was, it could not be cured by climbing mountains, running races or lifting weights. A little contemptuously he thought of his own weaker self that had suggested such a crude method. But what else was there?

Two things, he decided. One—to face it squarely. Do not resist, he told himself. There must be a pattern in these dreams, yes, there must be an end and a beginning. If he could find the clue, he could defeat the enemy. And if that did not work—he could always stay awake. In four or five days they should be across the frontier. In three, if necessary; but he did not want to hurry as Helen might think it strange. And once in Spain, he could relax. He could tactfully prepare Helen for the next stage of their journey—across the ocean. What did it mean? To stay awake for ninety-six hours. It had been done before. Somewhere he had read that adults stayed without sleep for over four days—without any ill effects. There were those crazy Marathon races and dances. And their participants had no help, could not use stimulants he could use. There were those pills . . . they should be handy.

There was another thing—he never had two of these dreams in one night. If the worst came to the worst, he could endure one . . . and afterwards still have a good sleep. Yes, this was a reassuring fact. He closed his eyes and settled down in the warmth of the bed. Ten minutes later he was asleep and this time no nightmares came.

XXXII

ON THE SECOND DAY IN PARIS Peter Whitney found his man. He spent an infuriating twelve hours being sent from pillar to post, passed from one department to the other, with Sergeant Ira tagging along philosophically, pausing now and then to make disparaging remarks about SHAEF. The remarks were funny and unprintable but they did not noticeably improve Captain Whitney's temper.

However, his quest seemed to have come to an end in the afternoon of the second day. He was sitting in a small room off the Place Pigalle, drinking bad coffee and fencing with Mr. Kladnik, who held a mysterious position in the Czech mission of inter-Allied liaison, whatever that meant.

"Yes, I have met your General Steele," M. Kladnik said, and inspected Peter's credentials for the fifth time with the same interest an avid fan would display in the last chapters of a crime story. "He is an excellent man but has a bad digestion."

Thus bluntly stated, it seemed to be a good description of Old Leatherguts. However, Peter was not paying a social call and he said, as politely as he could:

"We were talking of Karel Reznicek, Monsieur Kladnik."

"Oh yes, Reznicek. What did you want with him, now?"

"I wanted to discover his whereabouts."

"Why?"

"Because I wish to meet him."

"For what purpose?"

"My dear sir . . . I want to play checkers with him. I want to ask his advice on what tie to wear with a tuxedo. Don't you realise that my business is urgent?"

Kladnik was plump, rosy-cheeked and very self-possessed. Sarcasm rebounded from his pneumatic ego. But he had a sense of humour and he smiled while he pontifically folded his hands on his stomach.

"Captain Whitney, I am going to be frank with you. Has Karel Reznicek caused some trouble for you?"

Peter stared.

"Trouble? How could he? Well . . . he stole my girl . . . in a way. But that has nothing to do with my need to see him."

"You are convinced that this Reznicek is all that he seems to be? That he is a Czech? That he is a *bona fide* agent of the Czech armed forces?"

"Great Scott, man, I checked up on him myself. He is O.K."

Kladnik began to shake his head slowly. He was exactly like a porcelain mandarin.

"But . . ."

"Karel Reznicek is dead," the Czech said.

"Dead? But . . . when? And where is Helen . . . his wife? I mean, she must need help and . . ."

"The man whom this lady married is still alive, as far as I know," replied Kladnik. "You see, I don't know very much. What you have told me, was all news to us—but then, liaison is far from perfect between the various intelligence organisations. What I am trying to tell you, Captain Whitney, amounts to something rather serious. Two days ago we heard that the real Karel Reznicek was dead. We have not found his body but we have no reason to doubt our source of information. . . ."

He took a sip of coffee and made a grimace of disgust.

"It is a very long story and I don't want to burden you with all the details. Karel Reznicek was a patriot and a very useful and courageous agent of the Czech underground. He disappeared a short time before the liberation of Prague—the final stages of the fighting were rather confused. The day before yesterday the woman who had betrayed him to the Gestapo, came forward. Conscience is a weird and wonderful thing. She told us that he was dead. As a matter of fact, we had begun to suspect it a little earlier. You see, Karel Reznicek told this woman everything—except one small thing."

He paused dramatically and Peter wished M. Kladnik were less eager to resemble Orson Welles in "Journey into Fear."

"And what would that be?" he asked politely, providing the cue.

"That he had made arrangements with some of his comrades in Pilsen—to report there within a week after he had ended his last mission . . . unless he was dead."

"But how did you know if he did not tell this woman?"

"That's easy," smiled the plump Czech. "I was one of the men he was supposed to meet."

"And the woman?"

"She told us everything and then she committed suicide. A pity—she was a most ravishing creature."

"So the man who calls himself Karel Reznicek . . ."

"Must be an impostor. And not a Czech. Probably a Nazi. Possibly a dangerous and important person, using Reznicek's papers, suitably changed by forgery, to escape."

"But . . . good God, man, you don't know what you are saying!"

Kladnik smiled. These Americans were so over-excitable!

"If you don't believe me . . ."

"I do, I do! Only—it is so strange and pretty terrible. You see, this man, this impostor—he married, under the name of Karel Reznicek, a very great friend of mine. She is a fine girl and now she is helpless in the hands of this swine. I—I must do something to find them. At once. If I have to comb Paris from garret to cellar, if I have to . . ."

The Czech intelligence man smiled slowly:

"There is no need for such desperate measures, *monsieur*. And I would not worry about your lady-friend. I don't think this man would harm her. She is his best insurance—she may represent his best camouflage. And he may genuinely be in love with her. . . ."

"What? That double-dyed Nazi, that . . ."

"But we don't know for certain that he is a Nazi of any colour at all. Mine were all theories, idle guesses, *mon capitaine*. I suggest that we go to the Sûreté and put our facts before the Commissioner. The French police are not yet up to their pre-war standards of efficiency—but it is not difficult to send out a description of the couple, wireless it to all districts, and issue a general warrant. You don't happen to remember the number of the car?"

"No, I don't," answered Peter. "I only know that it was a black Mercedes, pretty big and battered. Of course, he might have changed its colour or taken to trains or . . ."

"Let us not be pessimistic, my friend. The cleverest man makes mistakes. And while this pseudo-Reznicek seems to be a very clever one, he cannot have travelled across Eastern France without having left some trace behind him. You are certain that he was at Strasbourg?"

"Yes, I think so," replied Whitney. "I am a little confused and not sure of anything—but he was there and . . ."

"Well?"

"The Nazi who was killed! The Nazi in the garage!

Obmann or whatever his name was . . . this fake Reznicek must have had something to do with his murder! He was asking for him at the desk of the Maison Rouge! But . . . would one Nazi bigwig kill another?"

"Captain Whitney, one of these days you ought to read a good book on the Nazi movement. What else have they been doing in their spare time except kill each other?"

"You are right and I am a fool. But now I am beginning to see daylight. Gosh, Kladnik, if we can only find them before . . ."

He turned away and the Czech with the round cheeks and the comfortable girth kept silent with elephantine tact.

An hour later Peter Whitney was sitting in a *bistro* that sold something called Pernod though it had only a faint resemblance to the pre-war article and its price had increased twenty-fold. Sergeant Ira sat beside him and mournfully inspected the steel table-top from which generations of drinkers had rubbed away the white paint.

"You sure this Czech told the truth?" he asked.

"Why shouldn't he? He is just as keen to catch that heel as I am."

"Yeah." Eads moved his jaws meditatively and rhythmically. His only weakness—practically—was peppermint gum. "But foreigners are funny. Why, I remember 'way back in prohibition times . . ."

"No, sergeant," Peter begged him. "Not now."

"Well, there ain't anything we can do, except wait. They promised to let us know if something came through. But would you mind very much, captain, if I did a little snooping on my own?"

"Not a bit, Eads. Go right ahead."

"Thanks, I will." The sergeant removed his small, wiry body from the uncomfortable chair and sauntered off. Any moment Peter expected him to pull a magnifying glass from his pocket or produce a couple of blood-hounds. No, Ira could not help him.

He was baffled and unhappy. Something had happened that had shaken his whole world to its foundations. He was helpless and yet his whole being cried out for quick, decisive action. If the man who called himself Karel Reznicek had come down the boulevard, he would have killed him—no, that would be too easy and too quick. Give him a beating, knock out his handsome white teeth, bash in his pretty profile, tear out his white-golden hair. He . . .

Until now Germans were *people* to Captain Whitney. You met them in battle, they had guns and you had guns and you shot at each other. They were not nice customers, true; but they fought with weapons you could understand and counter. Muscle for muscle, brain for brain, man for man, you gave just as good as you got. And you knew that you were riding a triumphant wave, that nothing could stop you getting to the crest. Later, the Germans became patients in a huge psychopathic ward. They had to be cured and kept from doing harm again—doing harm to anybody while they were in this dangerous state of lunacy.

But this—this man who had probably murdered Karel Reznicek or was responsible for his death—this man was not a human being, not an ordinary loony. You could not measure him by any normal or abnormal standards. He defied classification. There was nothing in Peter Whitney's experience that could explain a man who, with everyone's hand against him, paused to woo and marry a girl under the falsest possible pretences. When he thought of Helen, young Captain Whitney forgot all his law-book learning, all the tough and sophisticated things he had done and said in his life. His imagination worked overtime. He saw her murdered, he saw her being tortured, humiliated, helpless; and these were not pretty scenes. Sitting at the battered table in the Paris *bistro* he went through the agonies of hell. Because he was an American, he had been inevitably conditioned by Hollywood; and so he thought of Basil Rathbone and "Love from a Stranger"—and that did not make things one tiny bit better.

When he emerged from his own private hell, he felt empty and chastened. The only thing that remained was hate—hate of the nation that could produce men like this soft-spoken, handsome beast. Oh yes, Helen was right, Peter told himself—but what difference had it made? She had told him that there was no good or bad German—just the same paranoiac race, humble like Uriah Heep when conquered, sadistic and murderous when on top. She should have developed an instinct for smelling them out, for knowing from a hundred yards distance that a member of the *Herrenvolk* was approaching. But she did not. In three days she fell victim to this . . .

It was no use torturing himself, Captain Whitney decided. It was no use—yet how could he stop?

His vague suspicion of the man who called himself Karel Reznicek had begun when the tall, fair-haired man spun that story about mysterious Russians and plans of assassination. Or perhaps a little bit earlier, when "Karel" had explained glibly why he had denied his knowledge of English at their first meeting. It had thickened when the papers were stolen. Peter was now certain that this Nazi in disguise must have taken them. How? When? It did not matter. So he had two good reasons for wanting to catch him: Helen and his own neck. He *would* catch him if he died in the attempt. And what a wonderful settling of debts it would be!

He rose and walked back to Kladnik's office where he had told Sergeant Eads to meet him. Kladnik had no news. They spent the night together, smoking far too many cigarettes and drinking innumerable cups of a brew miscalled coffee. In the small hours they even started a game of poker. Sergeant Ira cleaned them out in no time at all. The Czech intelligence man acquired a new and considerable respect for Americans. Peter just sighed that if bad luck was riding a guy, he could never get rid of it.

When the telephone rang at half-past four in the morning, they were bleary-eyed and had reached the stage of doubting the evidence of their own senses. But they all three made a bee-line for the phone. Kladnik, for all his bulk, won the race, which was just as well for the voice at the other end of the line spoke Czech.

The plump man replaced the receiver and said:

"Yes, we've got in the first report from the Sûreté. They have been in Annecy for three days, leaving two days ago. Our friend seems to have no suspicion of danger for he registered as Karel Reznicek."

"And his . . . wife?" Peter asked.

"Madame appeared to be in excellent health. They did not give their destination when they left but it is thought that it would be in the general direction of the south-west."

"What do you think?" asked Whitney. "Is he making for Italy? Or Switzerland?"

"Hardly Switzerland," smiled Kladnik. "At Annecy the frontier is very near—yet they turned *away* from it. Nor Italy. I should guess—Spain."

"Well, what are we waiting for?" cried Peter. "Can I get a plane to Annecy?"

"I don't think so. But you have your jeep, *hein*? What about setting out after a good breakfast? Phone me from every stop on your way. That may avoid detours. And if they are caught, I'll join you. I'd rather like to meet *Pan* Karel Reznicek—whoever he may be."

Though Peter was impatient to start at once, Kladnik insisted on breakfast and Sergeant Ira seconded him heartily. About six they passed through Vincennes, on their way to the south. Peter tried to feel like a knight in armour, riding to the rescue of the captive princess, but he only felt sleepy and as full of hate as ever.

XXXIII

IN THE EARLY MORNING THEY struggled over the Col d'Izoard, using the snow-chains Horst bought at Briançon. The seven and a half kilometres of winding ascent took them over two hours. At Sainte-Marie they were told that the Col-de-Vars was blocked, but von Falkenau decided to risk it in spite of the advice of an old mountain guide. They got stuck a thousand feet from the summit and would have had to walk or spend the night in the icy wind if an American caterpillar truck had not given them a tow. Even so it was rather late when they reached Barcelonnette but Horst was determined to get to Nice. Up the Col d'Allos and down again to Beauvezer; another long climb to the top of the Colle Saint-Michel. At Puget-Theniers they stopped for dinner and it was past midnight when the lights of Nice greeted them as they drove down the Moyenne Corniche.

Their small hotel was near the Boulevard Carabacel and Helen was so tired that she went straight to bed. The long drive, however, had had the opposite effect on Horst; he felt wideawake and sat for another hour in the tiny *salon*, reading the local newspaper whose articles were studded with odd bits of American slang.

This was the last lap, he told himself; in two days they would be safely across the border. In his present alert state the terrors of the night seemed to be unreal and unlikely to return. He had come through a bad patch, he told himself; now it was over and he could relax. It was just as well that he had no need to use those pills—he had heard some ugly tales of their after-effects even if they did keep you awake for long periods at a time. No—and he stretched luxuriously—those fears and haunting spectres at Briançon must have been due to his weariness and the long strain. He knew that he could easily get through these last few days.

He strolled upstairs and found Helen asleep. Her face was a little flushed and she breathed rather heavily. Horst gave her a glance. Perhaps she had caught a cold—they had to stand for a long time in the snow when the car got stuck—or perhaps it was just weariness. He hoped that she would not become ill, it would be awkward if they were held up for any length of time—but then, even a week should not make a real difference. Karel Reznicek's identity, he told himself, was still a safe secret and he saw no way in which it could be uncovered.

When he got into bed, he felt how tired he was himself. The rhythm of the car throbbed in his brain, the bare rocks with their white-spattered brown and grey, rose in the darkness under his eyelids. He yawned and stretched his body full length, feeling drowsiness gradually creeping over him, numbing his mind, wrapping him in warmth and contentment.

That night he had two dreams, almost in immediate succession, like the two disjointed instalments of the same serial, with some of the connecting parts missing.

The first was short and simple. He was on some secret errand that was desperately important. As he set out, walking down an indistinct street, with the houses swaying wildly in some storm or earthquake, he was filled with the urgency and importance of his mission. He carried something under his arm but whether it was a brief-case, a loaf of bread or a hand-grenade, he could not tell. He turned into the vaulted entrance of a building with a sentry-box on each side; but the sentries had disappeared. If he walked through the passage and up the stairs, he would reach his destination in sixty seconds—it was as simple as that. But when he got to the staircase, there was a big sign in Gothic lettering right across it, saying; OUT OF ORDER. DANGER. NO ADMITTANCE.

He shrugged; there were the back stairs, he could walk up

those and it meant only a little delay. But at the bottom of the stairs, after he had crossed a large, dim courtyard with uneven cobblestones under his feet, there stood a man whose face he could not see and who pointed to the left. Aha, Horst thought, there is an ambush on the first landing, how kind of him to warn me; and once again he passed under a vaulted arch, emerging into another courtyard.

The rest was confused and increasingly menacing. Again and again he stopped at the bottom of stairs which were barred to him. More and more courtyards appeared, growing smaller and darker, until he was stumbling over boxes and garbage cans, low-strung clothes lines and other unidentifiable obstacles. And all the time the sense of urgency was with him; he had not much time left, and unless he could persuade the guardians of the staircases that his business was important and could not be delayed, he would lose . . . no, he was not certain what he would lose and what he was carrying under his arm. He told himself that he must keep his head, that if he panicked, disaster would follow—but still the courtyards and blocked staircases repeated themselves in endless succession until he could have cried in mortification except that he remembered that tears would give him away. Tears . . . it was ridiculous. At the next stairway he decided to risk all. He brushed the silent, formless figure aside and rushed up to the next landing. The corkscrew turn prevented him from seeing what was ahead and he stopped only at the last moment. The staircase ended and there was nothing there . . . no corridor, no more stairs. Just empty space, unrelieved darkness. A wall rose behind him so that he could not turn back . . . inch by inch it edged forward like the steel wall in that ridiculous story he had read—how long ago? he did not know. Inch by inch he was edged closer to the abyss and when he fell, he suddenly knew what was under his arm; a human heart, gory and soft to the touch, still beating he could not tell how and why, its rhythm filling the air as he fell and was jolted into consciousness again. . . .

. . . Well, it had not been so bad, he told himself as he lay awake in the darkness and listened to Helen's swift breathing. He looked at the luminous dial of his watch. Only half an hour had passed since he had marked the time, before he began to drift off to sleep. The image of the last staircase was still in his mind; he told himself, harshly, that he must not think of it. Something else instead . . . something pleasant and reassuring. Helen's face when he proposed to her . . . the gleaming white curve of her body . . . And then, other women: redheads and blondes, that black-haired Jewish girl in Posnan who had spat into his face when he took her . . . Shining mornings as he rode through the pine-forest, feeling his strength and superiority like a pliable yet impenetrable armour . . . The ancient and civilised aroma of Napoleon brandy swirling in the broad glass as he turned it between his hands. . . . The touch of ice-cold water on his skin after a night of hard drinking and wenching . . . There were so many pleasant things in the past and quite a lot to look forward to. . . . If he impressed these memories upon his mind, they would surely be transferred into his dreams—provided there was no way of escaping those dreams. But perhaps he had had his dose for to-night.

. . . *His last conscious thought was that it had worked—those pleasant images had been the right conditioning. Because when he closed his eyes, he was back on the stage of the* Kammerspiele *and nothing unpleasant could happen to him there. Had he not risen from the obscurity of an understudy to the glory of a star in three short months? Of course, it was his talent, that chameleon-like genius of acquiring any colour the part demanded; but even at twenty-one he believed in the maxim that Lady Fortune needed a little shoving, a little judicious guidance in the right direction.*

He stood in the wings watching Reinhold Below rehearse his great scene in "Götz von Berlichingen." Martin, the director, prided himself that he always chose his revivals aptly—he thought that in these confused and unhappy times while Munich seethed and groaned with the aftermath of the short-lived Bavarian Soviet Republic, the tale of the iron-fisted old knight who took the side of the people, would be most appropriate. It was a fine part, anyhow; and Reinhold was the right man for it even if he was only twenty-eight. A strange fellow, Reinhold; some said that he was over-sensitive, a good actor but an unbalanced human being. Perhaps because he had served through the war in U-boats and once had to endure attacks by three destroyers for almost twenty-four hours, he had brought back a slight nervous complaint from the long years under the sea. . . . He was affable enough to his colleagues, a most conscientious worker—even if now and then a trifle upset him and rehearsal had to be broken off. Martin handled him as a trainer would treat a high-strung thoroughbred. But Horst hated him because he was only Reinhold's understudy and Reinhold blocked his way to greater things of which he felt himself perfectly capable. He had talked to Martin but Martin was a fool—he considered himself the greatest stage producer after Reinhardt (sometimes, in his cups, even above *Reinhardt) and insisted that actors needed "maturing," that in three or five years Horst might make a good Mercutio or a passable Egmont—but that he must be patient.*

Yes, Martin was a fool; and Horst von Falkenau had been quietly amused and not a little satisfied when twelve years later the great producer was denounced as a Communist and beaten to death in Dachau. There was little patience in the Gestapo and their victims were given no time to "mature". . . .

He stood there on the stage, watching his rival and grudgingly admitting that Reinhold made a good job of the fire-eating robber knight. That scene where he denounced the feudal oppressors and then rushed from the council chamber . . . it was really well done. It left the audience shaken, reluctantly admiring; it cast a spell that helped over the somewhat lame and colourless later scenes. It even made an impression on the handful of people watching the rehearsal in the semi-dark theatre. Martin's bald head shone like a billiard ball in the dimness and when Reinhold finished the scene, he barked his approval.

It was then that Horst's cup of bitterness flowed over and that he decided to do something about it. "Götz" was to be presented to the Munich theatregoers in a week's time; after that, for at least a month, it would be played every alternate night—provided the revival was a success. And why should it not be? It had everything—a fine cast, imaginative scenery, good direction . . . everything except Horst von Falkenau, who had by now almost forgotten those dark and dismal months with the Freicorps *and wanted to be a successful actor. For Horst von Falkenau, struggling on a salary that inflation shrunk smaller and smaller every day, had exactly ten lines to speak in "Götz von Berlichingen"—and not very important lines at that.*

With the suddenness of the dream-world the scene changed and he was standing at the back of the stalls, watching the first night of the revival. His call was not till the fourth act—and though Martin liked everyone to be in their dressing-rooms, this time Horst had broken the rule.

There was fun and triumph to be enjoyed if he only waited patiently for a little. Again, grudgingly, he admired Reinhold's brilliance. He held the audience spellbound, every inflexion, every gesture was worked out with great artistry yet appeared to be perfectly natural. Slowly the play moved up to the climax when, at the end of his long speech, he would turn and rush from the castle hall in fury and contempt.

The speech had ended; the audience was rigid under the fascination of the old knight's harsh voice. Then Reinhold Below turned and rushed at the lath-and-canvas door.

But the door was locked.

He fetched up with a hard smack against the scenery. As yet no one had noticed that something was wrong. The set was realistic enough; at the wings only a very narrow slit was left, not enough for a man to pass through in a hurry—a slim person might have squeezed through the opening with some discomfort and in a rather undignified position. But Reinhold did not think of such a possibility. Again he attacked the door. It would not yield. It could not yield for Horst had himself wedged the two narrow wooden strips which held it in position and which were turned the right way when the scenery was put up. No one had seen him do it . . . there was no possible proof.

And now the audience noticed that something was wrong. A girl tittered, a man's voice called out:

"What's the matter, old fellow? Have you forgotten where the door is?"

Laughter spread in waves, swelled to a flood. Catcalls and ironical remarks flew from row to row. Reinhold had his back to the audience. It was a defeated, broken back. Martin's fat voice was heard giving a command to lower the curtain. But the curtain had stuck or perhaps the man who turned the handle, was not at his post. The sneering temper of the audience rose. These were cynical, lawless times in Munich; and any crowd quickly turned into a mob if it could find a victim. They shouted at him to dig a tunnel, to sprout wings and fly away, to scuttle himself. And then, slowly, silently, Reinhold turned.

That was how it happened: he had turned round and in his face there was defeat and madness. He was finished and he knew it. Before the curtain came down and mercifully hid his shame, he had collapsed and was clawing at the bare boards.

Yes, that was how, simply and effectively, Horst von Falkenau, the understudy, got his start in the Munich Kammerspiele. *And even now, in re-living his triumph in a dream, he was filled with a sense of pleasant anticipation as Reinhold Below slowly swung round to face his tormentors.*

But the face that stared across the footlights, shadowed by madness, was not Reinhold Below's. It was his own—it was Horst von Falkenau's. And as he cowered, split into two, one of his egos down in the turbulent, catcalling audience, the other up on the stage, he knew the mortification and self-contempt, the urge to scream and run, the choking feeling in his throat and the cold clutch upon his heart that Reinhold Below must have known before they came and took him away to a padded cell.

XXXIV

THE SLIMY HORROR CLUNG TO him and he felt that he could never shake it off. He would never wake to a normal and real morning; there was no return and no escape.

But into the deep well of unconsciousness a voice insinuated itself gradually. A voice he knew but could not place, calling a name he did not recognise.

"Karel! Wake up! Karel!"

He opened his eyes but he was still blinded. And his brain was covered with an opaque layer, a jelly-like substance. When he spoke, it was in the tongue that was his childhood's:

"*Was gibt's? Lass mich allein . . . ich mag das nicht. . . .*"

But as she repeated her cry in English, he summoned all his strength and shook off the paralysing daze.

"Karel! Wake up! You have been dreaming again . . . a nightmare. . . ."

It was better not to speak. He still could not trust himself and the rage that possessed him was directed just as much against her as against himself. She had no business taxing his strength, drawing on it, when he needed every ounce; she had no business barging into this most private struggle. But the next moment he clung to her, still silent; for she was anchor and a bridge back to sanity.

"Was it very bad?" she asked. She reached out and switched on the small bedside lamp.

He shook his head.

"No, it's all right. . . . Did I—speak or something?"

"You were shouting—quite loudly, too. I couldn't distinguish the words. It sounded like German—but perhaps it was Czech. Karel, don't you think . . ."

He noticed that her bare arms, pressed against his cheek, were very hot to the touch. She coughed and he felt her body trembling in a brief paroxysm. She turned away and put her free hand against her lips.

"What's the matter?" he asked. He was a little alarmed, but he also welcomed the opportunity to guide the conversation away from himself.

"Oh, Karel, I feel an idiot," Helen sighed, "but I think I am going to be ill."

"But . . . how do you mean? You feel unwell? Shall I go for the doctor? Or get you some medicine?"

It was an entirely new situation in Horst von Falkenau's life—playing nurse to a sick woman. For Helen must feel pretty bad if she confessed it; during their trip he had realised that she ignored physical discomfort and could remain cheerful when he had long become irritated. If her illness should prove serious . . . if it should hold them up . . . half a dozen surmises flashed through his mind and for a moment he forgot the problem he had to face himself. For it was no longer any use trying to hide his head in the sand—two of these damned visitations in a night . . . and what if all his nights, every sleeping hour should be turned into one long sequence of them? Perhaps it was all caused by the tension of having to play two parts—that of Karel Reznicek, to Helen and the world—and that of Horst von Falkenau, the man whom nothing could frighten or dismay, to himself. For when he analysed his own reactions to these dreams, he had to confess that he had not been quite frank even to himself; that he had shut off all the implications behind a curtain of defiance and belittling scorn.

Well, he still had sufficient reserves of strength—and it should not last long. A week could make no great difference and in a week he should be in Spain. That would mean safety and perhaps a doctor . . . but no, he had no faith in doctors where the mind was concerned and there was nothing wrong with his body.

When he asked Helen what he could do for her, she did not answer. He chafed her hands; they were dry and hot.

"You'd better take your temperature," he said. "Have

you got a thermometer or shall I ask for one from the people downstairs?"

"In my bag . . ." she whispered. "There is one in my bag. . . ."

She shivered violently and a soft moan made him thoroughly alarmed. What if she died? he thought, and the idea seemed to be fantastic in connection with anyone as vital and young as Helen. He fumbled in the bag, found the thermometer and coaxed her into opening her lips. He noticed that they were a little cracked, the soft red skin dried out by the fever.

While he ticked off the minutes on his wrist-watch, he decided that he would take some of those pills he had collected in the woods near Blamont. If he could spend about five nights without sleep, he should be all right. It was no weakening, he told himself; Helen needed him and he had good cause to stay awake. No, it was not a cowardly act—if, at the same time, he escaped those inconvenient visits from his past, that was of secondary importance. A little uncomfortably he felt that perhaps he was not entirely sincere about this; but introspection was a very new pastime for him and the sooner he ended indulging in it, the better it would be for both of them.

The Continental thermometer showed a little over forty degrees Celsius—high enough. He must get a doctor, he decided, even if it meant taking a certain risk.

"I am going out for a few minutes," he told Helen, unconsciously lowering his voice. "But I'll send up the chambermaid to sit with you. Will you be all right?"

Surprisingly, distressingly she clung to him.

"Please, don't go," she pleaded. "I am . . . I feel so queer . . . I want you here. . . ."

Gently he freed his hand from her hot clutch.

"I must go out to find a doctor," he explained. "I really won't be long."

She started to cry. It was a quiet, subdued sound in the somewhat airless room and the tears came slowly, surging from under her eyelids. He bent down and kissed her and was once again appalled by the dry heat that seemed to emanate from her whole body. Then he tiptoed to the door and hurried downstairs. He found an elderly woman who looked rather stupid but kindly and explained to her that Madame Reznicek had a chill; would she sit with her? Francine—that was the chambermaid's name—made little clucking noises and hurried upstairs.

The doctor, the receptionist told him, lived down the street—only a dozen houses away. "But he is rather old, *monsieur*," the man said. "Our young men are all away. He'll do his best, though."

Dr. Pascal was a dried-up, grey-haired wisp of a man who wore the little red ribbon of the *Légion d'Honneur* in his buttonhole and was prouder of his family name than of anything else. Within the first five minutes he informed Horst that he was a descendant of the great philosopher—and he could prove it, too. Horst restrained himself with difficulty from being very rude and warded off the doctor's attempt to show him his family tree. The surgery was more like a drawing-room with small gilt tables and chairs, a great mass of bric-à-brac scattered everywhere; but there was also a white enamelled business-like instrument cabinet and in the corner an X-ray machine.

"Young people are so careless," the doctor chattered while they walked the few dozen yards to the hotel. "They think their bodies will last for ever. Yet there is nothing more fragile, more vulnerable than the human organism. A few degrees difference in its temperature, the lack or surplus of infinitesimal doses of certain chemicals can destroy it rapidly. Now the other day I was telling a young student . . ."

"Most interesting," interrupted Horst without the slightest hesitation. "Shall we go up straight away?"

The doctor gave him an indignant glance but did not persist in telling his story. Upstairs Francine rose from beside the bed and whispered:

"She has been very restless. Calling for you, *monsieur*, all the time . . . and for her mother, too. . . ."

The doctor examined Helen who was semi-conscious; her big, feverish eyes fixed on Horst who stood at the foot of the bed.

"I am not sure," Dr. Pascal pronounced, "but it looks like pneumonia to me. Only one lung, though and she is in very good physical condition. Are you a refugee, *monsieur*?"

He is worried about his fee, thought Horst and hastened to reassure him: "I am travelling in an official capacity, doctor. Do you think there is serious danger?"

"Not if we can get some M and B quickly," Dr. Pascal said. "Perhaps the American hospital can let me have some."

"M and B?" repeated Horst. "I am afraid I don't know . . ."

"It is a new drug, developed by the British," Dr. Pascal

lectured him. "I am an old man, *monsieur*, but not a fool and always willing to learn new tricks."

"And how long will it be, do you think, before she recovers? I mean . . . I would like to make my plans accordingly . . . and if my wife cannot travel for a considerable time . . ."

"I am no prophet," Dr. Pascal protested testily. "She may be fit to travel in a week—though I doubt it—or a fortnight—or a month. Pneumonia is no joke, *monsieur*."

He prescribed a sedative, gave directions to Francine what to do about food and warmth, cold compresses and drinks; he promised to return in the afternoon with the drug if he could get it.

Horst walked downstairs with him. He wanted to ask a number of questions—but he was also afraid that the doctor would consider him a fool. So he said nothing except:

"I trust this will cover the cost of your visit," and handed the old man a folded note.

Dr. Pascal took it without looking at it. Surprisingly he reached up and patted Horst on the shoulder.

"Don't worry," he said. "She'll be all right. She *must* be. A woman, so young and lovely . . ."

"Thank you, doctor," Horst said stiffly. Suddenly he felt very tired. A low, steady humming within his skull seemed to fill the whole hotel hall, the whole building. He turned back and slowly climbed the narrow, steep stairs. He could not think in such a state, he decided. There was nothing he could do except wait—wait for the doctor, wait for Helen's recovery, wait for his own return to his usual balanced, sane self. But he *was* sane, of course he was; no one could deny that he was still able to act quickly and decisively. The way he dealt with that swine Obmann—that was not a madman's or a coward's way. . . . If he could only sleep without . . . But no, sleep was dangerous; in unconsciousness a lurking enemy was waiting for him he could not yet name and therefore could not eject.

Francine was waiting for him, a look of anxiety on her plump, motherly face.

"She is sleeping now," she said. "But the doctor said, give her these . . ." and she held out a few small white pills.

"You go and get something to eat," Horst told her. "I'll wait a little time at her bedside and if she doesn't wake by herself, I'll wake her and give her the pills."

The chambermaid nodded and disappeared. Horst drew up a chair and sat down, close to Helen. Her face was flushed now, her hair damp, clinging to her temples and forehead. He felt an almost irresistible impulse to smooth the strands of hair back; he stretched out his hand when she suddenly opened her eyes. They were dimmed with the fever but even so brighter than he could ever remember.

"I am going to die," she said slowly.

"Nonsense." His voice was sharp, in surprised protest. "Dr. Pascal will be back shortly to give you an injection and you'll be well in no time."

She did not reply and he thought that she had gone to sleep again. He hesitated, the pills ready in the small teaspoon; she spoke again:

"Karel . . . last night . . ."

"Yes, my sweet?"

"When I woke you—after your nightmare—you spoke in German. I know now. I am sure. Why did you speak in German, Karel?"

He laughed.

"What an absurd question! I was dreaming . . . and I haven't the faintest idea what language one uses in dreams."

"But you weren't asleep then. You——"

"Look here, Helen," he said firmly, "you must not worry about things that don't matter. I went to a German school when I was a child. I am bi-lingual or tri-lingual or whatever you wish. But now you are going to take these pills; later, Francine is bringing you some broth and you'll rest until Dr. Pascal comes."

She swallowed the pills obediently and lay back, her eyes closed.

"Don't go away, Karel," she murmured. "If I am alone, I'll die. My mother—it is funny—I have been thinking of my mother. If she were here—she would only fuss and wouldn't help a bit . . . but still if she were here, I . . ."

"You'll be well by to-morrow," Horst said. "And you'll see your mother soon. Don't worry, darling. I am here. I won't go away."

She remained silent, but the fever burned brighter and brighter in her cheeks. She tried to throw off the bedclothes and he had to tuck her in again and again for the room was none too warm and the doctor had warned him to keep her well covered. She was in a sleep that was half-delirium; she was muttering all the time but he could not distinguish the words.

Two hours later the chambermaid came back and he went down to eat something. As he was returning to the sick room, he met Dr. Pascal.

"I have got it," the doctor beamed. "These Americans are really wonderful. A young colleague even offered to come along and give the injection. But I told him that I was not so decrepit yet that I should not be able to find the vein. How is she?"

"Not much better," Horst replied. "She seems to be very restless."

"We'll see about that," Dr. Pascal declared cheerfully. "This stuff works wonders. Really wonders. They say, it saved Monsieur Churchill's life."

As they reached the landing, he stopped for a moment and said:

"They would not take any money, of course. I just gave them your name and nationality."

"Oh . . ." It was a non-committal sound. "But I don't think I introduced myself to you. . . ."

"That's all right," waved the old doctor. "I rang up the hotel and got it all from the reception clerk. I did not want to disturb you. I hope you don't mind."

"Oh no, not at all. They are certainly generous, those Americans."

The fever had risen and Helen was breathing heavily. It seemed cruel and senseless that her body should be attacked by something as humiliating and malicious as this sudden illness. Health belonged to her, was a part of her, like her hair or the little furrow between her eyes. Now she was helpless and Horst felt something he could not remember ever feeling before: compassion, pity, indignation—mixed with a formless fear that this complex emotion would weaken him in some way, endanger his plans, put obstacles into his way. Dr. Pascal quickly and deftly gave the injection; he said that if the fever rose another tenth of a degree Centigrade, they should send for him again—otherwise he would come early next morning to look at the patient.

Francine declared her willingness to stay up during the night; but Horst said no, they could share it; if she sat up till midnight, he would take the rest of the vigil. He went out for a stroll, found that he was just as restless walking as sitting down and returned to the hotel for the evening meal; Helen was asleep but the fever had not yet abated and Francine was busy with cold compresses and with bathing the girl's body in a solution of vinegar and water.

"I'll come back at midnight," Horst said when he had inspected his wife. "This room isn't big enough for the three of us. I'll find a place for a short nap in the *salon*."

Francine nodded and he went downstairs again. He wondered whether Dr. Pascal's optimism was justified. He wondered what he could do if Helen's recovery was slow. He wondered . . .

XXXV

HE WOULD NOT TAKE THE tablets. He would not trust his fate to something so dangerous and unknown. All his life he had kept away from drugs—even when he was in pain. He thought of Goering and the enormous dose he needed every day. Roehm, too . . . and all the others. Whether he had two or twenty of those . . . dreams . . . it did not matter. The humming in his head had gone; he was tired but he could think clearly again. *Nothing could defeat him that was within himself*—he repeated this sentence as if it were a declaration of faith, a solemn oath, a reaffirmation of some shining piece of wisdom. He would get over this alone. Goering's bright boys when they went off to bomb Coventry or Rotterdam—they needed these artificial aids to courage and alertness. But he . . . not Horst von Falkenau.

Francine had gone; she told him that just before he came up, she had changed Helen's bed-clothes as they were soaking wet with perspiration.

"It is a good sign," she said. "She is still on fire, the little one, but I think she is mending already. . . ."

Horst had nodded and sat down in the chair at the bedside. Helen was sleeping but in the dimmed light he could not decide whether her colour was more normal, her breathing less tortured. Dr. Pascal had said that they should not disturb her if she slept—that nature was doing its work best with the body completely relaxed. Nature . . . Horst grinned savagely. Nature or whatever it was, had played him a scurvy trick. . . .

The room enveloped him, like a shell. It was the container of his universe; suddenly he could not even visualise the corridor, the staircase, the hall, let alone the street and not far from it, the sea. The tiny noises of the night stopped at the threshold as if something had deadened all sound. He and the fever-stricken woman in the bed, the night-table and the dimmed lamp, the oblong of the wall opposite him, half-dipped in shadow: that was all. Once he had roamed freely across the heaths of his *Gau*; his plane crossed frontiers as if it were passing over a shallow furrow; he was driven three hundred miles a day or travelled from one state to another between breakfast and lunch. Europe was both spacious and small; spacious for those who belonged to the *Herrenvolk*'s masters; small for those who were hedged in by barbed wire, by passport regulations and deportation orders. But now this room seemed sufficient.

A slow, heavy stroke reverberated through the night. It was the clock on the nearby church tower, striking the half-hour. It was the only sound that had penetrated the protective shell. Strange that he had not noticed it before; but during the day the roar of traffic must have swallowed or minimised it. Now that the silence was absolute, the ponderous clangour caught his imagination. He glanced at Helen but the sound had not disturbed her. The prospect of listening to the clock, striking each quarter, was not unpleasant; it cut up the night into orderly segments, built steps for his brain upon which he could ascend.

He heard the third quarter strike and then the first of the twelve marking the hour.

. . . He was standing in the courtyard of Stadelheim. Above his head a dirt-encrusted bulb shed scanty light upon the cobbled archway. S.S. men and prison guards surrounded the victims of Adolf's purge. The commander checked their names, then they were led to the wall at the back of the courtyard. Here a few people stood, holding torches or fastening them into the loose, reddish soil.

Four men came first . . . among them a priest. Suddenly they realised why they had been taken out into the courtyard. One screamed that he had been promised, it was only for questioning; another embraced the legs of the priest, begging him to save his life. But the guards swiftly and brutally ended the scene and dragged them to the wall where the execution squad was waiting. Horst winced a little at the volley. He saw the four men collapse in postures that were more ludicrous than tragic—except for the priest for he, lying on the ground, lifted his arm in a final benediction. Then an S.S. man walked up to him and shot him through the head. A waste of ammunition, Horst thought; but then, bullets were cheap on this night. . . .

There was no break in time, no transition; but the courtyard had dissolved and he stood outside the Sanatorium Hanselbauer. It was a fresh, clear June morning; the birds were singing in the rose-garden and the new day was superbly contemptuous of whatever was coming.

A small group of men entered the building; ten minutes later they reappeared, driving a motley crowd of half-dressed S.A. leaders in front of them. The prisoners looked surprised, foolish and frightened. They were hustled into cars and driven off.

Horst moved forward to follow the Fuehrer into the sanatorium. Armed sentries had taken up their places in the corridors. He drew back a little as Hitler knocked on a door. A sleepy voice asked who it was and the Fuehrer gave his name. Inside there was a shout of joy; then the door opened and Roehm, in pyjamas, stood on the threshold. The Fuehrer with three others entered the room and the door was closed . . .

. . . Again the smooth yet abrupt transition. Somehow Wiessee had disappeared and he had returned to the Stadelheim courtyard. A group of prisoners was led from the cells. One was crying; all the others shouted, repeating assurances of innocence, begging for a chance to clear themselves. But a few minutes later the volley rang out . . . the first . . . the second . . . the third . . . after that he gave up counting. The afternoon passed imperceptibly, but he still stood in the archway, listening to the punctuation of the minutes by the barking, sharp-voiced guns.

Then Roehm passed him, his fat chest heaving, his eyes full of tears, perspiration running down his face. He passed so close to Horst that he could have touched him, but he saw nothing except the wall at the far end, bloodsplashed and mottled, the firing-squad and the little group of S.S. officials waiting. He cried out and threw himself at his escort, roaring like a wounded animal. The guards took hold of him, fastening his hands behind his back. He kicked out and they tied his feet together, then dragged him to the wall.

"Dogs, swine, dirty swine . . ." he shouted till the very last moment when the volley crashed out. . . .

Horst relaxed, with a sigh. He had been tense; he felt the rough surface of the wall against which he had leant, leaving a pattern of pressure upon his back. But now he was free; nothing more could come, nothing disturbing could happen. Some of the men who had died out there in the courtyard had been his friends and companions in the early days; one or two he had even liked or found amusing. But that did not matter. They were dead and he was alive; that was the important thing.

But as he turned to go, another long, shuffling procession approached from the direction of the prison. There were no guards to accompany them—a circumstance that Horst did not find strange at first. Swinging in a severe rhythm they came towards him—twenty or thirty men, all in uniform. He could not distinguish their faces, not even when they came much closer. Some mask had fallen over their features, freezing them in a uniformity that was grotesque and a little frightening.

They passed very close to him and now the first one spoke. Two words only:

"Du auch . . ."

He reached out to grab the man's sleeve but could not touch him. A barrier was between them, intangible yet unsurmountable.

The second passed and he, too, murmured:

"Du auch . . ."

On came the others in more and more rapid succession, and their murmured malediction merged into one whispered chant, like the soft response of a congregation to the priest:

"You, too . . . you, too . . . you, too . . . you, too. . . ."

The susurration of voices ebbed and rose again. The line seemed to be interminable. Horst covered his ears but the voices penetrated flesh and bone. In the delicate labyrinth they echoed and reverberated, until the two words could no longer be distinguished, but their sense was driven through the ears into his brain; his whole skull was filled with the sound. He opened his mouth to scream but it was a soundless protest. He felt as if he were back in the shadowy, ash-grey cave of many nights ago when he stood and waited for his enemy to attack, challenging him and knowing that he would never come.

Louder and louder the echoes grew until they merged into one vast gong-like, metallic sound which squeezed all other sound from the universe.

. . . He woke and still the strokes of the gong, the echoing clangour continued. There was a little interval now between them and he counted the strokes—one—two—three—four—five—six. . . . Then, a somewhat longer pause and a different, sharper stroke. After that, silence.

Almost in terror he glanced at his wrist-watch. It showed exactly one o'clock. Panic clutched him. He remembered now that he had heard the church clock strike the first of the twelve strokes on the hour. Between the first and the sixth stroke he had lived through more than a day. Between the first and the sixth . . . how many seconds could have passed? Not more than half a dozen.

He remembered suddenly the story in "The Arabian Nights." He could not recall the exact details—but dimly he thought of the caliph and the sage; how the sage wanted to show the futility of human endeavour, the narrow limits of our perceptions. The caliph immersed his head in a bucket of water—and between the time he put his head under the water and took it out again, he had lived through a lifetime of joy and sorrow, of love and hate. He had been poor, he had married and begotten children, he sang and got drunk, fought enemies and died; and all in that brief second spent with his head in the bucket of water. It must have been thirty years or more since he read the story; he saw the book with the heavy Gothic print and the black-and-white illustrations clearly. He had not understood the tale then, he had even thought it rather silly. But it was true and the thing that was happening to him was no new, unique experience. Dark were the vistas, incredible the depths which opened to a single human being within his own body and mind. And now he was truly afraid.

He turned his head and saw that Helen had awakened and was looking at him.

"Darling," he said and moved close to her, "how do you feel? Let me take your temperature. Then you must have these pills. . . ."

Her eyes were clear. Her damp hair tousled, she looked as if she had passed through some barrier, left a landmark behind her. Her voice, low and soft, was full of wonder.

"Who are you?" she asked.

The question hit him a square blow; was she getting worse? Was this some strange delirium?

"But Helen," he tried to explain, "you know me. You know Karel."

"Karel?" she repeated musingly. "Karel? Is that your name?"

"Come on, take these . . ." and he offered her the pills. "Just a sip of water. They'll make you sleep."

She stared down at the small white globules on his palm.

"Don't want to," she shook her head. "It's poison." She lifted a forefinger to her lips. "Sssh! They want to poison me. . . "

"Don't be silly," he argued. "You have to take these. They'll make you well."

"Are you a doctor?" she asked. Mechanically she took the pills and sipped the water he held out to her.

"Helen, you are not well," he said. "Perhaps it's the injection Dr. Pascal gave you. Don't you know me? I am your husband."

"Husband?" She inspected the word and found it distasteful. She wrinkled her nose. "I haven't got a husband. I . . . but Hans is dead," she cried suddenly in a strained voice. "Hans is dead and he cannot marry me. I don't want any other husband. I want Hans. I want to go home. I . . ."

Before he could move, she was out of the bed and half-way to the door. He caught her but she struggled and he had considerable difficulty in getting her back to the bed.

"Let me go," she sobbed. "Please, let me go. I don't know, who you are. I never did you any harm, did I? Please, don't keep me here. Please . . ."

He did not know what to do or say. If this was the crisis . . . should he fetch the doctor? But he could not leave her alone. He managed to get her under the bed-clothes; he shook up the pillows, made her lie comfortable and talked all the time, in a soothing, persuasive voice. She had started to cry and the flow of her tears dismayed him; it was a Helen he did not know. But gradually, as he chafed her hands and stroked her hair, her sobs became quieter.

"Nobody is going to hurt you," he was saying. "You'll go home in the morning. Everything's going to be all right. Just rest a little and try to sleep. It's a long journey and you need all your strength. Just rest. Close your eyes now, there's a good girl. Close your eyes. You are going to sleep now. Yes, sleep is the best thing. Sleep . . ."

Obediently she closed her eyes and he sighed in relief. He felt terribly tired. Suddenly he hurried to his suit-case which stood in the corner and took from it the small box—one of half a dozen he had collected from the woods near Blamont. He stared dully at the instructions, in small print and in German and swallowed three of the pills. He could not resist any longer. This was the only way. The double fight was too much for any single man.

Helen was quiet now. Horst walked to the window and glanced out. Day was breaking slowly, reluctantly. Gulls wheeled above the housetops. He sat down again and began his long vigil.

XXXVI

ILL LUCK SEEMED TO DODGE the new Sir Galahad who rode in a jeep. His temper grew steadily worse and Sergeant Ira needed all of what he called his "sunny disposition" to calm his irascible superior.

"You're getting just like Old Leatherguts . . . I beg your pardon, General Steele," the outspoken sergeant complained. "Haven't you heard of the Chinese saying? Softlee, softlee, catchee monkey. . . ."

"Sometimes I entertain myself with the various ways I would like to murder you, Ira," grunted Peter Whitney. "The death of a thousand cuts, that's the only thing the Chinese developed in which I am interested. So shut up."

Sergeant Eads shut up, according to regulations. They reached Annecy with the jeep's engine almost red-hot; they had to wait five endless hours until the French mechanic who had never seen such a monster, produced the necessary tools and parts for some emergency repairs. No other mishap held them up until they reached Saint-Michel-de-Maurienne where they burst a tyre—a rare occurrence with these sturdy vehicles—and were given the most pessimistic reports about the state of the Galibier pass. There had been a heavy snowfall in the night and even the Valloire was said to be blocked. Ira took one look at the captain's face and decided not to argue with a madman. If he was destined to freeze to death in an outlandish place with a name he could not even try to pronounce, that was *kismet*—a word he had learned at the local cinema in the Bronx which was addicted to pictures with sheikhs in them.

They struggled through Saint-Martin-d'Arc and up to the tunnel just above Valloire. But at Les Verneys they found a ski patrol who had just returned from the slopes of the Col du Lautaret. They had been searching, in vain, for a party of foolhardy *maquisards* who were in too much of a hurry to return to Briançon, their native place.

"If they are lucky, they die quickly," the sergeant in charge of the patrol said. "If not—it's even worse."

Peter asked him about the pass.

The bearded "old sweat" shrugged.

"In some places the snow, it is three feet deep . . . and soft. In other places it is one foot deep and frozen . . . like an ice skating rink. But mostly it is four feet deep and you could never get out of it. No, *monsieur*, you cannot joke with the Galibier. You must wait unless you wish to commit suicide."

Peter did not wish to commit suicide. He looked at his map and tried to puzzle out some way of getting to Nice without having to cross the Alps. There did not seem to be any. Even if they crossed into Switzerland . . . but that would mean extra papers and permits—and probably would take a week. He did not have a week left. If he wanted to catch the pseudo-Karel Reznicek, he had to move fast. Sergeant Ira was a very amusing companion but he had his orders. And Peter meant to keep that rendezvous with General Steele in Nuremberg, whatever happened.

Les Verneys has few amenities in summer, even fewer in the early spring. The only hotel is a wooden chalet and not too well heated. They shivered for two days and three nights and Sergeant Ira played poker with the local inhabitants. This time, though he taught them the game, he ended up with a net loss of eighty-five dollars and thirty-two cents. His temper did not get any sweeter through this elemental catastrophe.

It was all the more galling because they knew they were on the right track. The black Mercedes had been seen at Faverges and Albertville, at Epierre and Saint-Jean-de-Maurienne. There was no doubt about it: Karel Reznicek was heading for the Grande Route des Alpes. He had passed through Valloire three days in front of them. The Mercedes was a good car but Ira's super-jeep could catch up with it if they drove twenty hours a day—and Peter Whitney had no intention of dawdling on the road. Also, the fake Karel had no idea of the pursuit—at least so Captain Whitney hoped—and would probably stop every night during the hours of darkness. But all these advantages were washed out by the snow—four or three or six feet thick, it made no difference—that perversely blocked their way.

On the fourth morning after their arrival, the ski-patrol turned up again. It was still dangerous, they explained; but it could be tried. They would need snow-chains, a guide—and perhaps it was just as well if *Messieurs les Americains* also had a few French soldiers along to help them if they got into any trouble.

So off they went and after two-and-a-half days of nerve-racking travel they reached Puget-Theniers and began the long, slow descent to the Mediterranean.

XXXVII

FOR ALMOST TWENTY-FOUR hours now Helen's temperature had been normal, but she was still weak and Dr. Pascal frowned whenever Horst tried to mention the subject of travel. There was nothing to do but to wait and it was not an easy thing to do.

Four days had passed since that night of delirium. Ninety-six hours without sleep for him.

The doctor urged him to take a rest—though old Pascal did not know that he had stayed awake all this immeasurable length of time—and Helen begged him to take a second room and have a good sleep. He smiled and said that he was all right; an old campaigner, he could exist on short cat-naps. He was lying, for he craved sleep whenever the effects of the tablets wore off; but then he took a few more, gradually increasing the dose. For the first few hours it was wonderful—he felt alert, very much alive and thought that he could do almost anything. After that it was not so good. He had brief spells of dizziness, for minutes he became deaf and once he had what might have passed for a heart-attack with anyone else—but of course, his heart was as strong as a bull's. Worst of all, his brain refused to function for brief periods; his sense of timing and co-ordination went to pieces. He dropped things and missed small objects by inches when he wanted to lift or touch them. But he was not alarmed. It would pass. Helen would soon recover and then, in Spain, he could relax. He could relax . . . for he was still tense. Sometimes he was tempted, terribly tempted, to throw the small boxes containing the pills into the sea—to cut off his way of retreat and face the nights' terror once and for all. But he could not do it. He could not think very far ahead in these days. When Helen was well . . . when they could get across the frontier . . . when he could settle down without the constant pressure of anxious waiting . . . when . . . when . . . when . . .

He did not dare to take more than one dose of the drug a day; he knew really very little of its nature and it was unthinkable to ask for information. He went so far as to visit the Nice town library but he could find nothing that made him any wiser. Dr. Pascal? No, the old fool would ask inconvenient questions.

The only thing he could do was to remain alone as much as possible during the hours of depression and physical discomfort that followed the brief period of alert well-being. Every morning he stayed with Helen for a few hours; in the afternoon he went out and sought some lonely part of the coast, some hidden spot in the woods. Of course, he had to come back at nightfall and there was still the night to get over. But Helen, during her slow convalescence, slept a good deal and fell asleep early; he was free to wrestle with his demon.

Until the fourth night when weariness and despair overcame him in an overwhelming wave. He covered his sunken, bloodshot eyes with trembling hands. Yes, it were better to yield, he thought. Nothing could be as horrible as this: the fear of unconsciousness, the terror of what would emerge from the darkness, with slimy fingers and faceless head. But somehow the hours dragged on and he still clung to the tatters of his pride, the remnants of his strength. Then came the false vigour, the sense that the next day, the next night could not be so bad—that, at the worst, he would reach a state of indifference and torpor in which nothing would matter.

He was rocking to and fro when he felt a light touch on

his shoulder. He started, looked up and saw Helen standing in front of him.

"What is it?" she asked. "What is the trouble, Karel?"

He had never alluded to her strange delirious talk that night when she was just getting over the crisis; and she must have forgotten it.

His first impulse was dislike, almost hate. Why couldn't she leave him alone? But then he roused himself and even managed a crooked smile.

"You shouldn't be up," he said. "Go back to bed, Helen . . . you know what the doctor said about catching colds."

"I have my dressing-gown," she replied. "And it isn't cold at all."

She sat down, close to him; he felt the warmth of her body. But there was no desire in him, no stirring of his blood. She took his hand which trembled a little in hers.

"You are ill," she said.

"I am perfectly well."

"Then why don't you sleep? The last three nights . . . I woke up once or twice. Every time you were up. Don't lie to me, Karel. For better, for worse . . . we are married, you know. Perhaps it is not your body—though you look simply frightful, with those sunken eyes of yours . . . and you haven't shaved to-day. Tell me, dearest . . . what is it? Is it something to do with the war? With the things you had to suffer? Is something . . . haunting you?"

Woman's intuition, he sneered to himself. But he could not tell her. He could not even invent a lie to cover it all.

"Nonsense," he said dully. "And I did sleep every night. It just happened . . . I was worried about you. . . ."

"But I am almost well. In two or three days . . . if you wish . . . we can go on. . . ."

Two or three days. Forty-eight or seventy-two hours. He was too tired to translate it into minutes and seconds, but every moment he would feel and suffer separately.

"That's wonderful," he said mechanically. "The sun in Spain will do you good."

"But Karel . . . I must know what's troubling you."

"Nothing . . . nothing at all. . . ."

She pressed closer to him as if her nearness would strike a spark of trust in him.

"Perhaps you don't know yourself. . . . If you saw a doctor . . ."

"That old fool Pascal?" He could not keep the contempt out of his voice.

"No, but he told me of an excellent psychiatrist, a former assistant of Forel. He is a Swiss himself, staying in Nice for a few days. Why don't you go and see him—just to please me?"

"Good God, Helen," he said and pushed her away, "you sound as if you thought I was a lunatic."

She tucked her dressing-gown under her and gave him a quick, warm smile.

"Of course not, don't be silly. But insomnia can be very trying. And sleeping drugs don't always help."

Why can't she leave me alone? he thought again, almost savagely. Why must she go on prying and fussing? Sleeping drugs! He felt he could sleep for a week—a month, if he only dared.

"I have no insomnia," he said curtly. And he was speaking the truth. But he could not tell her . . . he could not . . .

"Don't you think you are behaving like a child?" Helen asked. Her voice was even and patient but he could feel that she had no intention of giving up the subject.

"Not at all. I—don't like fuss. You must understand that I have learned to be rather independent. I don't mean it unkindly—but really, there's nothing the matter with me and even if there were, I don't want to see some quack——"

"Please, Karel, don't be so stubborn. For my sake, as a favour—let this doctor have a word with you."

"No."

He was tired of fencing, of being polite. Yes, she was a lovely woman and he still wanted to keep her. But no woman—or man—would ever dictate to him or even offer unsolicited advice.

She got up with a tired gesture.

"You make it very difficult for me," she said in a strained voice. "But I must tell you because you force me into it: these last few days, ever since I began to recover myself, you haven't behaved . . . as a sane man would. . . ."

Horst jumped to his feet. Now he was angry.

"I think you're absurd. You are imagining things. I am well, I tell you, perfectly well. . . ."

"You don't act as if you were well."

"Stop it, Helen. I've had enough of this. I . . ."

"Don't try to bully me. You know I am right. Why do you persist in this ridiculous attitude . . . ?"

No woman had ever spoken to him in this tone. They were quarrelling, he thought, just like people in a play—question and answer, retort for retort.

"I don't want to discuss the subject," he said stiffly.

"But I do. We are grown-up people and . . ."

His irritation and weariness overwhelmed him. He could not bear it any longer. He had to silence her—but she would not remain silent. And so he struck her across the face.

Immediately he felt sorry—not for her but because he had lost his temper, fallen out of character, failed to carry his part. She stood there, facing him, her face very white, her eyes enormous in amazed indignation.

Horst von Falkenau turned on his heels and rushed from the room.

XXXVIII

FOR OVER TWO HOURS HE WALKED, blindly, hurrying—he did not know where. When dawn came he found himself on a rocky promontory, deserted even by the birds. He sat down under an overhanging rock and hugged his knees. It was the quiet, hushed hour just before sunrise, with the light filtered through a thin mist; everything muffled, wrapped in the wisps of cotton-wool clouds that drifted across the steely sky.

He felt the weariness seeping into his bones. And suddenly he remembered that he had left the pills behind. There was no way of recovering the strength and alertness even for a few hours unless he went back to the hotel. And he did not want to go back because he did not know what he could say to Helen. Some women, he knew well enough, liked to be beaten. But he doubted whether she belonged to this category. She had a strange pride he could not fathom. After a fortnight or more she was still a comparative stranger. He could foretell her reactions to his love-making, to his jokes, to the tales he fished out for her from Karel Reznicek's past . . . but beyond that?

He was angry with her at first, because she caused this

quandary, because he would have to prolong the period of pain and depression from which only those pills could save him—or go back and face her curiosity or compassion; he did not care which it might be. But slowly anger faded. She did not know. He speculated idly what her reaction would be if he told her—oh, not that he was Horst von Falkenau, a Nazi *Gauleiter*, masquerading as a Czech patriot . . . but if he told her about his dreams? She would insist even more strongly that he should see that doctor. And if he yielded to her . . . no, he could not completely trust himself any longer. Probably the Swiss psychiatrist was a charlatan like so many others, but what if he wasn't? What if by some black magic he could break down his defences and make him talk? That would be the end of everything—for Horst did not believe in the Hippocratic oath. If he betrayed himself to this stranger, the doctor would not hesitate to go to the police forthwith. . . .

Gradually he became aware of the reddening on the eastern horizon. Slowly the solemn ceremony of sunrise began. He could not bear the strengthening light and closed his eyes. Only for a moment, he told himself, only for a few seconds—he would not go to sleep, he would just rest his eyes and . . .

. . . A bonfire burned on the left, fed by small black figures who passed and re-passed between the church and the centre of the square. They were carrying shapeless bundles of wood, straw and faggots, piling them up around the blackened walls and at the same time replenishing the fire on the left. He was sitting on the roof of his car, idly playing with his riding-crop. He liked fires, he liked to watch the leaping flames, the glowing coals, the running, nervous fingers of fire hurrying up the ladders of the planks and logs of which the bonfire was built. And in a few minutes there would be a bigger and better blaze.

A group of soldiers appeared at the crossing leading into the square. They were driving a large crowd of people towards the porch of the church. There was no resistance; closely packed, men, women and children stumbled forward, silent and passive. They passed close to the car and Horst could see their faces which were empty of expression. Cattle, he thought, just cattle; but they might yet prove interesting subjects of experiment.

At the church door, other soldiers were standing, getting the crowd into some semblance of a queue, seeing to it that no one stopped or hung back. The people were still silent as they passed in small groups into the interior. It took almost ten minutes before they were all inside. The heavy oak door, studded with broad-headed iron nails, was closed and barred from the outside. A bundle of faggots was placed against it and straw was piled high until it all but covered the door.

A sergeant of the S.S. came up to the car and saluted.

'We are all ready, Herr General,*" he said.*

'No one is left in the village?" Horst asked.

"No one who is alive."

"Very well, you can proceed."

A dozen soldiers held torches to the bonfire; the pitch flared up. As if performing some complicated ceremony, they ran up to the church door and divided there, circling the building, touching their torches to the combustibles heaped up against the walls. Here and there it took a little time before the fire caught but soon the circle of flame had enveloped the base of the building. No sound came from inside.

Horst settled a little more comfortably upon the roof and steadied himself with his free hand. Above him the sky lost its smoky colour; as the fire rose, the clouds became tinged with a rosy hue that was rather attractive. He tore away his eyes from watching the changing play of colour overhead. The windows of the church had no shutters, but iron bars were securely fixed in the thick stone. He hesitated whether he should get off his grandstand seat but decided against it. He did not want his uniform to be soiled—and he could see from here just as well.

It was through the door that the flames penetrated into the church. As the dense smoke was blown aside by a gust of wind, a couple of heads appeared in the hole burnt through the wood. But they vanished again as the soldiers pressed as close as the flames would permit and pushed them back. A thin wail now rose like a column of smoke—the wail of children and women. And suddenly the windows sprouted arms and hands, heads and shoulders as some of the crowd pressed against them in their desperate search for air. They were beaten down with the butts of guns which the soldiers wielded like clubs.

There was something musical, rhythmic in the screams and shouts that came from inside the church. Horst, sitting on the car, shouted down to the driver to move back a few feet; the heat began to be uncomfortable. He still enjoyed the fire, its colour and its ever-changing tracery. As for the people inside, he felt neither pleasure nor compassion. An example had to be set, a group of evildoers punished, so that there should be no more sabotage, no more attacks on solitary German soldiers in the district. His job was to see that it was done. He had not come to gloat; it was an experience like any other. In half an hour he would drive away, satisfied that his orders had been carried out, and leave the rest to the local commanders.

But though the driver obediently backed the car away, the heat did not seem to recede. He felt his clothes growing damp, his hair clinging damply to his skull. He wiped his face and once again gave a brief command to drive to the far side of the square.

It made no difference. The noise inside the church now rose above the crackling of the flames and the shouting of the soldiers who had become intoxicated by the fire. But Horst was just as hot as before. His skin began to burn, the prickly heat climbed up his body, rising from his legs to his torso, his armpits, his neck. He jumped from the roof and entered the car. Angrily he ordered his driver to take him back to headquarters. But as they drove through the silent, deserted streets, he seemed to be on fire himself. He was, within a few moments, in agony. Enough of his self-control remained so that he did not cry out; he did not order the driver to stop. Higher and higher the temperature rose in and around him though he opened the windows and leant out to catch the cooling breeze. It did not help. The noise and the flames were left far behind; he wiped the sight and sound from his memory. What was this sudden fit? Had he been overtaken by some mysterious illness? At last he could not bear it any longer. He shouted to the driver to stop but the man either did not hear him or was wilfully refusing to obey. He tore open the glass pane and shouted into his ear—but still without effect. He felt as if his very bones were melting in the fire. He kicked open the offside door and jumped. He rolled into a ditch and scrambled to his feet with difficulty. There was a pond nearby and he rushed towards it, pursued by the fever that was in his body. Fully clothed, he plunged in. There was, he noticed half-consciously, a thin layer of ice at the edge of the pond. But the water was hot, scalding hot. With a shout of despair he tried to get back to the bank—but the heat seeped into his clothes, his flesh, his brain and he went under into a flame-coloured, incandescent hell . . .

. . . Horst von Falkenau woke and found that he was lying in the sun which blazed from a cloudless sky. A grave-eyed child of about five stood in front of him and regarded him with a mixture of curiosity and fear. Clumsily, he got to his feet and began to stumble towards the road running along the top of the steep slope. Several times he fell; sobbing and cursing, he dragged himself up again until he found a firm surface under his feet. He was somewhere on the road to Cannes, a few kilometres from Nice but he felt that the distance was endless and he would never make it.

The porter had to help him upstairs when he reached the hotel. Inside the room Helen sat quietly, still in her blue dressing-gown. When she saw him, she started to her feet with a cry of alarm.

"The pills . . ." stammered Horst, "the pills in the little box . . . on the desk . . . give me three, please . . ."

He swallowed them without water and lay back, with closed eyes, exhausted. Usually they worked within a few minutes but this time it was almost half an hour before he felt his strength returning. It would not be for very long, he knew; in a few hours he would have to begin the fight again. Helen had helped him to undress and supported his weight as he staggered to the bed; she watched silently as the colour returned to his face, his eyes were bright again and his voice clear.

"Helen . . ." he began and found the rest very hard to say, "I—I feel terrible about last night. You must forgive me."

"Don't speak of it now." She took his hand. "You were not yourself. And what's a little slap between husband and wife?"

She smiled and he was rather relieved. His apology was sincere only to the extent that he was sorry he had forgotten himself; the blemish of the desired perfection, the false tone in the part he played displeased him. And he wanted her forgiveness because he could not find the strength to woo her, to go through a long process of pleading and reconciliation.

But Helen was a strong-minded woman who never forgot her purpose.

"There's one thing, dear," she said, "and I hope you won't be unreasonable now. I want you to see Dr. Keller."

"Who is he?"

He was not pretending; he really did not remember.

"The Swiss psychiatrist I told you about. He'll be in

Nice for another week and I can make an appointment straight away, for this afternoon, if you want to."

He was too tired to argue; so he used delaying tactics.

"I'll see him if it makes you happy . . . but would you mind very much if I left it till to-morrow? It's just—I don't want to see anybody except you. And you aren't well enough yet to be out of bed yourself."

"Nonsense," she said briskly. "Dr. Pascal said I could go out if I wanted. But it's all right—we'll make the appointment for to-morrow. Now . . . you'd better try to sleep."

"I can't," he protested. "Let's go out and have a walk. I am wideawake. I feel really fine."

"You can't possibly . . . half an hour ago you looked as if you were half-dead. Please, darling, rest a little. . . ."

"But there is nothing the matter with me. Look . . . don't I look all right? Who wants to sleep at eleven in the morning?"

He kissed her and her lips kindled a flame in him he had not felt for some days. Their love-making was brief and fierce, almost as if they were enemies. His strength was not yet ebbing, the pills had given him a new lease of life. Perhaps it was all over, he thought, as he lay at her side and watched the soft line of her cheek. Such . . . visitations or disturbances of the mind can come and go suddenly. He felt warm and secure. She had been silent for a while. But now she asked:

"Karel . . . what were those pills you took when you came back?"

"Oh, I don't know," he evaded her question. "Something a doctor in the underground gave me—against fatigue and over-excitement and that sort of thing. I haven't the faintest idea what their ingredients are. . . ."

"And have you taken them regularly? I never saw . . ."

"Now, your ladyship, forget your days of hunting opium-smugglers. I am not a drug addict."

"No one said you were, silly. Still . . . these things can be dangerous. You'd better tell Dr. Keller about them."

"Yes, of course."

They went down to lunch where Helen was greeted with great warmth by the staff who had all been very anxious during her illness; Francine, who doubled duties in the dining-room and upstairs, served them with a beaming face.

"I'd like to write a letter," Helen said. "Are you sure you don't want to go up and lie down?"

"No . . . I want a paper and a little walk. I'll be back for tea."

"Very well, dear . . . but take care of yourself, will you?"

He nodded and strolled from the hotel. He bought a copy of *Le Petit Niçois* at the corner but did not look at it. For a while he walked on the Promenade des Anglais and then sat down in a sheltered spot. He still felt fine. The nightmare of the early morning seemed to be very distant. He put all thought of it resolutely from his mind. Leisurely he unfolded the paper which carried uninteresting news. But suddenly his eyes fastened on a small item printed in heavy type.

It gave the facts baldly. A dangerous individual, masquerading under the name of Karel Reznicek, was loose in the department of the Alpes Maritimes. There followed a reasonably good personal description, the call to all men of goodwill to denounce the fugitive if they could identify him and the offer of a substantial reward.

It was sudden and for a moment it completely caught him off his guard. He felt trapped; he looked around with haunted eyes to see whether anyone was watching him. There was no one in sight; and the dizziness that came over him, passed in a few seconds.

Almost he welcomed the shattering news. It meant that he was called upon to act, to gather all his strength, to fight something that was tangible instead of the misty wraiths of his dreams. If he had any doubts whether he could master this crisis as he had mastered so many others, they did not last long. He had to use all his audacity, all his ingenuity, to get out of this trouble. He folded the paper, put it into his pocket and started back to the hotel.

XXXIX

THE TRAIN TO PERPIGNAN WAS crowded but Horst von Falkenau had secured a seat in a corner. The rest of the compartment was occupied by a Basque family—father, mother and six children, their ages varying from sixteen to six months. They got in at Cannes and started to eat almost as soon as the train moved out of the station. The children climbed all over the seats, hung out of the windows, ran along the corridor, noisily demanded more food. A small girl of about seven climbed on to Horst's lap to see the landscape better, but he did not protest. A touching family scene, he thought; and in his shabby clothes, open-necked shirt and greasy *béret*, he was part of it. The child wriggled on his knees—but the child was a link with the others, it made him less conspicuous. He was still alert but he knew that weariness would come—and yet he could not relax for a moment . . . not for another day.

The little girl had dark eyes and brown hair. It was coarse hair, threaded with a cheap blue ribbon—but Horst wished it had been a different colour. He did not want to be reminded of Helen. He had put her out of his mind time and again—but she would not stay out. At other times he would have been quite ready to cut his losses and forget a woman as soon as she ceased to be useful or desirable . . . but this was different. . . .

In order to give his brain other material to work on, he went over the details of the last twenty-four hours. He thought he had organised the whole thing beautifully, without a hitch—but in this general state of his mind, vacillating between almost unnatural wakefulness and deep, exhausted depression, he could not be quite sure.

When he had read that little news item in the *Petit Niçois*, he had gone back to the hotel. Helen was waiting for him, looking a little thoughtful. He wondered whether she had seen the paper? But no, she was anything but a good actress—even if he was ignorant about a good many things in connection with her, he could always read her mind.

"Had a good walk?" she asked.

"Yes, a very nice one," he replied and sat down. "Did you write your letter?"

"Part of it . . . I was a bit restless and tired. I lay down and had a nap. Disgraceful habit."

He smiled and said evenly: "I have been thinking of what you said, Helen. Perhaps it is better if I see your Swiss miracle-man as soon as possible. Could you get in touch with him this afternoon?"

"Why, yes . . . it is only about fifteen minutes' walk to his apartment. I could slip round. . . ."

This was better than he expected.

"Would you? I'll wait for you here . . . I am rather tired myself."

She put on her coat and hat, talking all the time:

"I am so glad you are being sensible, Karel. I don't mind confessing, I was really worried. . . ."

"Don't get away with the idea," he laughed, "that I am really ill. I've just decided to humour you."

She came and stood in front of him as if offering herself for his inspection.

He took her into his arms. For a moment he felt sorely tempted to pour out the whole story. He was a good actor, he knew, and perhaps he could make her believe that she belonged to him, that these weeks had joined them together so that, no matter what he was, she could not forsake him. But the urge passed as swiftly as it had risen to the surface of his mind. He could not risk it. He remembered how she had spoken of Germans and Nazis, recalled her laughable dispute with that young American. Even if he succeeded, it would take too long. He hated to let her go. Of all the manifold possessions he had discarded since he slipped from the *Gauleiter's* mansion, she was the most valuable, the most important. But he could not keep her and he knew that to the hour of his death, he would remain a realist.

He was not concerned for a moment with what she would do or think after he had gone. He would not be there to watch whatever happened, therefore it did not concern him. What did concern him, was his own safety, his mission or whatever he called it—he did not bother to put it into words. But for the last time he drank in the sweet scent of her body, and his kisses were wild and hungry until she freed herself, laughing.

"I am not going to the end of the world, darling," she said. "I'll be back in no time."

"That will be too long," he said, and meant it.

When she was at the door, he called her back:

"I am a scatterbrain," he said. "I forgot to send two telegrams while I was out. Would you do it for me? And if you could buy one or two things . . . just wait one moment, will you?"

He scribbled two entirely imaginary names and addresses on a piece of paper and added some messages which were largely meaningless. That would keep her another fifteen or twenty minutes. He also made out a shopping list—choosing things that would take her into two or three different shops.

She nodded, glad to do something tangible for him—he had refused her help so steadfastly! She gave him one last smile and hurried from the room.

Feverishly he began to pack. He emptied one suit-case completely and sorted through all his belongings, selecting those that could in no way give away either Karel Reznicek or Horst von Falkenau. He changed into his best suit and went through his pockets. He came upon two sheets of paper and paused for a moment. . . . These were the sheets he had taken from that fool American. There was no fire-place in the room and to tear them up was to invite disaster. He was horrified at the discovery; for he had completely forgotten about them and that showed that something was wrong with his memory, his proudest possession. And then some perverse idea flashed through his mind. He sat down and scrawled a few lines on the back of the sheet that contained his personal description and record. He placed it in an envelope, sealed it and put a stamp on it—he had bought a few in the afternoon—and then slipped it into his pocket.

He met no one on the service stairs and reached the street unnoticed.

The rest was easy. In the Old Town he found a pawn-broker's shop and bought a greasy, second-hand suit with a *béret* to match. He gave a regretful thought to the Mercedes —but to use the car would be suicide. No, his best bet was to take a train to Perpignan. There was another "station" of the underground there—unless it had disappeared by some unfortunate accident as Gaston had at Strasbourg. But he refused to be pesimistic. Now that he knew what he had to do, every step he took, every word he spoke, was purpose-ful. He had been living too softly and comfortably, he thought, while in the lavatory of the railway station he changed into the soiled, shabby clothes and with a few quick strokes changed his appearance, making himself about fifteen years older than his real age. The fools, he laughed softly, who thought that they could catch him because they published an indifferent description in the papers of France. . . . He made sure that he had a box of the pills on him and his gun. No one paid any attention to him when he boarded the night train. He took a ticket to Montpellier; he could always say that he had changed his mind and pay the surcharge. Karel Reznicek's papers he tore into tiny pieces and flushed down the drain. He was nameless, commonplace —a man no one would look at twice. And the Basque family was a very convenient camouflage indeed.

But as the night passed and the train crawled on, his self-assurance gradually began to wane. The little girl, after bouncing up and down on his knee, had fallen asleep and his arm ached as he held her. He would gladly have returned her to her fat mother—but she, with all the others, was asleep; snoring filled the crowded compartment and he could not get the window open with his left hand alone. In the half-light, for most of the bulbs were broken and the carriage showed many signs of war-time neglect, he watched them, turning his eyes from one inert face to the other; he thought them obscene, devoid of all humanity. Sleep was the great stripper of masks, the supreme remover of pretensions and prides. He wondered how he looked when he was asleep and regretted that there was no way of finding out, for who would tell him truthfully?

But he, he was awake and that gave him a fleeting sense of power. He could rob or kill some of these people before they stirred into consciousness. He felt that he was the only human being awake in this train, perhaps in the whole universe. The headache that sent shooting pain through his skull, the stiff discomfort in his body—all that was the price he had to pay for his lonely superiority. Prometheus, he thought, must have felt the same when he was chained to the Scythian rock. But Prometheus was a failure—he stole fire and yet he could not escape the revenge of Zeus. . . . How silly, Horst thought, that these ancient symbols and fairy-tales should still haunt us in the twentieth century. Christianity and the Greek ideal of beauty, Kant and Rousseau—the rubbish of past ages, the trash of so-called intellectuals cluttering up even the most utilitarian mind. . . . Perhaps that was the real root of his troubles—that while he was a man of action, he had read and studied enough in his youth to carry this lumber of dead philosophers and prophets with him. . . . You could not erase lines you had spoken on the stage, sentences that leapt to your eye on a printed page and became stamped upon your brain. . . . Perhaps this useless flotsam was making it difficult for him to forget other things. If so,it was the damned irony of fate . . . but it still could not beat him.

Now that he was on his way—he had posted the letter at the *gare*—he permitted himself a brief consideration of Helen. She would get the letter to-morrow morning after a night probably spent in anxiety and in a wild search for him. What would she do? It did not particularly matter. Nor was he concerned with her future. Perhaps she would go back to that young fool Whitney; convert him to her views about Germany and the Germans, marry him and produce a brood of children. . . . But this thought could not be dismissed as easily as the rest. The idea was painful and infuriating. He had killed Anna because he did not want her to betray or encumber him—but he had another motive for the killing. She had been his mistress and he did not want to bequeath her to anybody else. Perhaps she would have been inconsolable—but that was not certain. It was a fastidious thought—no one should drink from his glass, no one should lie in his bed, no one should embrace his women if he could help it.

There had been a brief period during his walk back to the hotel after finding that piece of news in the *Petit Niçois*, when he had played with the idea of killing Helen. But he soon discarded it. It was unnecessary and . . . yes, he might weaken at the very last moment. The flight from Nice had been well staged and smoothly executed, but he no longer trusted himself completely. There was something he could not quite control, something within himself that had turned against him. Yes, he had better face it as it had always been his habit to face the facts. But time and freedom from strain would heal it, would seal the fissure through which this dark and intangible power reached out now and again.

He waited for the morning, for Perpignan; aloof and brooding, but not without hope while the small Basque girl breathed softly in his lap and the train crawled towards Spain and safety.

XL

NEXT MORNING, SHORTLY AFTER eleven, a battered and protesting jeep came rattling down the Avenue des Diables Bleus, turned into the Rue de la République and came to a halt in front of the Nice *préfecture* in the Place Garibaldi. Two men—one tall, the other small and wiry—climbed stiffly from it.

"I hope it's the end of the journey," yawned Sergeant Ira. "I'd like to lead a stationary life for a change."

Captain Whitney made no answer. His face, under the grime and weariness, was set and grim. If his trip had been in vain, if the chase should prove to have been fruitless after all . . . He had spoken to Kladnik a few hours ago and the plump Czech had told him that the frontiers were watched: no Mercedes with a couple travelling in it had been reported from anywhere. No, his quarry must still be in France. And at the thought that he might be within a few hundred yards of the man he sought, a fierce exultation filled him. This was the show-down, the final battle—and this time he would prove to his slippery opponent that he was not so dumb, nor helpless.

The *sous-préfet* was very friendly. Yes, of course they would make the necessary enquiries. Fifteen minutes later they had the required answer. Karel Reznicek and his wife had registered at the Hotel du Monde, near the Boulevard Carabacel. The *sous-préfet* told them how to get there, but pressed them to stay and have an apéritif first. Peter refused and had difficulty in doing it politely; he was half-way down the staircase before Sergeant Eads caught up with him.

"What are you going to do?" asked Ira as he switched on the engine.

"Listen, sergeant," Peter began, "this is very irregular. I didn't tell the Frenchman what I wanted with Karel Reznicek. Strange that he had not received the circular—but I suppose efficiency is not their strong suit. I am going to arrest him—I may have to bluff a little. You play along with me. And when we're on our way back, I'll stop in a convenient spot and . . ."

"Bump him off? You can't do that."

"No, you half-witted idiot. I just want to give him a taste of my knuckles. We can always say that he had resisted arrest or tried to get away. Are you game?"

"Sure, I am game. I'll even help you. At the unarmed combat school we were taught some useful tricks. Now if you twist the left arm in a certain way . . ."

"Thanks for the advice, sergeant," smiled young Whitney but his smile was not even skin-deep. "I think I'll get by on my own."

He burst into the hall of the small hotel and roared at the elderly clerk in his worst French:

"*Monsieur Reznicek . . . est-il ici?*"

The clerk stared and shook his head dumbly.

"But I was told he had registered here!" shouted Peter. "Don't lie to me."

"Monsieur Reznicek left yesterday," the old man said. "But *madame* is upstairs. We have great trouble with her. If *monsieur*. . . ."

"What's her room number?" demanded the young captain.

The clerk gave it and Peter rushed at the stairs as if he were charging a machine-gun emplacement. Sergeant Ira plodded behind.

On the landing they ran into a plump, motherly looking woman—it was Francine, the chambermaid. She stood in front of a closed door, pleading with someone inside to let her in. Peter glanced up and saw it was the number he had been given downstairs.

"What's the matter?" he asked.

"It's terrible, *monsieur*," wailed Francine. "*Madame* . . . she won't admit me. She won't even answer. But I know she is in there. I gave her the letter myself. She has but two days ago left her sick-bed. But when the letter came . . ."

"What letter?" asked Sergeant Eads.

"I do not know, *monsieur*. It had a French stamp and I think it was posted in Nice, but of course I did not open it."

Peter pushed her aside and knocked. There was no reply. He turned back.

"Sergeant, go and make some enquiries about the Mercedes. Find out where it was garaged. Go to the station and see whether they have seen anyone answering to the description of Reznicek board a train. Then come back here. Hurry."

Sergeant Eads saluted and turned on his heels. Peter knocked again. Then he called out:

"Helen . . . it's Peter . . . let me in, please. . . ."

There was a little pause, then the door opened.

He took one look at Helen's face and stepped inside, closing the door behind himself.

The beauty was still there, the beauty of line and curve but drained of all colour, Her eyes were lifeless or perhaps what life was in them, was hidden. They were almost like the eyes of the blind and Peter was once again filled with hate and helpless rage that this had happened to her. He did not know what it was that had made her so pale, so still, so lifeless. He made a move to touch her but she retreated a step or two and stared at him worldlessly. He had just enough brains not to follow her.

When he spoke, it was the conventional thing he said; almost like Stanley's "Dr. Livingstone, I presume?" For he said, and his voice sounded false and forced:

"Helen . . . thank God you are all right."

She replied and her voice was huskier than he remembered it, huskier and tinged with some tremendous restraint as if she could not trust herself to relax an inch:

"Yes . . . I am all right."

"I came as soon as I could," Whitney continued. His words were foolish and empty, he knew; but what could he say, not knowing what had happened? "Is he—is he gone?"

She sat down, her hands hanging inert, her whole body robbed of vitality.

"Yes."

"But what . . ."

"I must tell you," she said as if giving herself an order. "He is not a Czech. He was masquerading all the time, playing a part. His real name is Horst von Falkenau and he was a Nazi *Gauleiter*. He used me as he used you and everybody else to get away. He . . ."

Her voice broke then but still the tears did not come. What could he do or say? The wisest thing was to keep quiet, to hear her out.

"He wrote a brief note before he went away," Helen continued. "He said that he was not sorry, that these two weeks had been worth the danger and the risk. And he left two sheets of paper behind."

Peter Whitney's heart gave a sudden jerk as if someone had hit him hard in the ribs.

"Two sheets?"

Helen held them out and he was hard put to avoid snatching them too abruptly. He was bewildered. Why did this man—what was his real name? Falkenau?—relinquish his prize? Was it some strange streak of foolhardy bragging . . . was it some hidden motive? He glanced at the papers and saw that they were the documents stolen from his brief-case. It had been Karel Reznicek, after all . . . but he should not call him by that name, think of him as the Czech patriot whose character he had taken. A grudging admiration rose in him for Horst von Falkenau who had carried his part with such superb arrogance and life-like confidence. But the next moment this feeling was swamped by the old hate, the old fury. What did these pieces of paper matter compared to Helen. And Helen . . .

"You know what I have been doing ever since I got the letter?" she asked in the same dull, lifeless voice. "He posted it before he left Nice. I spent the whole night looking for him—he had sent me out on a fool's errand so that he could get away—running to the police, getting up a search party. He—he had been acting strangely for some time. I thought he was ill. But probably he was just worried how he should get rid of me . . . how he should get away. I think he is making for Spain—unless that was a lie, too, like all the other things. . . . But you know what I did? I took three baths . . . and then came back here and scrubbed myself again and again. . . . It is so foolish . . . I felt like Lady Macbeth . . . I felt as if I had committed a murder. . . ."

"Stop, Helen! It's crazy to . . ."

"Yes, a murder," she nodded. "I killed Helen Fleming, all by myself. Wasn't I clever! Wastn't I the perfect murderer! Peter, you'd better get away from me. I—it may be catching. I can never again talk to normal people, touch a child, go in a crowd. I can never go back home. I . . . I wish I had the courage to kill what little there's left of Helen Fleming."

It was an old-fashioned method but Peter remembered having seen it used on women before, and with good effect. He lifted Helen from the chair. She winced and struggled but he held on to her arms grimly. Then he began to shake her—shake her hard until her teeth began to chatter, her hair came tumbling into her face and her knees went limp.

Her weeping was not soft or rebellious. She cried as perhaps no woman would cry in front of a man, however indifferent she was to him—with a wild abandon that frightened Peter a little. He was sufficiently worldly-wise to know that tears came easier to a woman than to the weakest man; but this was not sorrow, nor rage; it was the weeping of hopeless defeat.

"Listen, Helen," he said, kneeling at her side, feeling in advance how inadequate and clumsy anything he could say would be, "listen, honey. You walk in the street and someone throws mud at you. Your dress gets dirty, maybe even your hand or face, too. Does it make you any different? You can wash it off, can't you? What is a fortnight compared to a life time? If you were one of those women who are waited on hand and foot, who have never been useful in their lives . . . I could understand. But you had a job. You still have it. I don't know what you're thinking about the Krauts now and I don't care. You can't hate them any worse than I do. But you are still Helen Fleming. You haven't killed her. No one could. No one could kill someone who was so fine and brave and intelligent. Gosh, I am a dumb clerk from a law office, but even I know what you meant to anybody who ever met you. Listen to me. It will be hard , I know. It will take time to forget. But it's nowhere written in the book that you can't forget it. You know what I mean when I say that more evil, more horrible things have happened to women all over Europe, all over the world. It isn't that I want to belittle what—what has happened to you. But they bore up under it because they had something to live for."

She lifted her head and looked at him. There was a little more life in her eyes. Her lips trembled.

"What's there to live for? You know . . . I must be frank about this . . . when I got the letter it wasn't so much the discovery of who he was . . . but the feeling that I had been used and thrown aside like an old shoe, a worn-out tennis ball . . . I guess I thought too much of myself. He never mentioned with a word what he thought . . . what I should be expected to do . . . or feel. . . . He just went off and if it had served his convenience, he would have killed me or dragged me along. A slave girl or a concubine, a beast of burden or a . . ."

Peter waited till the new paroxysm of crying spent itself.

"How—how did you know?" she asked.

"I discovered in Paris that he was an impostor. He had

to get away from here, to leave you because the hue-and-cry was up. I wonder that he stayed so long. And what you say about your being discarded . . . it's all foolish, Helen. You know, it is."

"But I . . ."

The door opened and a whole crowd of people burst into the room. There was Sergeant Ira trying to keep pace with the *sous-préfet*; there were two policemen, old Dr. Pascal and another medical-looking gentleman with a small grey beard; and behind them all, like a big sheepdog, Kladnik. It was his voice that boomed above the babble that filled the room:

"Captain Whitney, I think we ought to leave now. I have a car outside. Our man, I am sure, was making for the Spanish frontier."

Helen had drawn back to the farthest corner of the room. Dr. Pascal elbowed his way to Peter's side. He introduced himself and added:

"This lady is my patient. She needs good care. My eminent colleague, Dr. Keller, promised to help me with her case. If you are a friend of hers, would you please explain to these imbeciles that she is not a criminal?"

Peter stared helplessly at Helen at whom the *sous-préfet* was firing questions with the rapidity of a machine-gun. He turned to Kladnik:

"Can't you do something? She is in no state to be questioned. That unspeakable swine . . ."

"But of course," and Kladnik bowed as far as his waistline would permit. He cleaved his way to the *sous-préfet* and drew him aside. Their conversation was in whispers and lasted for ten minutes, but at the end of it the official left the room and took his policemen with him.

Dr. Pascal and his colleague closed in on Helen. But Peter was not through with her yet. He told Kladnik to wait.

"I must go," he told her. "You stay right here. These gentlemen will look after you. And when I come back, we'll talk about—about the other things. I warn you, if I don't find you here, I'll be awful sore. There's no telling what I might do."

She was a little dazed but slowly, almost incredibly, she smiled. It was enough. Peter took Kladnik's arm and called out to Ira. Before he left the room, he turned back and gave Helen a last look. She was sitting quietly in the corner, her hands folded. Professor Keller was talking to her and she was listening . . . that was good. But Peter wished he did not have to go.

XLI

HE KILLED THE SPANIARD JUST after midnight. It was too easy, yet it did not go as smoothly as he had thought. Not because the fat wine merchant from Tarragona was a difficult man to finish off but because of his own condition. He had taken some more of the pills as soon as he got off the train in Perpignan but their effect wore off after a couple of hours.

The Spaniard was a gross fool, half-drunk; he boasted of his prowess as a business man and as a lover of exquisite women and his lies on both subjects were blatant enough. He patronised Horst who introduced himself as a French ex-prisoner-of-war, trying to get back to his village in the Pyrenees. They drank together and a little skilful steering of the conversation brought forth an offer of a lift to the frontier.

When they sat in the ramshackle car, an ancient Fiat, an almost unbearable weariness came over Horst as so often before. At first he consoled himself with the thought that it would be soon over—that he was free now, unencumbered by the need to pretend to Helen, the necessity of playing a double part. But it did not help. Perhaps he should have waited a little longer; they were still on the outskirts of Perpignan when he reached out and turned off the ignition key. The motor coughed, spluttered and died; the fat wine-merchant looked at him and saw, even in the semi-darkness, murder in Horst's eyes.

Von Falkenau caught him—he could not use his gun—but the greasy, soft flesh was slippery and the man wriggled from his grasp. The next moment he was out of the car, yelling lustily. But Horst had followed him a second later and with a flying tackle landed on his back, one hand clamped over the Spaniard's mouth, the other around his neck.

He tripped up the man and they rolled in the gutter which

was full of rotten bits of vegetables, nameless filth, slimy and wet. The wine-merchant was fighting for his life but he was obese and his muscles had no strength. Once Horst got his hands around his neck, it was soon over.

No one had moved around them, there was no sound, no light. He bent down to lift the body on his shoulder but dizziness welled from the darkness and he had to sit down suddenly, close to the corpse. With closed eyes he rocked to and fro until the pendulum within his brain seemed stilled. He staggered back to the car and dumped the dead Spaniard into the back seat. He drove on, slowly, breathing heavily, until he had left the town well behind. Then he turned off the road, towards a clump of olive trees. Screening the windows of the car with a rug he found in the luggage boot, he switched on the small roof-light. With considerable trouble he propped up the dead man on the back seat so that his face was plainly visible. He searched him and found his wallet and his passport, duly visaed for leaving France. This was what he had expected.

He put his suit-case on the front seat and took the small flat make-up box from it. He could not do very much—yet this had to be his masterpiece. Quickly, with practised skill he worked until he had transformed his face at least to a reasonable replica of the rather blurred passport photograph.

He stripped Carlos Albuera—his papers gave him that name—to his skin, then put on his clothes over his own. This gave him some added girth though far less than the dead man had. Next he disposed of the body—by simply dumping it behind some bushes. He did not care who found it or when . . . by that time he would be in safety. He was bathed in perspiration by the time he had finished the distasteful job. A pity he could not find the "underground station" in Perpignan; they must have got cold feet or had been caught. But this was almost as good. Carlos Albuera returned to his native Spain. Karel Reznicek had disappeared. Horst von Falkenau was nowhere at all.

He did not want to cross the frontier at night. Inspection was always closer—men were suspect in the darkness whereas the light of the day made people look more innocent. He had at least six hours to kill—but he wanted to get away from this spot. He could not be far from Argelés sur Mer and he felt suddenly hungry.

One little wineshop was still open and when he proved

that he had some English money, they gave him a bowl of potato soup and the remains of a scraggy hen. He drank a pint of harsh red wine and killed time talking to the ancient patron who had the same grievances against General de Gaulle that he had had against Pétain, Léon Blum, Reynaud or Daladier. But finally the old chap started to yawn and Horst took himself off. He sat for a while in the car; then he decided to drive on, very slowly and if necessary, fill out the time just this side of the frontier.

A few hundred yards from the wineshop the first attack came upon him. It started with a violent shiver; his heart was gripped in a cramp that sent tears into his eyes. He must have lost consciousness for a few seconds but some instinct made him stop the car just before he did. At least an hour passed before he recovered from his weakness. He was bathed in sweat and as he stumbled from the car into the cold night air, he shivered again.

It was unthinkable that he should fail now, when he had got so far. It would be ridiculous, an anti-climax. If Fate or whatever it was, had any sense of fitness, it would not do this to him. There was no sense of proportion left, nothing outside the pain and the tremendous relief when it had gone.

He drove on again a few hundred yards and the second attack came. With trembling fingers, when it was over, he searched for the pills and swallowed half a dozen. It usually took fifteen minutes for them to do their work—but this time nothing happened. Alertness and strength did not return; he felt just as weak as before. He was afraid to take any more. Perhaps if he waited . . .

. . . He was certain that he had kept his eyes open, that he had not relaxed for a moment. Yet here he was, once again a spectator, in the forest clearing he knew so well.

Others must be here with him but he could not see them. As far as his senses could tell, he was alone with the other man—the little Jew in the middle of the clearing. A thin, shabby little Jew, looking like the caricatures Streicher published in his paper, with long hair, drawn into corkscrew sideburns down his temples, a misshapen nose. Only his eyes were large and bright. His caftan was green with age and stiff with dirt. His hair was matted with blood; bareheaded he stood there for a moment and then started to dig.

The little Jew was digging a grave. He worked clumsily and with unnecessary effort; as he lifted the spade, the earth slipped back again and again into the hole. There was no trace of those who forced him to do this; and however slowly he worked, gradually the hole grew and his figure became shorter.

Suddenly he lifted his head and spoke. It was a sing-song voice and the words seemed to strike at Horst's brain quite independent of the Jew; as if he knew in advance what he was going to say, as if the words ran parallel in his mind.

"Sound the great horn for our freedom," sang the little Jew, "lift up the ensign to gather our exiles, and gather us together from the four corners of the earth. Blessed art thou, O Lord, who gatherest the outcasts of thy people Israel. . . . Restore our judges as at the first, and our councillors as at the beginning: remove from us sorrow and sighing; reign over us, O Lord, thou alone, in kindness and tender mercy, and justify us in judgment. Blessed art thou, O Lord, the King of judgment. . . . And for slanderers let there be no hope; and let all wickedness perish in a moment, let all thine enemies be speedily cut off, and the dominion of arrogance do thou uproot and crush and cast down and humble speedily in our days. Blessed art thou, O Lord, who breakest the enemies and humblest the arrogant. . . ."

A little silence, punctuated by the flashing of the spade and the moon that had risen somewhere, casting a clear light upon the scene. Horst hooked his arm around a fir-tree. The little Jew was not up to his knees in the hole he had been digging. But his voice rose again:

"Let our prayer come before thee, hide not thyself from our supplication, for we are not arrogant and stiff-necked, that we should say before thee, O Lord our God and God of our fathers, we are righteous and have not sinned; verily we have sinned. . . . We have trespassed, we have dealt treacherously, we have robbed, we have spoken slander, we have acted perversely and we have wrought wickedness, we have acted presumptuously, we have done violence, we have framed lies, we have counselled evil, we have spoken falsely, we have scoffed, we have revolted. . . . We have turned away from thy commandments and thy judgments that are good, and it hath not profited us. But thou art righteous in all that hath come upon us; for thou hast acted truthfully, but as for us, we have done wickedly. . . . What shall we say before thee, O thou who dwellest on high, and what shall we declare before thee, thou who abidest in the heavens? Dost thou not know all things, both the hidden and the revealed?"

The voice ceased abruptly. But Horst wanted to hear more.

This was a voice that covered the misshapen nose, the corkscrew curls, the shabby caftan. It was a splendid, great voice, rising from the depth of the earth. It spoke words of humility and pride, of confession and trust. The heaped-up earth now hid the little man up to his shoulders. Occasionally the spade still flashed, the pile of wet soil visibly grew. And just when Horst wanted to move, to step closer, the chant arose again:

"O my God," sang the little Jew, digging his own grave, "guard my tongue from evil and my lips from speaking guile; and to such as curse me, let my soul be silent, yea, let my soul be unto all as the dust. Open thou my heart to thy Law, and let my soul pursue thy commandments. And as to any who devise evil against me, speedily make their counsel of none effect and frustrate their design. Do thou it for the sake of thy Name, do for the sake of thy right hand, do for the sake of thy holiness, do for the sake of thy Law, that thy beloved ones may be delivered. O save with thy right hand and answer me. Let the words of my mouth and the meditation of my heart be acceptable before thee, O Lord, my Rock and my Redeemer. He who maketh peace in his high places, may he make peace for us and for all Israel, and say ye, Amen. May it be thy will, O Lord our God and God of our fathers, that the temple be speedily rebuilt in our days, and grant our portion in thy Law. . . ."

Now even his head was almost covered by the mound of earth. And hands, disembodied, huge and hairy hands came out of the darkness of the trees and shovelled the loose soil upon the little Jew. They pressed him down into the hole he was digging. And tall, shining black topboots appeared and trampled down the earth. But the voice was still unsilenced:

"Thou knowest the mysteries of the heart, O Lord; unto thee alone belong both revealed and secret things. We come with words wherewith to crave thy favour; heed not our wickedness nor our wrongful acts. We come this day like unto one who feareth and hath dread; thou who art exalted, being merciful, yield loving-kindness for thy sake. Strict justice deal not unto dust and ashes; see! our end is the worm. If we have erred and the sin is veiled from us, art not thou alone he who perceiveth faults? So judge us not as one who acteth designedly; and, in an acceptable time, list thou the confession of our lips. Pardon us on this day our sins, whether known unto us or unknown; whether committed presumptuously or in ignorance, both in relation to positive and negative commands. Deliver us from

the punishment of excision and death; have compassion upon this clay, the work of thy hands. . . ."

When silence fell again, Horst felt that it was unbearable without the voice. But nothing disturbed it, the forest was breathless and expectant. He could not endure it but he knew somehow that his voice would not help. The answer, the salvation was in that little mound of earth, wetly glistening with the freshly upturned soil. It was in the grave which the little Jew had dug for himself and into which his voice and his eyes were trampled. Horst staggered forward and began to dig with his ten fingers, feeling the mud clinging to his skin, feeling that however frenziedly he worked, he made no impression on the soft earth which yielded only to harden again the next moment. It was all in vain and he sobbed, cursing God and Man; and then he woke and the world of reality around him was full of the same silence and the same terror.

XLII

THE SUN'S GLARE, IN THE LATE afternoon, was just as blinding as the noontime dazzle. It was reflected from the white rocks, the straight white road, the white bridge.

Carlos Albuera, wine merchant, of the town of Tarragona, had passed through the French customs. The barrier was still open. The Spanish frontier guard gave a cursory examination to his papers; they seemed to be in order. The sergeant, a tall, black-browed Catalan, nodded to him to drive on.

But the car did not move.

On the other side of the barrier, still on French soil, a large, dusty car drove up and stopped with screaming brakes. Three men jumped from it—an American officer, a sergeant and a portly figure in civilian clothes. They hurried up to the little hut that housed the French frontier guards and began to shout and gesticulate. The Spanish soldiers craned their necks and tried to listen; but as they were about fifty yards away, they could not catch any of the words.

And now the occupant of the battered Fiat climbed stiffly

from the driver's seat. He stood at the side of the car, swaying a little. His face was grimy, his eyes flat and dead.

"Are you unwell, señor?" asked the sergeant but he received no answer.

For Horst von Falkenau, erstwhile *Gauleiter*, General of the S.S., wearer of six decorations for bravery, this was Waterloo and the end of the road. He knew that he was not asleep, that this could not be one of his nightmares. Every small detail was sharply etched in the scene: the bluish tint of the sergeant's jowl where the strong beard did not yield to the razor; the white bridge, the red-and-yellow colours of the barrier, the small crushed stones of the road. And equally sharp was the throng of people blocking the road to safety, the road into Spain.

Anna was there, her buxom fairness just as ripe and desirable as it had ever been. Kemmerich, his loutish face pale and determined, stood side by side with Obmann, who still wore the garish tie as a gag, bisecting his features. Reinhold Below and the Spanish wine merchant, Aunt Agatha in her stiff black shiny dress, Kowalski and his family, with the servants a little distance behind them. . . . There were others whose faces he could not distinguish, closely packed, rank upon rank, in serried lines. This was no nightmare, no unearthly visitation. He was no Macbeth to struggle with bloody ghosts, no murderer in some cheap novel being haunted by the spectre of his victims. He was Horst von Falkenau and he had been betrayed. He had conquered and outsmarted all, nothing and nobody could stand in his way. But there was the enemy inside him, cunning and invisible, he could never find or get to grips with; an enemy that at this very moment was whooping and laughing in his brain; an enemy to whom he had to surrender. . . .

Something snapped in his mind; a blinding light, a great, rushing noise filled the world. With a hoarse shout he turned. He did not hear the amazed cry of the sergeant. He started to run back across the bridge, shedding his cumbersome clothes as he went. He saw nothing but the road under his feet and even so, stumbled and staggered, but rushed on, drunkenly and aimlessly. One of the French soldiers reached out to halt him but it was no use. He ran and as he ran his face grew lax and child-like; the white gold of his hair streamed out like a mane. And when he fell, spent and almost at peace, he was no longer a man. His slobbering lips, his colourless, blinded eyes were like an animal's. He twitched and lay still; as Peter Whitney and Kladnik hurried up to him, he was a lump of inanimate flesh in their hands. He offered no resistance, as they carried him to the car.

"This is our man," Peter Whitney said when the big limousine backed up to the bridge and then jumped forward, roaring towards Perpignan. "But why on earth . . ."

"I don't know," Kladnik sighed. "It doesn't matter. I don't think it will make much difference, my friend. But sometimes, you know, I wonder whether we, in this enlightened century, are as clever as we think ourselves to be. . . ."

The man who had no longer a soul, sat rigid and silent on the back seat. And no one else spoke for there was nothing more to say.

THE END

London, December 1944—July 1945